The Mid-Cape Open

By: F. Edward Jersey

ALSO BY F. EDWARD JERSEY

(non-fiction)

Softwhere

(fiction)

Paines Creek Mystery

ObitUCrime

Cougar Attack

Unfinished Business

Monomoy Mystery

The Mid-Cape Open

A Cape Cod Adventure

By F. Edward Jersey

Copyright © 2012 by F. Edward Jersey
First Edition January 2012

Cover © 2012 by F. Edward Jersey
Edited by Wendy H. Jersey, Diane Kelley and Victoria L. Jersey

ISBN-10: 1470021684
ISBN-13: 978-1470021689

This book is dedicated to all the golfers out there who have the desire and passion for the game.

The Mid-Cape Open

Chapter 1

Every now and then, an opportunity comes along for an average person presenting a once in a lifetime opportunity. Just such a situation happened to Joe Campbell. Joe was a diehard golfer. He would play a round of golf whenever he could, it didn't matter how cold it was or how wet or windy. Joe was addicted to the game.

After a long winter, merchants in the Mid-Cape area of Cape Cod looked for ways to jump-start the spring/summer season of business. To that objective, those merchants got together with representatives of a number of golf courses on Cape Cod to sponsor an amateur-only golf tournament, to be called *The Mid-Cape Open*. To draw in a good group of golfers, a first place prize of $5,000.00 along with a number of other prizes were donated by many of the businesses. Some of the more notable included airfare to Nantucket or Martha's Vineyard including two nights lodging, a season pass to the Melody Tent in Hyannis for the current year, and ten dinners at ten restaurants for two.

The golf tournament format included qualifying tournaments accompanied by recognition ceremonies at various Cape Cod establishments. Each qualifying tournament offered prizes appropriate for the level of competition. Any amateur golfer could sign-up to compete. An entry fee of fifty dollars was assessed for each golfer competing in each qualifier round.

The rules for participants followed standard golf protocol. Any golfer who played on any professional or semi-professional golf association could not participate. Each golfer had to sign a form declaring the golfer's amateur status.

Joe had no problem with the rules, although he had always dreamt of being a professional golfer, Joe Campbell's game rarely reflected a score under ninety.

Joe lived in West Dennis on Center Street. During the spring, summer and fall, Joe worked his landscaping business cutting lawns and doing general grounds maintenance for a respectable client base he had built up over the past few years. Winters were slow and Joe would pick up whatever work he could find. Sometimes it was snow plowing, sometimes repair work inside a house of one of his landscaping clients. When Joe read about the open in the Cape Cod Times, he thought he might enter. The newspaper listed the various establishments and businesses sponsoring the tournament. Joe was familiar with most of the names listed. Sundancers, in West Dennis, was identified as the headquarters for the tournament. Joe frequented Sundancers from time to time and decided to stop in after work to get more information.

After cleaning up and showering, Joe dressed in jeans and a long sleeve flannel shirt and went to Sundancers. The April evening was rather cool, in the mid-forties; frost was expected overnight. Joe drove into the parking lot, parking in one of the many open spaces. Sundancers had only recently re-opened after the long winter layoff. Joe took up a stool near the windows.

Darlene Crowe, who liked to be called Dee, was bartending.

"Hi Joe, what will it be?"

"I'll have a Bud Light, please."

"Sure."

"So how are things going Joe?"

"Pretty slow right now Dee. I expect business will pick up once the weather warms."

"Yeah, we're a little slow now as well. The weekends are pretty good, but mid-week we only get the regulars."

"So what did you do for the winter, Joe?"

"Not much work-wise. There weren't too many jobs available. So I spent most of my time working on my computer trying to come up with some software for the landscaping industry."

"Really? I didn't know you were into computers?"

"I kind of got interested in them a few winters ago. I took a class two winters ago and learned how to program. It's actually pretty cool."

"You said you are working on something for the landscaping industry?"

"Yeah, I've come up with a program that lets the landscaper interact with a client, designing the landscape virtually for the client."

"That sounds pretty interesting."

"You take a picture of the area to be designed, then using the software, you design what you want the final product to look like."

"What kind of things can your software do?"

"Well, you can illustrate a wall, plants, build a deck, put in a garden, things like that."

"You'll have to show it to me sometime. A lot of people come in here and I overhear them talking about making improvements."

"That's a good idea Dee. I'll bring my laptop in the next time I come in."

"Please do."

"Say Dee, is Harry in?"
"Yeah, he's in the office. You want to see him?"
"Nothing urgent. I'll wait until he comes out."

Dee got Joe's beer and placed it on a coaster on the bar. Then she went to the other side of the bar to wait on another patron.

Harry Adams was the managing partner of Sundancers. His family owned the bar/restaurant and most days he could be found there. Twenty minutes later, Harry walked out of the kitchen into the bar area. Harry talked to a few patrons around the bar and eventually came around to where Joe was seated.

"Hey Joe."
"Harry."
"How's business Joe?"
"About the same as yours. Slow."
"Hey Joe, I met with a number of the other merchants in the area recently to talk about how we might jump start the business season. I think we came up with a pretty good idea you'd probably be interested in."
"What did you come up with?"
"We're going to sponsor a golf tournament for amateur golfers."
"I read about it in the paper."
Joe reached into his pocket and pulled out an article he had cut out of the paper. He showed it to Harry.

"Yeah, that's it. What do you think?"
"As a businessman or as a golfer?"
"Both."
"Well, I have a pretty good customer base already so I'm not sure it would help me much, but it's a good idea. As a golfer, I'm interested. You know how much I love golfing."

"You should enter Joe. The prizes are good."

A few guys came into the bar before Joe could respond. Joe, recognizing the three and, pointing at the last one who came in, said, "Well, if Tommy Anderson enters I don't have a chance."

"Joe, everyone has a chance."

"Harry, Tommy has beaten me in every game I've ever played against him. It didn't matter if it was golf, basketball or even bowling. I have never been able to beat that guy."

"Yeah, I remember when you two were in high school. Tommy was a natural at every sport. Too bad the guy couldn't stay off the stuff. He could have been a pro."

"If I only had half his talent," Joe said taking a sip of his beer.

"Joe, why not enter anyway? It's only a few bucks and you never know."

"Oh, I know. I'm not sure I want to give Tommy another reason to throw it in my face."

"You sound like he's made you his whipping boy."

"Just watch the next time you see him talking to me."

"Say Joe, I'm playing golf tomorrow at Bass River, care to join me?"

"What time?"

"I like to play early in the morning. It should start to warm up by 9:00."

"I could be there by 9:00."

"Then I'll see you there."

"Who else is playing?"

"Just Tony. You want to invite a fourth?"

"Yeah, why don't you ask Tommy?"

"Might be interesting, if you can stand the competition this early in the year."

"I might get to see how his game is before deciding on the tournament."

"Joe, I wouldn't let Tommy's play interfere with your decision to play in the tournament. Play for the love of the game, and who knows, we're all a little rusty after the winter break."

"You're probably right. But I still might get some ideas about how good or bad Tommy's game might be."

"You might. I'll invite him and we'll see."

"Ok Harry. I'll see you there."

As the two were talking, another car pulled into the lot. A very attractive woman got out. She had long flowing blond hair. She was dressed in a pair of dark denim skinny jeans, black boots, a white blouse and a light black leather jacket. Closing the door to her BMW, she strolled through the door. She turned right and took up the stool next to Joe and Harry.

"Hi Harry."

"Carol."

"How are you Joe?"

"I'm fine Carol. And you?"

"Good."

"I thought you were down in Florida?"

"I did go there for the winter. Now it's time to get back into the swing of things back here, get the house open, clean things up."

Harry looked to the kitchen and could see Chef Antonio "Tony" Davis waving to him. He excused himself and went to the kitchen leaving Carol sitting alone next to Joe.

"So you're back?"

"Yes. My last year has been hell. Florida re-energized me. I think I'm ready to get my life back to normal."

"I heard about what happened to you last fall. That was terrible."

"It was, but things have a way of working out. Thanks to Katherine Sterns, I got my money back. Too bad what happened to her."

"She did have a run of bad luck from what I gather."

"If you mean losing her first husband in a freak accident, losing her baby in a fall down stairs, being robbed of a large sum of money, or being accused of attacking her friends all in addition to the death of her fiancé and then dying out on the ocean and washing up on the south shore of Monomoy Island, you're right. I don't think I could have gone through half of the things she did."

Dee approached the two.

"Carol, I haven't seen you in a while. How have you been?"

"I'm fine Dee. I've been down in Florida."

"Good to see you. What will it be?"

"A dirty martini."

"Extra olives?"

"Yes, please."

Dee went to make the martini. When Carol turned back to Joe, Tommy Anderson had taken up the stool on the other side of Joe. Tommy had a piece of paper in hand that he laid in front of Joe.

"Joe, you thinking about entering this tournament?" Tommy tapped the article from the newspaper he had put in front of Joe.

"I'm thinking about it."

"Don't bother. I'm entering. If you want to lose, go ahead but don't expect to win the big prize."

Joe didn't respond. He picked up his drink and took a pull. Tommy got up and left the copy of the newspaper article in front of Joe. Carol picked up the paper, and read it.

"Joe, you entering the golf tournament?"

"I'd like to, but Tommy beats me at everything."

"I wouldn't let it stop me. You just need to find an advantage."

7

"Well, Harry has asked me to play golf tomorrow and he intends on asking Tommy to join us. Maybe I'll get to see what Tommy's game looks like this year."

"That's the way to think Joe. Gather information and then figure out how to use it to your advantage."

"Carol, he's beat me at everything we've ever competed in since our school days. I'm not sure it's even worth it."

"Joe, don't be so hard on yourself."

"He even beats me with the women."

Carol put her arm on Joe's shoulder, "If you want some coaching on how to best Tommy, just let me know. I'm an expert at getting even. Katherine took me under her wing after Frank Jenkins died. She taught me quite a few things."

"What did you have in mind?"

"Why don't we get together sometime. I think I can help you out."

"Let me think about it."

Joe motioned to Dee. When she came over he said, "Dee, can I get a shot? Make it a Jack."

"Sure Joe. I heard Tommy talking to you and I agree with Carol. You shouldn't let him get to you."

"That's easy for you to say."

"Just the same, don't let him psych you out."

Joe threw back the shot and took another pull on his beer.

Tommy came back over to the two.

"Carol, got any plans for tonight?"

"I thought I did but it looks like I'm free." She looked at Joe with a slight frown.

Joe didn't respond.

"Why don't we finish these drinks and go to your place?"

"Sure Tommy. Let's go to my place."

8

Carol finished her martini. Tommy paid his tab. Carol paid her's and the two got up and left. As Tommy was getting into his car, Harry saw him as he walked back into his office.

"Hey Tommy, I'm playing golf tomorrow morning with Tony and Joe. Care to join us?"

"Sure, what time and where?"

"Bass River, 9:00."

"I'll be there. I'll show Joe what he's up against if he's even thinking about entering that tournament."

"Tommy, you don't change."

"Just getting the upper hand."

"We'll see. See you at 9:00."

Tommy got into his car, started it up and left, following Carol's car out of the lot.

"Joe, you could have hooked up with Carol" Dee said, putting a fresh beer in front of him.

"I don't know."

"She asked you to ask her out."

"You think so?"

"Joe, I know her. She was on the prowl."

"Yeah, but Tommy..."

"Tommy nothing. You let him get to you."

"You're probably right."

"Fill out the entry form. You never know, and you've got plenty of time to practice."

"Maybe you're right."

"Joe, just do it."

Joe picked up the article, folded it and put it in his pocket. He finished his beer, paid his tab and went home, alone.

Chapter 2

When Joe finally left Sundancers, Harry walked over to Dee, "What happened to Joe and Carol?"

"Tommy Anderson."

"Yeah, Tommy has been getting the best of Joe for years. He stopped coming in here for a while. I think he found a new place to hang out."

"So why's he coming back around now?"

Harry held up the article for the golf tournament. "Joe's an avid golfer. I've played a few rounds with him. He's intense on the course and very competitive. My guess is he was trying to find out if Tommy had signed up for the event."

"I overheard Tommy telling Joe he's entering."

"Joe might not enter if that's the case."

"That's too bad. Do you think Joe's good enough to win the tournament?"

"If he put together all his good rounds, he might be able to win. Joe's problem is inconsistency. One day it's his putting, another day it's his long game."

"If Joe played his best all around game do you think he could beat Tommy?"

"Only if Tommy doesn't play well."

"I hope he enters. He needs something to cheer him up."

"I'm playing golf with the two of them and Tony tomorrow. It should be an interesting morning."

"For them or you?"

"Joe has had it tough for the past few years. He married young and didn't have a pot to piss in. Then his wife ran off with some guy she met at a bar."

"How's he with the women?"

"Until now, even the cougars have avoided him. His poor luck and depressed attitude had been known by everyone. No one wants to hang around someone who's under a black cloud all the time."

"Well, if it means anything, I overheard Carol talking friendly to him."

"Really?"

"Yeah, I heard her tell him they should get together."

"I'm not sure that would be in his best interest. Her conduct from last year is still pretty fresh in my mind. One night when Katherine was working here, she told me she had become good friends with Carol. The two had spent a lot of time together while Katherine was in seclusion after her fiancé died. I think Katherine taught her everything she knew before she died."

"I think she's over the disappointments and given the conclusion of the Charles Chamberlin thing, she should be over her revenge quest as well."

"Wasn't Chamberlin the guy who took large sums of money from a number of widows here in the Cape Cod area?"

"Yeah, that's the guy."

"You might be right about her changing Dee, but if Carol is anything like Katherine, then that woman is capable of anything."

"Harry, are you still bothered by Katherine?"

"She and the other Cougars hurt my business big time last year. I don't want a repeat."

11

"I think the untimely death of Katherine really slowed her down."

"I guess."

"Were you involved with Carol?"

"I was referring to the impact on my business."

"Say Harry, remember those silky playboy pajamas?"

"What pajamas?"

"You know, the ones I found in your safe."

"Yeah."

"Carol's about the same size as me wouldn't you say?"

"I don't know."

"I know Katherine thought the pajamas were her's. She told me so when she saw them at my house once. I kind of forgot about them until recently. Carol had a shopping bag with her when she came in and she showed me a pair of new pajamas that looked just like the ones I found in your safe. Maybe the ones I found in the safe were Carol's."

"Then how did they get in my office?"

"I don't know, you tell me."

"I thought they were Katherine's and Ed Phillips put them there. I still have them. I'll bring them in and show them to her the next time she comes in and see if they were her's."

"Dee, they might look like something she once owned but that doesn't prove anything. You've had them for some time. Didn't you wash them."

"Sure but what does that mean?"

"Then there probably isn't any possibility of identifying them positively as Carol's."

"You're probably right. I was just thinking those pajamas might be able to help answer some of the mystery."

"Dee, you should just let it go."

"Ok. Harry, we're getting a little low on singles in the register. Can you bring out another pack?"

"Sure."

12

Harry got up and went to his office through the kitchen.

Tina Fletcher had been seated at the bar near where Harry had been seated. She motioned to Dee to come over to her.

"Dee, can I have another drink?"

"Sure Tina."

"I heard you talking to Harry about Carol. You know I think he had something with her."

"He did get a little defensive."

"And what about those pajamas?"

"I found a pair of pajamas in the office safe one night when I was closing last fall. When I asked Harry where they came from, he said someone must have left them there."

"But in the safe?"

"That's what I thought."

"He gave you the pajamas?"

"Yeah, when I brought them back into the bar after closing he told me I could have them. As I remember, he even told me to try them on."

"Did you?"

"I did. Right there in front of him."

"Then what happened?"

"Nothing. He watched. I tried to entice him but he didn't bite."

"You think he was pre-occupied?"

"Now that I think about it, he was."

"Maybe there's an unpleasant story behind those pajamas and Harry couldn't get it out of his mind?"

"Could be."

"You should show them to Carol since they look like the ones she had in her shopping bag and see what she says."

"I might do just that. Last year, Katherine had come by my house and saw them on the clothesline. She thought they were hers and had been taken from her the night she was attacked at her home."

"Really?"

"Yeah. She talked to Harry about them, but I didn't hear anything else about it. I had forgotten about them until today."

Dee finished making Tina's drink and put it in front of her. She walked around the bar making sure the other patrons were all set and then came back to Tina.

"Tina, what do you think about Joe Campbell?"

"Joe? He seems like a quiet guy. I don't think I've ever seen him with any of the women in here."

"Me either. I think he was badly affected by that slut of a wife he had. She treated him like crap."

"I didn't know her well. She was a few years behind me in school."

"I did. She cheated on him a number of times as I recall. Then one afternoon, Joe came home early from playing golf and caught her in bed with another man."

"What did he do?"

"Nothing. He came to the bar and had few drinks. She ended up running away with the guy and moving off-Cape."

"No kidding."

"Joe mostly stopped coming in shortly after that. Today's the first time I have seen him in at least a year."

"Do you think he's looking for a woman?"

"I heard him talking to Harry about a golf tournament. Plus, Carol practically invited him over. He didn't bite."

"I'll have to talk to him the next time he comes in. I'll find out."

"I'm sure you will."

Another patron at the other end of the bar motioned to Dee for another beer. She left Tina to take care of the other patrons.

14

Ed Phillips saw Tina sitting by herself at the bar. He walked over to her.

"Hey Tina, what's going on?"

"Ed, young Ed. Now what are you up to?"

"I heard you and Dee talking about Joe Campbell. What was that all about?"

"Oh, nothing. Dee was just telling me about Joe and his misfortunes."

"What did she say?"

"I don't really know Joe, he's a lot younger than me, but Dee said his wife ran off with another man. She said he used to come in here quite a bit but hasn't been around much for quite a while."

"Yeah, he was really down about the wife. It was just as well though. She wasn't a good wife."

"Did you know her well?"

"Yeah. I went to school with Joe and his former wife Jessica."

"So you knew her?"

"Oh yeah, I knew her."

"I think she was the same age as my younger sister. Was she as bad as Dee said she was?"

"Let's just say she had a reputation."

"Did you ever hook up with her?"

"A number of times. She was very active, even after they were married."

"Really?"

"I remember one time after we played Joe's softball team the teams were going to a bar to have a few drinks. Jessica had been at the game watching. When Joe said he was going with the guys to a bar for a few drinks, she asked me to come over to their house. I made up an excuse with the guys and did go over to their house. She made it worth while."

"Did he ever find out?"

"Not with me, but one of the other guys on my team went to their house after another game. On that occasion, Joe

15

only stayed at the bar for one beer and then went home. He caught her naked in bed with the guy."

"Then what happened?"

"She ended up running off with the guy and getting divorced from Joe."

"You know, my younger sister had told me something about a girl she had gone to school with doing something like that. It must have been her."

"I've known Joe for many years and he was really affected by the breakup with Jessica. It affected him even more than always losing to Tommy in everything they competed in. I'd hate to think what he might do if he ever found out I slept with Jessica."

"Why, is he a violent person?"

"I know he has a temper. You never know what a person will do when something like that happens."

"You're right."

"So Tina, do you have any plans for the night?"

"I do now. Why don't we go to my place?"

"Sounds like a plan."

Ed called Dee over and asked for his tab and Tina's.

"Thanks for picking up the tab Ed." Tina said, whispering in his ear.

"No problem," Ed replied.

He took a fifty out of his wallet and laid it on the bar. "Keep the change Dee."

The two left Sundancers together for the night.

Dee turned to Ron, "Looks like Ed will get lucky tonight."

"Looks like it," Ron, the night bartender, replied, turning around to provide the waitress station with a couple of beers.

Chapter 3

Joe Campbell grew up on Cape Cod. His parents were both teachers in the Dennis and Yarmouth school districts. Joe's dad, Joe Senior, taught mathematics at D-Y High. Joe's mother, Helen, taught fifth grade. Joe attended Dennis schools and then D-Y High. He played on all the major sports teams as a slightly above average athlete. His academic acumen was just average. When Joe graduated high school, his grades were insufficient to get him into college so he started his own landscaping business on Cape Cod. The year after graduation, Joe married his high school sweetheart, Jessica Broadmore.

The two made their home in Dennis, renting a house just off Airline Road. Joe worked very hard at building up his landscaping business, taking on a number of vacation homes owned by off Cape people. He had been selective focusing on clients who had upscale vacation homes that were in the rental market, and preferably those that had more than one home. This technique provided Joe with a good client base from which to run his business.

It was in grade school where Joe first met Tommy Anderson. A few years later, Tommy and Joe were classmates at D-Y High. Tommy was the star athlete on the basketball, baseball and golf teams. As teammates in basketball and baseball, they got along but on the golf team, the two were very competitive. Tommy got all the sporting awards. Tommy was MVP of the baseball team, captain of the basketball team and the leading amateur golfer in the mid-Cape area. Only once during their entire high school careers did Joe have a chance to beat Tommy at golf. During a state championship tournament, Joe had the round of his life going. Through fourteen holes, he was two under par. Tommy was three over par. As a team, they were beating their opponents by nine strokes. Before they could finish the round that day, a thunderstorm came up and golf was called off for the rest of the day. When the tournament resumed the next day, Joe couldn't do anything right. He ended up in fourth place. Tommy on the other hand did everything right. He birdied the last three holes and posted the lowest score of the tournament. Joe and Tommy beat their competition, but Tommy got all the praise and the MVP trophy.

It was like that in every sport. Joe was always the bridesmaid. The also ran. The runner up.

Dee had been talking with Ron one night at Sundancers about Joe Campbell. She told Ron about a confrontation she remembered between Joe and Tommy.

"A few years out of high school, Joe had been sitting in Sundancers with his wife, Jessica, having a beer. Tommy Anderson came into the bar having just returned from graduating college in North Carolina. Tommy was in a celebratory mood," Dee recalled. She said the dialogue went something like this.

"Joe Campbell, how the hell are you?"

18

"I'm fine Tommy. How 'bout you?"

"Just graduated from UNC. Voted the top golfer in the NCAA."

"Good for you Tommy. So are you going pro?"

"That's my plan."

Joe excused himself for a few minutes to visit the men's room. He got up and walked in the direction of the restroom sign.

Tommy looked over at Jessica, "How are you Jess?"

"I'm fine Tommy."

"You know Jess, you could have been making the trip to the PGA with me if you hadn't got caught up with Joe."

"Tommy, Joe's doing just fine."

"Maybe so, but is he as good as me?"

"Tommy, Joe doesn't know about you and me so don't say anything."

"Just tell me, is he as good?"

"He does ok."

"So he isn't as good?"

"Tommy."

"Jess, why don't you come over to my place and I'll show you a good time before I go pro?"

"That's alright Tommy. I'm a happily married woman."

"Married maybe, but happy? Probably not."

Joe returned from the restroom. As he sat next to Jessica, Tommy asked Dee to give them all another drink and to give him a shot of Jack as well. Dee got the drinks. Tommy sat with Joe and Jessica for the next half hour reminiscing about their high school days and about his superiority. After four drinks accompanied by shots, it was pretty clear Tommy was inebriated.

"Joe, isn't Jess fantastic?" Tommy said slurred.

"You're drunk Tommy. Why don't you go home?"

19

"Sure. Can Jess come with me?"

"I don't think so. She's my wife."

"That never stopped her before," Tommy said reaching around Joe and putting his hand on Jessica's arm.

"Don't," Jessica said pulling away from Tommy's grip.

"Jess, you want me. You've settled for less for so long. It's time for you to have a real pro," Tommy said as he fell backwards almost knocking his stool over.

"Joe, do something," Jessica said looking angrily at Tommy.

"What would you like me to do Jess, he's drunk."

Just then, Tommy stood behind Jessica and put his arms around her under her arms. His hands were on her breasts, "Just how I remember them."

Joe stood and landed a punch squarely on Tommy's jaw. Tommy fell back, out cold before he hit the floor. Harry came running out of the kitchen in time to stop Joe from going any further.

"He put his hands on my wife," Joe said standing in a fighting position.

"Joe, why don't you and Jessica leave? I'll take care of Tommy."

"Sure Harry. But if he touches her again, it's going to be more than a punch."

"Don't make threats Joe, just leave."

Joe and Jessica got up and left.

"What did he mean when he said just as he remembered them?"

"It was a long time ago Joe. We weren't even dating."

"Have you been with Tommy?"

"Let's just say we knew each other when we were in high school."

"I thought I was your first?"

"Please Joe, don't be so naive."

"Did you sleep with him?"

"No more questions Joe."

"I can't believe this. He even slept with my wife. That guy has beat me at everything, even you."

"Like I said Joe, it was a long time ago."

"I can't believe it."

The two got into their car and left. Joe's disappointment and depression was clearly evident.

After Joe and Jessica left, Harry got Tommy into a chair. Dee brought over a wet towel. She rubbed it on Tommy's face. He came around and asked what happened.

"You passed out," Harry said handing Tommy a glass of water and aspirin.

"Why does my jaw hurt so much?"

"You must have hit it when you hit the floor" Harry said taking the glass from Tommy.

"What are you going to do with him now Harry?" Dee asked.

"I don't know. He's too drunk to drive home."

"Want me to take him to his house?"

"Sure. I'll bartend while you're gone."

"I should be back in twenty minutes."

"Ok."

The two took Tommy out and put him into Dee's SUV. She drove Tommy home. When they got to his place, she helped him into the house. They walked to the bedroom and Tommy sat on the edge of the bed.

"Can I have a glass of water?" Tommy asked.

"Sure, let me get it for you."

"She went to the kitchen and got a glass of water. When she came back, Tommy had shed all his clothes and was lying on top of his bed naked out cold. Tommy was indeed well endowed. Had he been awake, she would have joined him. Instead, she put the glass of water on the nightstand and pulled a cover over him. She locked his door on her way out and returned to Sundancers."

"Did you get him home alright?" Harry asked when Dee returned.

"Yeah. He took his clothes off and passed out on his bed."

"He probably thought he was going to get lucky."

"Maybe, but he passed out. I put a cover on him and left him there."

"Good choice. Thanks for taking him home Dee. I appreciate it."

"Don't mention it Harry. I did get a little reward out of it."

"What was that?"

"I got to see Tommy naked."

"Was it worth it?"

"Sure was. I know what the cougars are talking about."

"So you think you want to get to know him more?"

"Let's just say he has the whole package."

"He might, but his drinking is going to get the best of him."

"Maybe."

Then Dee went back to waiting on the people at the bar. Harry returned to his office.

"Wow," Ron said. "You recall that much detail?"

"Ron, I remember everything."

"I'll keep that in mind."

"Remember Ron, you have a history as well."

"Ha. And Joe and Tommy have a history as well."

"There's more, a lot more."

"You'll have to tell me about it sometime."

"No sense bringing up the past."

"What about sports?"

22

"Oh, the two were always competing. Tommy seemed to always get the best of Joe."

"You think the rivalry is still alive?"

"If Joe enters that tournament, we'll see."

"He took the article with him. My guess is he's thinking about entering."

"Should be interesting."

"Harry said the entry forms should be here in a few days. We'll see if Joe takes one."

Ron and Dee want back to waiting on the patrons at the bar.

Chapter 4

Carol and Tommy got to her place about fifteen minutes after leaving Sundancers. Carol knew what Tommy wanted and she had similar thoughts. The two sat on her couch talking for a few minutes.

"Carol you have a nice place here."

"Glad you like it. Since I got back all the money Charles Chamberlin stole, I've been able to re-do the place more to my liking."

"I heard about you and the other women being caught up in some scheme Chamberlin had. Then I heard Katherine Sterns got all your money back for you and the others."

"Yeah she did. She told us to expect our funds to be returned, and she made good on her promise."

"Yeah, but she died doing it."

"We never really got an answer as to what caused her death, but yes; she did die right around the time we got our funds back. So did Charles."

"Does that bother you?"

"Not about Charles, but it does bother me about Katherine. She and I became good friends when her fiancé Frank Jenkins died. I learned quite a bit from her."

"What kinds of things did she teach you?"

"I'd rather not say."

"Did any of them have to do with sex?"

"Why do you ask?"

"Oh, Katherine was very good at certain things."

"So you slept with her?"

"I'd rather not say" Tommy said slyly.

"Tommy, I don't want you comparing me to Katherine, and especially in bed."

"Don't worry Carol. I wouldn't do something like that."

"That's what all you guys say."

"Oh, someone else is comparing things?"

Carol stood up, "I'm gonna make a drink. Do you want one, or a cold beer?"

"What are you having?"

"Captain and diet coke."

"I'll have one too."

"You pick a CD out while I get the drinks."

"Sure."

Carol went into her kitchen. She took two glasses out of the cupboard and filled them half with ice. Then she poured Captain Morgan into both glasses filling them a third of the way. Next, she added Diet Coke filling them most of the way to the top. She opened a drawer and retrieved a small bottle from the back. She took one blue pill out, broke it up and put it into one of the glasses, the one with a picture of a bull on the outside. She picked up the glasses and returned to the living room.

Tommy had found a CD marked 'Mix for Fun' and put it in. The volume was up, but not too much.

"That's a little loud, don't you think?"

"I like it that way," he said as he took the glass with the image of a bull on it from Carol. He sipped the drink.

"Tastes good."

"You like rum and coke Tommy?"

"I do."

"Well, this one is special."

"It is? How so?"

"It's made with something special."

"Like what?"

"Love."

That was all Carol said and then she unbuttoned her blouse and moved in on Tommy. She took his shirt off while he unhooked her bra. Then, the two kissed while their hands explored each other's bodies. It didn't take much and the two were naked lying on the couch. As Tommy held her close, she couldn't help but notice he was aroused.

Carol took matters into her own hands driving Tommy crazy for about twenty minutes. When he told her he couldn't take it any more, she stood up, took his hand and led him to her bedroom.

Carol instructed Tommy to lie on his back on the bed. As he did, she moved on top of him, kissing him as she moved. She reached into her nightstand, taking a small jar of lubricant out. She applied a healthy amount to Tommy and then she took control.

After a while, she lay down next to him, allowing him to explore her body. Tommy was still ready.

"Want to go again?" he said.

"I'm spent Tommy. Maybe later."

"What was that stuff you put on me?"

"Just a lubricant."

"Wow, I'll have to get some of it."

26

"Tommy. It isn't the lubricant. It's just the chemistry."

"Oh, between you and me?"

"Something like that."

She squeezed him and then got up to clean things up.

"Now what?"

"That's it for tonight Tommy. You can stay if you want, but I'm tired."

"I'll stay. Maybe we can do it again later."

"Maybe."

Carol never said anything to Tommy about the pill she put in his drink. At 8:00 am, the two showered. Tommy was ready to go again but Carol told him she had things to do and it would have to wait. She dressed and went to the kitchen to make coffee knowing she had left him wanting more. This was too easy.

When Tommy came into the kitchen, she said, "Tommy, why do you tease Joe so much?"

"What do you mean?"

"You know, like you were teasing him at the bar last night."

"Joe and I go back a long way."

"So what, but why do you go after him? I thought you two were friends."

"We are. But Joe just leaves himself open as a target. I don't know, maybe it's just left over from when we were kids."

"I like Joe, Tommy. You should be nicer to him."

"You like him. Do you want to sleep with him?"

"Maybe."

"Hey, I slept with his ex and she told me I was better than him in the sack. So if you're thinking about sleeping with him, take me instead. It'll be a step up."

"See, that's just what I'm talking about Tommy. You're slapping Joe down and he isn't even here."

27

"Well, I did sleep with Jessica."

"Tommy, some day, someone will be better than you. And you'll know how it feels."

"Maybe, but it won't be from Joe Campbell."

"People change Tommy."

"Not that much."

"Careful what you ask for."

"So Carol, when can we get together again?"

"I'll let you know Tommy."

"Don't wait too long. I may have to stray."

"Tommy, you'll do the dog if the dog will have you."

"I don't have to stoop that low. Now if you were talking about Joe."

"Stop right there Tommy. You need to stop picking on Joe."

"What's he going to do?"

"I don't know Tommy, but you have to back off. It's not attractive."

"Me change? Don't think so."

"Ok, don't say I didn't warn you."

"Now you're sounding like Katherine."

"Like I told you, she taught me a lot."

"Now that worries me."

"Don't worry Tommy. It's a waste of your time, because it won't help you out in any way."

"I'm going to have to get going soon Carol. I'm playing golf with Harry, Tony and Joe at nine."

Carol looked up at the clock. It was 8:30.

"You better get going or you'll be late."

"No problem. I've got my clubs in the car and it'll only take me a few minutes to get to the course."

Carol could see a bulge in Tommy's pants. She touched him in the area, "What are you going to do about this?"

Tommy wasn't used to this situation especially after the night before.

"I don't know.   This has never happened to me before."

"Hope it doesn't get in the way of your game."

"Oh, it won't."

The two finished their coffees, and Tommy left. Carol had things to do too, and started her day.

Chapter 5

That same day, Harry had a poster in the window of the bar for the Mid-Cape Open. It identified the three qualifying rounds to be played at Bayberry Golf Course in Yarmouth, Dennis Pines in Dennis and Bass River Golf Course in Yarmouth. The poster said the top thirty amateur golfers would qualify for the tournament. Entry fee would be $50 per golfer per qualifier round. A list of prizes was identified with the top prize being $5,000.

A stack of entry forms along with the tournament rules and regulations was next to the poster.

Qualifying rounds would be played on three consecutive Saturdays starting the first Saturday in May. Each qualifying round would be limited to a maximum of 36 golfers. The ten golfers with the highest scores from each qualifier would earn the right to compete in The Mid-Cape Open. Signup was on a first come-first served basis. Entry forms along with the entry fee had to be submitted at Sundancers no later than on the Friday preceding each qualifying round. After each qualifying round, a buffet reception would be held at one of three different sponsor restaurants. The low scorer would get a plaque and assorted gift certificates from area merchants.

Bayberry Hills Golf Course is located in West Yarmouth. The golf course consists of three nine-hole courses. The original 18-hole course is made up of what's called the Red Course, a 3259-yard par-36 from the blue tees and the White Course, a 3264-yard par-36 from the blue tees. The third nine is called the Blue Course composed of a 3120-yard par-36 from the blue tees. The Blue course is more like a links course. The land had been reclaimed from the town landfill. The tournament would be played on the Red and White courses.

The second qualifying round would be held the second Saturday in May at Dennis Pines Golf Course. Again, the best ten scores would qualify the golfers for the actual tournament.

The Dennis Pines course is located in East Dennis. The course is an 18-hole, 7000-yard, par-72 from the blue tees.

The course has a few challenging holes. Hole number eight is a 422-yard par-4. The hole is long and fairly narrow. A golfer must hit a straight tee shot over 250 yards in order to safely reach the green in two. The 10th hole can be a difficult 351-yard par-4. The fairway consists of a steep slope leading down to water. A golfer has to hit a long drive and straight to get by the intimidating grade. Hole twelve is a 513-yard par-5 dogleg right hole that takes most golfers three shots to reach the green. Very few golfers are capable of achieving eagle on this hole.

The third and final qualifying round would be held at the Bass River Golf Course across the river from Sundancers in Yarmouth. Ten more golfers would qualify for the tournament scheduled for Memorial Day weekend.

31

The Bass River Golf Course is a fairly short course of 6,129 yards from the blue tees. The course can play tough as some of the holes regularly have a prevailing breeze off the water requiring golfers to consider adding an additional club to shot selections.

The course starts off fairly easy with a 204-yard par-3. There isn't much in the way on the 1st hole and the fairway is wide open. The 2nd hole is a straightaway 310-yard par-4. The 3rd hole is the first hole where a golfer will face the prevailing breeze. This 425-yard par-4 is the number one handicap hole on the course. Most golfers end up playing this hole longer than it actually is. The 4th hole is a picturesque hole overlooking the Bass River. At 366 yards, this hole is very manageable. The 5th hole is a 358-yard par-4 containing a two-tiered green and a very large bunker on the left side. The 312-yard 6th hole is also a two-tiered green but easily a birdie opportunity for better golfers. The 7th hole is a 129-yard tight fairway hole. Discerning golfers will add one club to the drive. The 488-yard 8th hole is the first par-5 on the course. The 9th hole is the course signature hole. It has water all along the left side. The hole plays mostly up hill and the green has a severe slope from left to right. Reaching the green in one can be fairly easy. Making a putt, even a short one can be a challenge.

Hole ten is a short 258-yard par-4. Golfers can be aggressive on this hole. The 406-yard par-4 11th is the second most difficult hole on the course. The 12th and 13th holes are back-to-back par-5s. The 12th plays pretty easy while the 13th requires a golfer to stay on the left side of the fairway in order for a second shot to have a chance of reaching in two. The 14th hole is a 165-yard par-3 requiring a golfer to navigate a deceiving ravine. Hole fifteen comes back across the same ravine going the other way. Hole sixteen is the last par-5 on the course. This 484-yard hole has out of bounds on both the left and right side of the fairway. Hole seventeen is a short

325-yard par-4 with a small two-tiered green. The 352-yard 18th hole is a straight away open fairway hole.

The tournament would consist of four rounds of golf to be played over two weekends. The first round would be played at Dennis Highlands Golf Course. Round two would be played at Bayberry Golf Course. The third round would be played at the Red Jacket Resort course at Blue Rock. Even though Blue Rock is an executive par-3 course, it is considered one of the best in the country. Scores should be low, but Blue Rock might provide for some interesting drama leading up to the final round to be played at Bass River Golf Course.

Blue Rock golf course is a 2890-yard par-54 from the blue tees. The course will force a golfer to manage the short game, as all holes are par-3. Four of the holes are over water. Two holes are long par-3s. The greens are fast and some of the fairways are tight.

The winner of the tournament will be the golfer who posts the cumulative low score totaled from all four rounds. There will not be a cut after the first two rounds since the four rounds are being played on different courses. In the event of a tie, the golfers with the tied score will play sudden death holes sixteen, seventeen and eighteen in reverse order until one golfer posts a score lower than the other contenders for any hole played. If more than two golfers end regulation tied, then only golfers with the lowest score on each sudden death hole will continue to compete.

Chapter 6

Harry, Joe and Tony were waiting by the course starter when Tommy showed up. Tommy ran into the pro shop, paid for his round and joined the others.

"What happened to you Tommy? Did you forget we were playing golf today?" asked Harry.

"Nah. I stayed at Carol's last night and one thing led to another. I may be late, but I'm happy."

Joe rolled his eyes.

"Hope you brought your game Tommy," said Tony.

"I always bring my game. What are we playing for?" he asked.

"How about $100 per man for low gross?" Harry responded.

"Sounds good to me," said Tommy.

"I don't know," said Tony. "You guys are way better than me."

"Ok Tony. We'll give you a stroke on all par-5s," said Harry.

"Then I'm in," Tony responded.

"Count me in too, without the strokes" said Joe.

"Joe, you don't want strokes?" Tommy taunted him.

"No. I'll play straight up."

"What? Have you been practicing?"

"I just keep in shape Tom," Joe said confidently.

"We'll see," Tommy snickered.

Everyone handed Harry $100. He put his on the pile and put it all in his golf bag, counting it in front of everyone beforehand.

"May the best golfer win."

The starter indicated they could go to the first tee. Joe rode with Tony, Tommy rode with Harry. At the 1st tee, Harry used a tee to determine the order of play. He threw the tee into the air landing in the middle of the four golfers. It pointed to Joe. Then he did it two more times. Joe would hit first followed by Tony, then Harry. Tommy would tee off last.

Joe placed his Top-Flite ball on a tee between the blue tees. He took his driver, took a few practice swings and hit the ball. It went straight and long, about 280 yards.

"Wow Joe, nice hit," said Tony.

"Someone's been practicing," Tommy added.

"Good hit Joe," Harry added.

Next, Tony hit his ball about 240 yards to the left side of the fairway.

"I'm a little stiff," said Tony.

"Limber up a little more next time," said Joe.

"You're getting strokes Tony. Don't worry," was all Tommy said.

"I'd be happy with that shot Tony. I don't know what you don't like," said Harry.

"I just want to be competitive," responded Tony.

Then Harry took the tee box. He decided on using a fairway wood instead of a driver.

"What? No driver Harry?" questioned Tommy.

"I need to play a few holes before I break out the big dog," said Harry. "If I tried to hit my driver too early, my ball would end up in the woods."

His shot went about 210 yards right down the center of the fairway.

"Nice shot Harry," Joe said.

Then, Tommy took out his big driver. It looked like a monster club.

"What the heck is that?" asked Tony.

"You'll see," was all Tommy said.

He took a few practice swings starting out slow and finishing with a fast hard swing. Then he addressed the ball. Tommy took the club way back. When he started forward with the club, he grunted and swung the club as hard as he could. He made ball contact and his Nike ball took off. The other three golfers watched as Tommy's ball went higher and higher, way out down the fairway. At the end of the flight, the ball had a significant curve to the right. It ended up on the edge of the woods about 310 yards out from the tee box.

"Should have been straighter," Tommy said.

"Still, you hit the crap out of that one Tommy," Tony remarked.

"Same old Tommy," Harry said to Joe as they walked back to the carts.

"Looks like he can still play," commented Joe.

"We'll see," said Harry.

They all found their golf balls and readied for a second shot. Tony hit his just short of the green. Joe had a wedge shot landing about ten feet from the pin. Harry hit his shot to the edge of the green. Tommy was last to hit.

Tommy took out a 4 iron as he had about 90 yards to the hole but had hanging tree limbs in front of his shot. When he tried to hit a bump and run shot, he caught the ball squarely and it took off flying 30 yards past the green landing under a bench by the next tee box.

When Tommy saw where his ball landed, he declared, "I get a free lift from here, don't I, since this is a manmade object?"

"I don't know about that," questioned Tony.

Harry looked to Joe, "What do you think Joe?"

"Go ahead Tommy; take the lift but no closer to the hole."

Tommy picked up his ball and dropped it about three feet from the bench. He took out his wedge. When he hit the ball, it flew right over the flag, stopping a few feet from the pin.

"Now, that's what I'm talking about," Tommy responded.

"You still have to make the putt," said Tony.

"No problem."

Harry was first to putt. He hit the first putt about twenty-five feet ending up about a foot from the hole.

"Nice par Harry," commented Joe.

"Thanks."

Next, Tony who had hit his second shot to just about fifteen feet away from the hole, ran his putt about two feet past the hole. He then missed the 2-footer ending up with a bogey.

Joe putted next, sinking his putt for a birdie.

Tommy being Tommy said, "Hey Joe, everyone gets lucky sooner or later."

"Let's see you make it Tommy," Harry said to him.

Tommy addressed his ball. The shot fell a few inches short of the cup. He had scored a bogey.

"Looks like you still tee off last Tommy," Tony said jokingly to Tommy.

"I'll get better," Tommy replied walking to the golf cart, and slamming his putter into it.

They played the next few holes with similar results. Joe was playing well. He got par or birdied the holes. Tommy had a par, three bogeys and a double. Tony was three over and Harry one over par.

At the 6th tee box, Tommy said, "I don't understand why I'm so tight with my long shots and so stiff with my putts."

Tony chimed in, "Maybe you need to get your rest before you play golf instead of courting the women."

"Who me?" Tommy reacted.

"I'm just saying," Tony remarked.

"Must be not enough practice this early in the season," said Tommy.

"You talking about the women or golf Tommy?" Harry asked.

Tommy laughed. "Women? Me? Never. I'm referring to golf."

Harry turned to Joe, "See Joe, even Tommy can have a bad day. You should enter the tournament."

"I don't know. I'll think about it."

The rest of the round continued to produce the same results. When the round was done four hours later, Joe had shot an 81, Tony a 90, Harry an 88 and Tommy a 97.

Back at the clubhouse, Harry said, "Let's go to my place and have a drink. Joe, you're the winner."

He handed Joe $400 from his golf bag, and four headed off to Sundancers.

At the bar, Harry brought them all a drink. The four sat at the bar talking about the round of golf. Tommy didn't say much to Joe about his play, but Tony wasn't going to let Tommy's play get away so easily.

"Tommy, why don't you tell Dee how your round of golf went today?" said Tony.

"Ha, ha. So I didn't play so well."

Dee came over to Tommy, "Tommy, you're having a bad day?"

"Just my golf game. I couldn't do anything right."

"Why don't you show us that fabulous swing of yours Tommy?" laughed Tony.

"Funny Tony. You didn't do much better."

"Yeah, but I didn't claim to be the best golfer since Tiger Woods. You did," said Tony.

"Why don't you two knock it off? Don't turn a good day into a fight" Harry, the peacemaker, said.

"Oh, I don't know Harry. Its kind of fun turning the tables on Tommy for once," said Tony.

Dee turned and faced Joe.

"You're not saying much Joe."

"He won our bet today. He played real well," said Harry.

"Well Joe. See? I knew you had it in you. You should enter that golf tournament."

"Playing one good round is one thing. Putting four together to win a tournament would be a first for me."

"Plus, you'd be competing against me Joe. And we know how that's worked out for you in the past," said a defiant Tommy, even after Joe had just blown his socks off.

Joe didn't respond. He just listened quietly while contemplating his beer. It must have been Tommy's demeanor, because now Joe was convinced he'd give the tournament a try. The guys sat around for another half hour reliving the game. They would laugh and boast about one shot or another. Tony took every opportunity to put Tommy in his place bringing up one bad shot after another. After a while, the talk changed to other subjects. Harry had a few chores to address in his office so he excused himself. Tony said goodbye and went home for the day. Joe continued talking to Dee, and Tommy saw some women he knew at the other end of the bar, so he went down to talk to them.

"Hey Tina."
"Tommy."
"Who's your friend?"
"Tommy, this is Mary Higgins."
"Mary, Tommy Anderson."
"Hi Tommy."

Tina said, "I overheard you talking with the other guys about playing golf today Tommy. How'd you do?"

"I didn't have a great round today. Kind of stayed up too late last night."

Mary took a sip of her martini. "Oh? What kept you up so late?"

"I had a date."

Dee overheard him talking to the two women, "Yeah, with Carol."

Tommy looked at Dee with a frown. She wasn't helping his cause.

"So you're not interested in staying out again tonight are you Tommy?" asked Tina.

"I think I need my rest."

"I'm kind of tired myself," said Mary. "I think I'll be going home pretty soon."

Tina looked at the two, "Suit yourselves, but I'm out for the night." She looked around the bar to see who else might be up for some action. There weren't too many people there. She saw Joe at the other end of the bar. "Maybe Joe Campbell is interested in some action," she said.

"Really Tina?" said Tommy.

"Hey Tommy, you're calling it a day."

"Yes I am."

"Then don't say anything bad about Joe. I'm sure he'll be up for having a good time. After all, he did beat you guys today didn't he?"

"That he did," responded Tommy.

"Then, Joe it is," said Tina. She picked up her drink and walked towards Joe.

Tommy paid his tab. Mary did the same. They started to walk out the door together. When they got outside, Mary said, "Why don't we get some rest together?"

"I don't know. I'm kind of tired," Tommy replied.

Mary looked down at the front of his pants. It wasn't hard to detect the bulge. "It looks to me like you might want some company."

Tommy touched himself, "Why not? Your place or mine?"

"Follow me Tommy. I live about twenty minutes from here."

"I'm right behind you."

Chapter 7

After Tommy and Mary had left, Tina sat at the bar next to Joe. She joined him just as Dee was encouraging him to sign up for the tournament, again.

"Joe, I agree with Dee. You should enter. And I hope it ends up being you and Tommy competing for the prize and you beat him."

"Tina, there are slots for one hundred and eight golfers in the qualifying rounds in the tournament. From that group, the top thirty will compete in the actual tournament. There's no guarantee I would even make it past the qualifying round."

"That's no way to look at it Joe," said Dee. "Harry said if you put together a good round like you're capable of doing, and did today, you could qualify and even be a real contender."

"Harry said that did he?"

"Yeah, he said you're a pretty good golfer."

Tina added, "Didn't you win today? That proves you can compete with Tommy."

"I guess."

"So just do it Joe. I'd like to see someone put Tommy in his place," said Dee.

"Me too," added Tina.

Joe got up and walked over to the stack of applications. He took one off the pile, asked Dee for a pen and began to fill out the application. While he was writing, Carol Tindle came in and took up the stool on the other side of Joe.

"Hi Tina," said Carol.

"Carol," replied Tina.

"Can I have a dirty martini?" Carol asked Dee.

"Sure."

Dee went about making the martini.

Carol put her hand on Joe's leg, "So you're going to enter?"

"Why not? It's only fifty bucks."

"Plus, Joe beat Harry, Tony and Tommy today," said Tina.

"Good for you Joe. Now win that tournament."

"It might not be that easy Carol. Yes I did play well today, but what are the chances Tommy, or all the other golfers who enter will play worse than me?"

"Joe, you beat Tommy today. You can do it again. You know what they say, one game at a time."

"I don't know. Tommy had a bad day."

"What do you mean bad day?"

"He couldn't putt. Most of his long shots were left or right. He couldn't hit straight. It was like his body wasn't in shape."

"Or maybe it was something else," said Carol.

"Like what?"

"Let's just say Tommy might not have been himself playing today."

"Oh, he bragged about being with you last night and said it affected his game."

"Oh, I'm sure his being with me last night affected his game," said Carol.

"What, did you give him a workout?" asked Tina.

43

"That and some," said Carol.

"Well, I can't count on that happening to Tommy again every time we play a round."

"Why not?" asked Carol.

"Because Tommy always beats me."

"Except for today," Carol said.

"Yeah, except for today."

"Joe, I think Carol and Tina are on to something. You can beat him" Dee chimed in.

"And what about the other twenty-eight golfers should Tommy and I make it past the qualifying rounds to the tournament?"

"Worry about it when it happens. Until then, just do your best," said Carol rubbing Joe's leg.

Tina saw Carol's hand and did the same to Joe's other leg. Dee came back over, "One of you should help Joe celebrate his victory."

"I think that's a good idea," said Tina.

"Me too," added Carol.

Tina looked at both Carol and Joe, "Joe, have you ever been with two women at the same time?"

Joe was kind of taken aback. He would be lucky to end up with one of the women and now, if he understood the proposition correctly, both women wanted him.

"No. Not really," was all he could say.

"Joe, why don't the three of us get out of here and help you celebrate your victory properly," said Carol finishing her martini.

"I don't know."

Tina stood up, taking Joe's hand as she did. She turned him around. Carol stood from her stool and took his other arm, and the two led him out the door.

"But I didn't pay my tab yet," Joe could be heard saying as they led him away.

"Don't worry about it Joe," Dee shouted. "Harry said it was on him."

44

"See Joe, your day just keeps getting better and better," said Tina.

Outside Sundancers, they got into their cars and followed Tina to her place. When they arrived at her house, the three went in. Tina made martinis for them while Carol sat on the couch with Joe. While Tina was in the kitchen, Carol put her hands on Joe's chest and then kissed him passionately. Tina brought the drinks into the room and sat on the other side of Joe. While Carol sipped her martini, Tina turned to Joe and kissed him. Joe wasn't sure how to react. His male hormones started to kick in. Carol and Tina both noticed.

"Let's take this to the bedroom," said Tina.

The three stood, with Tina leading the way to the bedroom. Once there, both women took off their clothes and then they both helped Joe with his. While Tina was kissing Joe, Carol took a pill out of her pants pocket, crushing it and putting it in Joe's drink, but Joe hadn't see her do it. Carol picked up her martini and made a toast.

"To Joe's victory."

"Yeah, to Joe's victory," added Tina.

"I guess," said Joe.

The three finished their martinis. The women turned their attention to Joe. They worked him over pretty good, and in no time, Joe made love to both of them. He couldn't believe his good fortune but Carol could. When they had finished, Joe had a smile on his face.

"That was fun," said Tina.

"We should do it again," added Carol.

"I can't believe it," Joe commented.

"See Joe, you can do almost anything when you put your mind to it," said Tina.

"You just have to find your edge," said Carol.

"I guess. Carol and Tina, we don't have to say anything to anyone else about tonight, do we?"

45

"You're secret is safe with me Joe," said Tina.

"Joe, Dee did see the three of us leave together. I'm sure she'll ask us what happened after we left Sundancers," said Carol.

"Can't we make something up?" asked Joe.

"Oh, I think if we told everyone exactly what we did, no one would believe it," said Tina.

"Especially Tommy Anderson," commented Carol.

"Well, don't say anything to Tommy, please," Joe begged.

"Oh, we won't say anything to Tommy," said Tina.

"Thanks. Both of you. For everything."

Carol started to get dressed, and as she did, she said, "I've got a few things to do. Why don't the two of you keep each other company for a little longer."

"Sounds good to me," said Tina.

"Oh, I don't know," Joe said.

Tina pulled the sheet over the two of them. She put her arms around Joe pulling him to her. By the time the front door to the house closed, Joe and Tina were moving in unison. The two kept it up for another half hour. Joe couldn't believe his luck, let alone his stamina.

When the two finished, they cuddled in Tina's bed for a while eventually falling asleep. The next thing Joe remembered was the sunlight shining on his face and waking up in Tina's bed, naked, with her, also naked.

Joe, facing Tina, kissed her lightly on the lips. She started to stir.

"Good morning," Joe said sheepishly.

"Morning Joe," Tina said rubbing her eyes.

"Thanks for last night, Tina."

"You're welcome. It was fun."

"Sure was."

"Joe, why don't you jump in the shower while I start a pot of coffee."

"Ok."

Joe went into the bathroom turning on the water in the shower. Tina went to the kitchen and put on a pot of coffee. While it was brewing, she went to the bathroom, slid the glass door open and joined Joe. The two took turns helping each other wash. They made love right there in the shower.

"Wow, Tina. That was great."

"Joe, haven't you ever made love in the shower before?"

"No. And I have never been with two women at the same time before."

"See. There are still good things in life you can learn from."

"I get your point."

"Joe, you should listen to Carol more closely. She could help you out more than you think."

"You think?"

"I know. How do you think you were able to rise to the occasion so much last night and this morning?"

"I don't know. This never happened to me before."

"You had some help."

"If you mean you and Carol, you're right."

"That and a little extra help from Carol."

"What do you mean?"

"She gave you a little extra edge last night."

"I don't understand?"

"She put a Viagra in your drink."

"I don't take Viagra."

"You did last night. And it definitely worked."

"You think the Viagra made it possible to be with both of you at the same time?"

"And again this morning."

"I'll have to get some of those for myself."

"You're missing the point Joe. You didn't even know your performance was being altered."

"Yeah, and for the better."

"That's one way of looking at it."

"Is there any other way?"

"Joe, when the Viagra did its thing, it had a marked effect on you, and you didn't even know it was happening."

"Oh, I knew something was happening."

"No, you knew the result, not the cause."

"That's what Carol is trying to tell you. Some things can dramatically alter the desired outcome without the person being affected even knowing."

"How does knowing this help me?"

"It's all in how you use the information."

"Carol used her knowledge to get your performance enhanced."

"I guess."

"You could use that kind of knowledge to help you in achieving your goals."

"Like what?"

"Like winning that tournament."

"How?"

"You could do things to impact your competitors."

"What, give them all Viagra?"

"That and other things."

"Such as?"

"Oh, putting laxatives in cookies and giving it to them."

"What?"

"I'm just saying Joe. You need to think out of the box."

"I don't know."

"Look Joe, talk to Carol. She's a lot more devious than I am. She has ideas."

"Have you two talked about this?"

48

"Not much. But we did talk about it a little when it became clear you needed some help to beat Tommy."

"I just want to beat him fair and square."

"Joe, don't be naïve. Tommy has been using psychological warfare on you for years. Every time he brings up your past, he's doing it to you."

"Hey, I never thought of it that way."

"See, he uses what he knows as an edge. You need to do the same."

"I'm not sure."

"Talk to Carol."

"I will."

The two got dry and dressed while drinking their coffees. Joe thanked Tina again for the good time and the heads up and left Tina's.

Chapter 8

Later in the day, Joe stopped into Sundancers. Dee approached him, "What'll it be Joe?"

"I'll have a beer."

"Sure thing,"

Dee went and poured a beer. While she was gone, Harry saw Joe and came over to him.

"Joe, what happened to you last night? I came back in from my office and you were gone."

"He got a better offer from Carol and Tina," Dee said as she put the beer down in front of Joe.

"So, you did a doubleheader last night, Joe. You dog," Harry jokingly said.

"Yeah, something like that."

Joe took the tournament application out of this pocket along with a fifty, and handed them to Harry.

"Good for you Joe. You should enter," said Harry.

"That's what everyone's been telling him," added Dee.

"I'll give it a try."

"That's all you can do," responded Harry. He took the money and application and put it in his shirt pocket.

"I'll enter you when I go back to my office."

"Thanks Harry. How many other golfers have entered so far?"

"I have twenty-one so far and we've only been taking entries for two days. I think this tournament idea's gonna be a big hit."

"And that should translate into more business," said Dee.

"That too," added Harry.

"Well, I'm at least entered into the qualifiers," said Joe. "Did Tommy enter?"

"He said he's going to, but I haven't seen anything yet."

"Oh well," Joe said kind of dejectedly.

"You'll do fine," said Dee.

"I hope so."

As they were talking, Carol came into the bar and took up the stool next to Joe.

"Harry, Dee," she said as she sat.

"What will it be Carol?" Dee asked.

"A dirty martini."

"I should have known," Dee said as she started to make the drink.

"How are you doing this afternoon Joe?" Carol whispered into Joe's ear, but not quietly enough to keep Harry and Dee to hearing.

"A little tired and a little sluggish, but otherwise fine," Joe responded picking up his beer.

"Two women can make a man a little tired and a little medical magic can definitely make a man sluggish," she said as she picked up her martini.

Dee looked at Harry and rolled her eyes. She thought she had an idea of what went on last night even if Joe was a little elusive about it.

Harry went back to his office to enter Joe into the tournament spreadsheet.   He waved the application at Joe as he left.

"Thanks Harry."

When Harry had left, Carol said, "Good for you Joe."

"I'll give it a try."

"We'll give it a try," Carol said and took another sip of her martini.

Dee overheard Carol's comments, "So Carol, you're going to help Joe with the tournament? What are you going to do, caddy for him? Teach him some strokes?"

"That's an interesting idea, but I think I can help him in other ways."

"I'm sure you can."

Then Dee had to go to the other end of the bar as two waitresses were waiting for her at the service bar.

When Dee had moved, Joe said, "I think my golf game is like my game with women: both unpredictable."

"Joe, you did all right last night."

"You think so?"

"Tina and I were both left satisfied."

"I still can't believe it. I usually have a tough time with one woman, let alone two."

"Well, you had some help."

"I know the two of you made it happen."

"That plus a little extra."

"What do you mean?"

"Viagra."

"So what Tina told me was true."

"What did Tina say?"

"She said you put Viagra in my drink and that's what gave me the ability to do what I did. When did you put the pill in my drink?"

"Joe, I put one in your martini. Hey, I know how guys usually react after sex. I was just hedging my bet."

"Well, it worked."

Carol smiled at him, "Sure did."

All Joe could do was say, "Wow."

"Look Joe, there are a lot of things you could do to improve your chances."

"With women?"

"With women, golf, almost everything,"

"Tina said I should talk to you about things like that. What would improve my golf game?"

"Making sure you have the edge."

"What could I do?"

"Remember that round you played with Tommy a few days ago?"

"Yeah."

"Well, you had some help beating him."

"What do you mean?"

"Tommy came over to my place the night before. I put a pill in his drink just like I did to you last night. You saw the results."

"You mean Viagra made Tommy play poorly?"

"That and him being with me for the night."

"I know what you mean. I can't get jump started, and I sure as hell would suck at golf today."

"Joe, there are lots of things you could do to make sure you have the advantage. I like to play golf too. Why don't you and me play a round and we can talk about some of my ideas."

"Sounds interesting. When do you want to play?"

"How about Monday?"

"Ok. I'll set it up."

Carol stood. She turned to Joe, "I've got a few things to do Joe. Call me when you get the tee time."

"I will."

"See you later." Carol kissed him gently on the cheek.

"Bye."

"See you Dee."

"Bye Carol."

Chapter 9

After Carol had left, Joe was drinking his beer when Dee came over to him.

"So Joe, you had a busy night last night."

"Kind of."

"I caught some of your conversation with Carol. Sounds like the two of them are taking you under their wing."

"We're just friends."

"Just be careful Joe. These women can be very sneaky."

"I will."

"So Joe, what else is going on with your life?"

"Oh, remember how I told you I spent quite a bit of time over the winter working on some new computer software for my landscaping business?"

"Yeah."

"You've got to see it. It's really neat."

"I'd like to see what you've put together."

"I have my laptop in my car; want to see it now?"

"Sure. We're not too busy, bring it in and you can set it up right here on the bar."

When Joe had gone to his car, Ron Jessup, the other bartender on duty at Sundancers said to Dee, "Joe's leaving already?"

"Nah, he has something he wants to show me. It's on his laptop. He just went to get it out of his car."

"On his laptop, huh? What is it, pictures or something?"

"Joe says he's been working on a computer program for his landscaping business. You need to get your mind out of the gutter."

"What did I say?"

"You didn't have to. I've worked with you too long now. I know what you're thinking."

"I was just asking."

"Sure."

"Here he is," said Ron.

"Can you handle the bar while I take a look at what Joe's got?"

"No problem."

Joe returned from his car with his laptop. Dee had cleared a space next to Joe's beer for him to set up the computer and he turned it on.

"So what's the purpose of your software Joe?"

"It's hard to get a customer to visualize what their property might look like when contemplating a makeover of their property. My software makes it easier for someone to make improvements by being able to see the changes visually before spending money or putting a shovel in the ground."

"Is there a big market for something like that?"

"Sure is. Imagine how much easier it would be to undertake a project where you can see what the alterations might look like before actually doing the project. Plus, my software can estimate the cost of materials and labor and can provide a list of area vendors for purchases."

"I can see how someone might find that appealing."

"Yeah, and the software can actually order the materials plus schedule most of the work that needs to be done."

"How accurate is your software for prices and scheduling?"

"It's been used by over thirty customers so far and each one using the software up front and committing to projects laid out using the software all came in within fifteen percent of the proposed cost and twenty percent of scheduling."

"That's pretty good Joe. You know how things are here on Cape Cod. Once a project is signed up, it can drag on forever."

"Yeah, I know. But part of the deal in signing up to use my software requires suppliers to commit to certain performance standards."

"And you actually got people to commit?"

"Sure did. My first thirty clients generated over $400,000 in projects. Some of it was actual landscaping work my firm did and a large part came in from usage fees for the software and royalties."

"Just how does it work?"

"I can take a picture of a client's property, upload it to the software, and then the client can use the software to make virtual improvements to the property. At anytime, the client can select some or all of the virtual improvements and request a quote. My software can isolate the request and prepare plans, inventory lists and price quotes for labor and materials."

"Sounds complicated."

"It's pretty technical, but my software is tied into a number of local businesses for prices. Once a client picks a project, the documentation can be printed and scheduled with any of the other businesses tied in to the software. It's all Internet enabled so project details can easily be transmitted to any supplier who has the same software at their end."

"Wow, Joe. You've really thought this thing out. It sounds like there might be a market for your software."

"Yeah. I've talked with a few big firms about the software and so far, they've been interested but none of the big companies has gone any further than that."

"What kind of companies have you contacted?"

"I've signed up over fifty businesses on the Cape already as business partners. Most of them are local suppliers of landscaping products or services. Recently, I talked to some people at the hardware store over on Route 134 about distributing the software to other stores in their chains off Cape and letting them set up the same arrangement with landscapers in their respective areas. They seemed real interested. They liked the fact the software interacts with all aspects of a project and helps the client manage the whole effort."

"I can see how a big chain would like something like your program. What kind of money can you license the software for?"

"I told the hardware store people I'd license them the software for $25,000 per store for a period of three years. Each store would be able to distribute copies of the software to landscapers doing business with them under the agreement. The software they distribute would steer the users back to their chain stores."

"Wouldn't that give everyone access to your program?"

"Anyone they authorized."

"How many hardware stores are there in their chain?"

"Hundreds."

Joe could see Dee thinking.

"Let's see if one hundred stores took you up on your offer, you'd get millions."

"Wouldn't that be nice?"

"Joe, you'd be rich."

"Well, it hasn't happened yet."

"I think you're on to something though."

Joe spent the next half hour showing Dee exactly what his software could do. He had before and after pictures of landscaping jobs he had undertaken. He showed Dee how the virtual image worked and then showed her the finished project.

"Joe, this is really good."

"Thanks Dee."

"You keep at it and you'll go places."

"Oh, I will."

"And entering that tournament is just another step in your future successes."

"Glad you think so."

"I do. And so do Carol and Tina."

Joe thought to himself for a minute then replied, "Oh yeah, Carol and Tina."

"Didn't you have a good time?"

"I sure did."

"Joe, I'd say things are looking up for you."

"That's what Tina said."

"Did you show her your software also?"

"Nah, only my hardware." The two laughed.

"Joe. You're naughty."

"I'm sorry Dee. I shouldn't have said that."

"That's ok Joe. I've heard worse. Say Joe, you want to go out some time?"

"You and me?"

"Yeah."

"Sure. I'd like that."

"How about next Tuesday. It's my day off."

"Ok. How about I pick you up at your place, say seven."

"I'll be ready."

Joe turned his laptop off. He finished his beer, paid his tab and said to Dee, "See you Tuesday."

"I'm looking forward to it."

Joe picked up his laptop and left.

On his way home, Joe called Bass River Golf Course and set up a tee time for Monday 10 am. Then he called Carol. He got her voice mail.

"Carol, we have a tee time for Monday 10 am. I'll pick you up at your house at 9:30. Call me if that time isn't good for you."

Joe closed his phone. He had a smile on his face as he drove home. Things were definitely looking up for him.

After Joe had left, Ron wanted to know what Dee had thought about the software Joe had showed her.

"So what did you think about what Joe had?"

"He's invented something that might be worth big money."

"Like what?"

"He wrote a computer software program for his landscaping business. He's licensed it to other businesses and has it set up to bring customers, landscapers, suppliers and other companies together in proposing projects. His software estimates the costs and proposes actual schedules to get the work done. Then if a customer likes what he sees, he can select all or part of a proposal and initiate the project."

"Really? Joe did all that?"

"Yeah, he did. Joe could be on to something big."

"Wouldn't that rub Tommy Anderson the wrong way."

"Sure would."

"Well, we'll see where all this goes."

"We'll see. Thanks Ron for handling things while Joe and I talked. He really is a nice guy."

"No problem Dee. We're not very busy."

"Thanks anyway."

Chapter 10

Joe pulled into Carol's driveway just before 9:30 on Monday morning. The sun was out, skies clear and the morning temperature around fifty degrees. Carol had already put her golf bag and golf shoes by the front steps, so Joe put the car in park, opened the back and put the clubs in. As he closed the back to his SUV, he heard a familiar voice.

"Mornin' Joe. Ready to play?"

Joe turned to see Carol coming down the steps. She was dressed in a short black golf skirt, a white golf shirt covered by a black and white hounds tooth golf jacket and a pair of sneakers. Joe noticed her socks were the same hounds tooth pattern as her jacket. Carol had her hair back in a ponytail covered by a black visor. She had on her sunglasses, and Joe thought to himself she looked good, real good.

"I'm ready. Do you think you might get cold dressed like you are?"

"If I get cold, I have something in my bag I can always put on."

"Ok then, let's get going."

The two got into his car headed towards Bass River Golf Course. The parking lot at the course was about half full. While Carol changed from her sneakers to her golf shoes, Joe went into the pro shop, paid for their golf and returned with a cart. He loaded both sets of clubs onto the cart and then put his own golf shoes on.

"We're on the 1st tee in 15."

"I like to have a few minutes to warm up. Do they have a putting green?"

"Yeah. It's right by the club house."

They stopped their golf cart next to the putting green. Carol got out beginning a stretching routine first without a club and then with a golf club in hand. Joe just stood and watched her. She was beautiful, and the sun shining on her blonde hair made it almost sparkle. After another five minutes, Joe heard the starter call out his name to take the tee.

"Campbell, party of two."

"That's us Carol. We're up next."

She confidently walked over to their golf cart, put away her putter and got into the cart. They drove to the 1st tee.

The starter was someone Joe knew, Ben Shaw.

"Joe, its ninety degree rule on the back nine today."

"Got it Ben."

"You can tee off as soon as you're ready."

"Thanks Ben."

"Are you practicing for that May tournament?"

Carol looked at Ben, "He's warming up."

Ben couldn't take his eyes off Carol. Joe didn't notice, and took out a seven iron. He walked up to the 1st tee box. Ben walked with him. The two were about thirty feet from the golf cart where Carol remained seated.

Ben said to Joe as Joe put his ball on a tee, "Wow Joe, she's a real looker."

"She sure is."

"You think you'll be able to keep your mind on your game playing with her?"

"I don't know. She's a real distraction."

"Well, good luck."

Joe took a few practice swings and then addressed his ball. He took the club back and swung hard. He made contact and his Top-Flite ball took off. It landed on the green, 165 yards away and about ten feet from the hole.

Carol used her 7-wood from the ladies tee. She made solid contact, landing her ball about two feet past Joe's.

"Nice shot Carol."

"It'll do."

"You're ahead of me."

"So it seems. But it only matters if we put it in the hole."

The two put their clubs into their bags and drove to the green. Taking her putter out of her golf bag, she said, "Looks like we'll be even after one Joe if you can sink your putt."

"Hey, you have to make yours also."

"True, but I don't have any pressure on me."

"You think I do?"

"I do."

Joe was first to putt. He lined up his ball. Carol had marked her ball and was standing right behind Joe. She wanted to see his ball so she could learn how to play her's. As Joe struck his ball, it went straight at first and then curved about two inches to the left, just missing the hole. Joe tapped in for a par. Carol, having gone to school on Joe's ball, lined her's up just outside the right hand side of the cup. She hit the

64

ball, and at first, it looked like it would miss the cup but at the last second, it moved left dropping into the left side of the hole. She had made a birdie.

The 2nd hole was a pretty straight, 282-yard open hole. All Joe had to do was keep the ball in the fairway. Joe took out his driver, and again, he took a couple of practice swings. Then hit his ball well over 250 yards. It ended up on the right side of the fairway into the rough.

"See Joe, that's what I'm talking about. I'm a distraction."
"Nah. I'm just a little stiff. I'll be ok once I loosen up."
"Stiff huh?"
"I'll loosen up."

Joe walked back to the cart, put his club away and drove to the ladies tee. Carol got out, put on her golf glove and walked up to the tee. She slowly bent over facing away from Joe placing her pink ball on a tee. As she did, she made sure Joe was watching.

Carol took a few practice swings and then addressed her ball. She had a smooth delivery striking the ball, and sent it right down the center of the fairway about 200 yards.

"Nice," Joe said as she admired her shot.
"It'll do."
"You have nice form Carol."
"You think?"
"I do."

Carol got into the golf cart, and they started down the fairway. Carol took out a pitching wedge for her second shot and again hit her ball straight down the fairway, landing just short of the green. The ball continued to roll another twenty feet ending up about fifteen feet from the hole and on the green.

"Wow! Nice shot," Joe commented.
"Like I said, it'll do."
"I hope I can do that good."
"Joe, see right there? You're setting yourself up for something less than success."
"What do you mean?"
"You're already thinking the wrong way. If you believe in your game, you shouldn't say anything until after you have taken a shot. Otherwise, your mind will be trying to overcompensate for a perceived bad shot."

They arrived at Joe's ball. He took out a pitching wedge, took a couple of practice swings and hit the ball. It went pretty high, right over the flag landing on the edge of the green about thirty feet from the hole.

"That's not so bad," said Carol.
"Guess I put a little extra into it."
"Probably trying to impress me."
"Maybe."
"Remember what I said Joe. Attitude and body language can say a lot."
"I guess. Is that some of what you were talking about when you said you could help my golf game?"
"Oh, there's way more than that. You'll see. I'll point out a few things while we play."
"I can't wait."

Joe was further from the hole, so he putted first. He walked around the green surveying his putt. Then he went through his putting routine. When he hit the ball, it was right on track for the hole. It fell a few inches short. Then he walked up and tapped it in. Par.

Carol addressed her ball. She had a smooth delivery and sank the putt. Birdie.

"Nice hole Carol."

"Like I said, it's all a mindset."

"That, and you play a good game."

"That I do."

They went to the next tee. It was a 391-yard par-4. The 3rd tee almost always faced a prevailing breeze. Joe took out his driver again, but this time, he slowed down his swing. He hit his drive straight down the fairway about 280 yards.

"Nice drive Joe."

"Thanks."

"See? I can tell you're settling down."

"Maybe. But I didn't get the distance I wanted."

"That's negative thinking Joe. You hit a good drive. It's straight and a good distance. Be happy with the game you're playing."

"I'd have to be better than that to beat Tommy Anderson."

"I don't think so Joe. Remember what I said, attitude and mindset."

"Yeah, I heard you."

Carol hit another drive a little over 200 yards again, straight down the fairway. They each hit their second shots straight, with Carol ending up about a hundred yards from the green and Joe about twenty yards short of the green. Carol put her 8-iron on the green about twenty feet from the hole for a third shot. Joe used a 7-iron to bump and run his ball to around four feet of the hole.

"Now you're getting it Joe. You're relaxing."

"Yeah."

Carol putted first, just missing the hole. She tapped in for a bogey.

Joe, suddenly feeling cocky said, "Looks like I can tie it with this one."

"We'll see."

Joe did his routine for putting. Just as he was taking his putter back, Carol lifted up her golf shirt to expose her breasts. Joe saw them as he followed through on the putt, and his ball went five feet past the hole.

"Why did you do that?" he asked.

"Just proving to you about mindset.

"That isn't fair."

"Joe, are you getting it? Tommy has been doing a job on your mind for years. I just got to you in a few seconds. You need to be focused. If not, you see what the result is. A bad shot" Carol said as she pointed her putter at his ball.

"Ok. You're getting through to me. But Tommy won't be flashing me on the golf course."

"Hey, I'm just using the tools I have to get a result. And it worked."

"Sure did."

Joe addressed his ball again and made the putt. Both had a bogey.

"So Carol, what other things could I do to improve my game?"

"It's not only improve your game, but improve your chances to win. My flashing you didn't improve my game, it just improved my chances of beating you."

"I see. So I should flash Tommy if the opportunity presents itself?"

"That would be too obvious, but there are other things you could do."

"Like what?"

They had arrived at the par-4 4th tee. Carol walked past the tee box to the wood line. There, she pointed at some shrubbery.

"See that Joe. It's poison ivy."

"Yeah."

"Do you get a rash if you touch poison ivy?"

"Yeah."

"A lot of people do. Maybe Tommy Anderson does."

"So."

"So, if he had poison ivy rubbed on his golf clubs, he might get a rash."

"But he wears a golf glove."

"Does he wear it when he putts?"

"No."

"So rubbing poison ivy on his putter might give him a rash."

"How would I do it?"

"Oh, you look for an opportunity during the round. When it presents itself, you rub it on his club. In a few holes, it'll do its job. Obviously using it during or before the qualifying rounds would be best."

"Wow. I never thought of doing something like that."

"Joe, stick with me. You can do a lot more than that."

They played holes five, six, seven and eight with Joe getting pars on five and six. He got a birdie on the 7th and a bogey on the 8th. Carol got a bogey on five, a par on six and seven and a birdie on eight. They arrived at the 155-yard 9th hole. This hole is the signature hole of the golf course. It overlooks water on the left. The green is severely sloped from left to right but it is a par-3.

Carol went first. She hit a smooth eight iron just past the hole. Joe, using a 9-iron, put his ball right next to the flag.

"Good shot Joe."

"Yours is just as good Carol."

69

"I still have a putt to make. You have a tap in."

"I'm sure you'll make it."

"Joe, look at that green. It has a big slope in it and I'm above the hole."

"Wasn't it you who said its all mindset? Think positive?"

"Sometimes skill has to come into play as well."

"Well, let's get up there and see what we can do."

The two got into the golf cart and drove to the green.

Carol surveyed her putt three or four times and then addressed her ball. She aimed about two feet to the right of the hole and hit her ball. It made a big curve and dropped right into the center of the hole.

Joe had a putt of two feet. He walked up to the ball and half leaning in, hit it. The ball lipped the cup, went around it three quarters of the way and stayed out.

"That ball should have dropped," he said in disgust.

"You got cocky Joe."

"No. I rushed the shot."

"So you learned something else now, didn't you?"

"Yeah. Nothing is guaranteed."

"Good for you Joe."

They played holes ten and eleven with Joe getting a par on both. Carol got a par on ten and a bogey on eleven. Walking up to the tee on hole twelve, Joe said, "This is the easiest par five Carol. We should both be able to birdie this one."

"Well thank you Joe. I appreciate you considering my game to be that good."

"You've done pretty good so far. In fact, I think you're kicking my butt."

"I told you, I like golf."

"Yeah, but you didn't tell me you were this good."

"I think I told you that as well. In fact, I think I showed you just how good I can be"

"We talking about golf?"

"Yeah, and other things."

Carol smiled, took out her driver, and then walked up to the tee. She took a few practices and then hit her ball just over 200 yards straight down the middle.

"Nice shot."

Then, Joe hit his ball right down the middle over 250 yards away. Carol put her arms around Joe, pulled him in to her, and kissed him. "Very nice," she said. Then, she turned and walked back to the golf cart.

They both hit their second shot. Joe's landed on the green. Carol's landed about 50 yards short of the green. She chipped on, ending up about a foot from the flag. Joe had a long putt of over fifty feet and needed to navigate a slight slope in the green. He addressed his ball. When he hit it, the ball went ten feet past the cup. His next putt found the bottom of the cup for a birdie. Carol's short putt found it as well.

"You called it Joe. We both got birdies."

"We've got another par five coming up. Let's see if we can keep this going."

They played hole thirteen. Both of them got a bogey. When they got to hole fourteen, Joe said, "There's a ravine on this one and the next hole. Try to hit to the top of the hill just before the ravine. Then you can reach the green on your second shot."

"Ok. Thanks for the advice."

Carol took out a fairway wood and hit to the top of the ravine. Joe used an 8 iron and did the same. When they arrived at their balls for the next shot, Carol looked down at the bottom of the ravine, "I'm sure glad my ball didn't end up down there."

"Yeah. You can't get any real direction from down there to the hole."

"Sounds like you've been there before Joe?"

"I have."

They both hit their second shot. This time, both of them were just short of the green. They chipped on and one putted for par. They played the next few holes at par. Standing on the 18th tee, Joe said, "You're up Carol. I need to get a birdie and you need to play very poorly on this hole or you win."

"Joe, I've already won. And so have you. Just getting out and playing has been fun. It doesn't have to be a competition."

"Then why play?"

"That's just how you guys think. Everything has to be a win-lose."

"What's wrong with that?"

"It's a mindset Joe. You have to keep things in perspective."

"Oh, like having fun, but learning, too?"

"Yeah, something like that."

Carol shot par on eighteen. Joe got a bogey but Joe's head was loaded with quite a few ideas he didn't have when the round started.

Finishing up on the 18th green, Ben watched the two walk off the green. He walked over to Joe, "Did you have a good round Joe?"

"Yeah. I shot a 85."

"Not bad."

"How about your partner?"

"She hit a home run."

"Oh, not a good golfer, huh?"

"Oh, she's pretty good. She shot a 84."

"You're kidding me."

"No I'm not. She's pretty good."

"Where you off to now?"

"We're going to stop into Sundancers and have a drink. I owe her."

"Well, have a good time."

"Will do."

Joe walked to the cart.

"I heard what you said Joe. Thanks for the compliments."

"No, thank you Carol. You opened my eyes in ways I would have never thought of."

"I'm just glad to help Joe. You can count on me."

"Thanks."

They put their clubs into Joe's SUV heading to Sundancers.

Chapter 11

The two took up stools by the windows at the bar. Dee came right over them.

"So how was the round of golf?"

"Not bad," said Carol.

"Not bad? Carol, you beat me by one and I thought I was having a pretty good round."

"Carol, you beat him?" Dee asked.

"Let's say I play an unconventional game."

"You played great Carol," Joe came back at her.

"I didn't know you were such a good golfer," said Dee.

"I used to play on the golf team at college. And I played quite a bit before my husband died."

"I should have known you'd have something like that up your sleeve," said Joe laughing.

"Carol, maybe you should enter the tournament," said Dee.

"I couldn't compete from the back tees. I only beat Joe because I hit from the front tees and he hit further back."

"But I used the white tees, not the blue. So, I should have been able to be competitive."

"Oh, you were competitive Joe. You were just out maneuvered."

"What did you do to him Carol, seduce him or something?"

"You could call it something like that."

Joe laughed. "Yeah, something like that."

Dee had to attend to other patrons at the bar. When she had walked away, Carol said, "Remember some of the things we talked about on the course Joe. You could certainly use some of what you learned out there today to help you when you compete."

"I got your point Carol. You definitely taught me a few things out there today."

"There are other things you could consider. We should talk more and plan your strategy for the tournament."

"You think I should have a strategy?"

"I do. You'll need to have one and a solid game plan for everyone you are competing against."

"That would take a lot of time."

"Not that much. But you would have to think about each match and clearly define your strategy and plans for each one. You don't know who you're playing against yet. But when you do…"

"I hadn't given it much thought."

"Joe, that's why you always come in second."

"I guess."

"Let's plan on meeting before each match when the pairings have been released. I can help you think things out. Plus, I might even be able to help you with some of the things you could do to improve your chances."

"You'd do that for me?"

"Sure I would Joe. What are friends for?"

"Ok. Then I'll plan on getting together with you before the tournament."

The two drank for another half hour talking about their round of golf. Eventually, Carol said she wanted to go home as she had a few things she needed to do. Joe paid the tab and they left.

When they had left, Dee said to Ron, "I'll bet she helps Joe out. I just don't know if he'll be able to handle her strategy."

"Yeah, she can be pretty aggressive. Whatever happened to the innocent Carol we knew when her husband was alive?"

"Katherine Sterns," was all Dee said.

"Maybe. That and the money she inherited when he died."

"She's a wealthy woman."

"And a real looker."

The two went back to bartending. About two hours later, Joe came back into the bar.

Ron got Joe a beer and placed it in front of him.

"So Joe, Dee told me about your round of golf with Carol."

"Yeah. We played Bass River. She's a good golfer."

"So I heard. I knew she had other physical skills, I just didn't know golf was one of them."

"She's real good with the putter."

"I think I've heard that one before."

The two laughed.

"That too," Joe responded as he picked up his beer and took a drink.

"Dee says you're entering the golf tournament Harry and some of the other merchants are putting on."

"Yeah. Why not."

"Hey, you might even win."

"I'd have to play my best."

"I think anyone who wins a tournament has to play pretty well. Even though it's only open to amateurs, some of these guys are pretty good."

"Like Tommy Anderson."

"Yeah, Tommy's pretty good. He might have been able to be go pro if he'd been able to control himself."

"I know all about Tommy. We've been competing for years and he's always beat me."

"Anything can happen Joe when the pressure's on."

"That's what Carol said."

"She's a smart woman."

"That she is."

"She knows how to get things done and how to get what she wants."

"You can say that again."

"Joe, I've known Carol for a few years now. She used to be a shy, quiet person as a younger woman. She married young. Her husband was very successful and died young. She inherited quite a bit of money. Then, Charles Chamberlin took some of her inheritance under the guise of investing it for her. She ended up getting the money back after Katherine Sterns figured out how to get the money back from Chamberlin. Katherine took Carol under her wing for some time, kind of teaching her the ropes of being a wealthy, attractive woman. Then Katherine died and here we are today."

"She's told me about some of the things she learned from Katherine. Some of its intimidating."

"Well, just remember, she's had an aggressive coach. If you knew Katherine, you'd know what I mean."

"Yeah, I think I know what you're talking about."

"And Carol has money. If she gets into trouble, she could buy her way out."

"I hadn't considered that point."

"Just be careful. Guys are straightforward, but women are very cunning."

Joe picked up his beer and took another drink. Ron turned and walked to the other end of the bar as another patron was waving him over. As Ron walked away, the door opened and in walked Tommy Anderson. He had a piece of paper in his hands. He selected a stool, two away from Joe. Dee saw him coming in and went over to him.

"Hi Tommy, what'll it be?"

"Nothing yet Dee."

He opened the paper he had in his hand. It was a completely filled out application for the tournament. He took out his wallet producing a fifty.

"Dee, can you call Harry in his office and ask him to come out for a minute?"

"Sure."

Dee picked up the phone, "Harry, Tommy Anderson is here and he'd like to speak with you for a minute. Ok, I'll tell him."

"Tommy, Harry said he'll be out in a few minutes."

"Then I'll take a Bud when you get a chance."

Dee drew a Bud draft placing it in front of Tommy.

Tommy turned to Joe, "You getting into the tournament Joe?"

"Yeah."

"It should be fun. Like old times."

"Maybe I'll beat you this time Tommy."

"That's the right attitude Joe. But it'll take some talent as well."

"Oh don't worry about me Tommy. I'll be ready."

"Joe, this is Tommy you're talking to. Let's see, how many times have you won anything against me?"

Joe picked up his beer and took a drink. "People change," he said.

"Sure they do," Tommy said as he picked up his beer.

"What makes you so sure the tournament would end up being you against me anyway Tommy?"

"It's being played on courses we've played hundreds of times going way back to high school," Tommy replied.

"Even if we make the cut, there'll be twenty-eight other guys vying for the same goal," was Joe's comeback.

78

"I can't think of anybody around here who might be serious competition," said Tommy.

"Maybe someone will surprise you," Joe responded.

"We'll see."

Dee came back over to Joe and Tommy.

"You two already arguing about who's gonna to win the tournament?"

"Tommy thinks there's no one around who can compete with him."

"That's the way I see it," said Tommy.

"Well, you're both in it, so we'll know in a few weeks," was all Dee added.

Harry walked through the kitchen and approached Tommy.

"What's up Tommy?"

"Harry, I wanted to give you my tournament entry form and fee."

Tommy handed Harry the paper and fifty dollars.

"I'll get you entered."

"Keep the money handy Harry. I'll be back to pick it up when the tournament's over," Tommy said in a cocky tone.

"There'll be other golfers in the tournament Tommy. You'll actually have to win to collect."

"I'm not worried."

"What about Joe?" Dee asked.

"Are you kidding me," Tommy sarcastically said.

"Yeah, and the other twenty-eight golfers," said Harry.

"Got anyone entered so far you think can beat me Harry?" Tommy asked.

"Oh, there are a few surprises," was all Harry said.

"I've been king in sports in this area for years," boasted Tommy. "Bring 'em on."

Tommy saw Tina and some other women seated in the restaurant side of Sundancers. He picked up his beer and walked to the back room.

"That guy's cocky," Dee said to Joe when Tommy had walked away.

"He's also won just about everything there is around here in sports," said Joe.

"That may be. But he was a younger man, too. You'll just have to go out there and beat him Joe. Saturday is the first qualifier. Just go do it. Someone needs to put him in his place," Dee said turning to see if anyone else at the bar needed anything.

"He'll get his someday. I hope. See you in a coupla hours Dee," Joe said as she walked away. She turned over her shoulder, smiled, and waved.

On Tuesday night, Joe picked up Dee at her place. They went to Chapins Restaurant for dinner followed by a walk on the beach. They talked about a lot of things while they dined and later when they walked. Even though Dee knew about some of Joe's activities with Carol and Tina, she didn't press him for anything more than dinner and the walk.

When Joe dropped Dee off at her place around 9 pm, Dee said, "Joe, I had a good time."

"Me too."

"We should do it again."

"I'd like that."

Joe stood at Dee's door in an awkward way. Dee moved in close to him and kissed him. He returned the kiss.

"Maybe next time I'll have you come in."

"I'd really like that."

"Good night Joe."

"Good night Dee."

Joe left. He had a smile on his face.

Chapter 12

On Saturday morning at 8:00 am, Joe made his way to the Bayberry Golf Course in Yarmouth. He, along with thirty-six other golfers, would compete in the first qualifying round.

Joe parked his SUV in the second tier of the parking log, put his golf shoes on and took his golf bag out of the trunk. A worker from the course stopped behind his vehicle.

"You in the tournament?"
"Yeah."
"Throw your bag in the back and get in. I'll take you up the hill to the pro shop."
"Sure."

Joe locked his vehicle and as they got to the clubhouse, Joe saw his nemesis, Tommy Anderson standing by the putting green talking to other golfers.

"Crap," Joe said.
The driver giving him a ride said, "Did you forget something in your car?"
"No. It's nothing."

"Well, let me know if you need anything."

"Thanks for the lift."

Joe took his clubs out of the back of the cart, laid them in the rack at the bag drop and went into the clubhouse. He walked up to the signup table.

"Name?"

The woman sitting at the table was probably forty, but was smiling and could have been younger. Her eyes were a vivid blue, and under her baby blue visor looked bluer. Joe stood there for a few seconds just looking into them.

"Name?" she laughed.

"Joe Campbell."

She looked his name up in the pre-signup sheets she had in front of her.

"You're paired up with Len Simpson. Your tee time is 9:15."

"Thanks."

Joe went outside, picked up his clubs and walked down to the putting green. Tommy Anderson saw him coming down, "So Joe, you're in."

"I told you I thought I'd give it a try."

"You should make it through the qualifier Joe. Ten of the thirty-six guys here today will make it to the tournament and you're better than most of these guys."

"Thanks for thinking so Tommy. I didn't think you thought much of my game."

"Joe, we're talking about this qualifier, not the tournament."

Joe got the message. He took his putter out along with a few balls and walked onto the practice green. He saw his playing competitor, Len Simpson, at the back of the green practicing. He had met Len some time ago and even played a round of golf with him at Bass River Golf Course once, so he walked over.

"Hey Len. Guess we're paired up together."
"Yeah. Should be a good time."
"What do you think of the competition?"
"I don't think either of us should have any trouble making the cut."
"Well, good luck."
"You too."

Joe spent the next twenty minutes practicing putts and loosening up.

At 8:30, the starter started calling out names for the qualifying round to begin. Tommy Anderson was in the second group. All the other golfers waiting for their tee time stood behind the 1st tee watching the early groups tee off. Tommy walked up to the white tee box, put his ball down on top of a big tee. Then he took a few practice swings. Everyone on the tee box and surrounding area was quiet. He took his big driver back and hit his ball high, straight and long on the 395-yard par-4 1st hole. The hole is a slight dogleg to the right about 250 yards out and Tommy's ball went at least that far.

Tommy turned to the crowd, "Now that's how it's done."

He put his driver away and picked up his bag.

Joe, standing with the crowd alongside the 1st tee, spoke to Len, "He's always bragging."

Len said, "He did hit a nice shot."

"I'm not saying he's not a good golfer. He just likes to rub it in."

"I know the type."

The two watched the next few golfers tee off. At 9:10, the starter announced, "Simpson and Campbell, you're up next."

Joe and Len flipped a coin to see who would hit first. Len was first to hit. He took a few practice swings, and then addressed his ball. He hit a long ball that drifted a little right as it rounded the corner 250 yards down the fairway.

"Nice shot Len," Joe commented.

Then it was Joe's turn. He took a few practice swings. He addressed his ball. When he took his driver back, he thought to himself, "Just swing slow, make contact and get things started. Be in control."

Joe's swing was smooth. He made contact sending his ball straight down the fairway about 260 yards.

"Good shot Joe," Len said.

"Thanks."

The qualifier had started for Joe. He picked up his bag and walked down the hill with Len. Joe hit a fairway wood for a second shot landing at the edge of the green. Len's drive had gone over 300 yards so he hit a nine iron for a second shot putting his ball about ten feet from the cup. Joe two putted and Len made birdie.

"What a good start," Len commented with excitement in his voice.

"Yeah. I'm happy with my start," said Joe.

"Then let's do this," said Len as the two fist bumped and walked to the 485-yard par-5 2nd."

"Right on."

They walked up to the 2nd tee. From the tee box, they couldn't see the green as the fairway bends quite a bit to the left.

"Len, you going to hit another big drive on this one like you did on the 1st?"

"Nah. It'll take me three to make this green. I might be able to do it in two but I think I'll play it a little conservative and be sure I don't screw up."

"That's sound thinking. I'll do the same."

"You know Joe, I'll bet Tommy Anderson hit it for all he could. He's an aggressive player."

"You don't have to tell me. I've been competing against him all my life."

"So you know how aggressive he can be."

"Yeah."

"He'll run into someone someday who beats him at his own game."

"A friend of mine was saying the same thing. She said Tommy's recklessness would catch up with him."

"Let's hope it catches up with him in this tournament."

"Wouldn't that be nice?"

"Sure would."

Len teed his ball up first. His shot went straight down the right side of the fairway out about 265 yards.

"That's a nice shot Len."

"Conservative, but nice."

Joe did the same. Their balls ended up about two feet apart. They picked up their bags and walked down the fairway. Len took out a 5-wood for his next shot.

"I can usually hit a five 210 to 220. That should get me near the green."

He hit his shot and it landed a few feet short of the green.

"Nice," Joe said.

Next, Joe took out his 3-wood.

"Going for it Joe?"

"We hit about the same Len. I think I need a little extra club."

Joe took a few practice swings. When he made contact with his ball, it took off on a low flight heading right towards a sand trap on the right side of the hole. His ball ended up in the middle of the trap.

"I should've paid attention to your shot Len. I got too aggressive."

"You can get your ball out of that trap pretty easily Joe. It's just a pitch. I wouldn't worry about it."

"Yeah, you're right."

They picked up their bags and walked up to the green. Len used his wedge, hitting his ball to fifteen feet from the hole. Joe used his sand wedge but he got all ball. It sailed to the backside of the green.

Len said, "Those shots could have been better."

"You're right about that. Let's make these putts."

Len ran his putt a few feet past the hole and sank the short tap-in for a par. Joe almost sank his thirty-footer that lipped out at the last second. He tapped in for par as well.

They played the next few holes each getting pars. When they got to the 505-yard par-5 7th, Joe said, "You're one under Len. I'm at even par. You think our scores will be enough to qualify?"

"I sure hope so. We'll have to check when we finish the 9th hole and see where we stand."

"Yeah, it's not like the PGA where they have running scoreboards throughout the course."

"We have to enter our halfway score with the starter when we make the turn, so he'll know."

"I just hope we're in."

Len teed up his ball. He hit his driver pretty hard sending his ball over 300 yards straight down the fairway. The 7th is a pretty straight hole, just long. Joe was next to hit.

He teed his ball up and took a few practice swings. When he made contact, his ball went down the left side of the fairway about 305 yards.

"Nice hit Joe."
"You too Len."

They picked up their bags. Walking down the fairway, Len said, "We should get a little aggressive on this next one. You don't get too many of these."
"Good point."

Joe was first to hit. He selected his 5-wood. When he made contact, his ball hugged the left side of the wood line bending back to the right as it approached the green. It landed about thirty feet from the cup.
"Nice Joe."
"I left the face open a little and it paid off."
"Sure did."

Len hit his shot right at the pin. It almost hit the stick as it landed, rolling a few feet past the cup.
"That was real nice," Joe said.
"Thanks."

The two picked up their bags and walked to the green. Joe was first to putt. He took quite a bit of time surveying the green looking at his potential shot from a number of angles. Then he addressed his ball. At first, it went to the left, then back to the right eventually heading right at the cup. It stopped one inch short of the cup.
"What a shot!" Len shouted with excitement.
"Thanks."
Joe tapped it in for a birdie.
Len then hit his putt in for an eagle three.

Len said to Joe, "Well, we definitely took advantage of that hole."

"We just have to keep it up."

They both shot par on numbers 8 and 9. As they made the turn, Len walked over to the starter to record his score. He was two under par. Joe walked over and gave his score of 35 to the starter.

"You two are doing pretty good," the starter said.

"How about the other guys?"

"Only a few groups have come through so far. Only Tommy Anderson is doing better than you two."

Joe sarcastically said, "Oh, what's Tommy shooting?"

"He shot a 32 for the front nine."

"Wow," Len said.

"That's so Tommy," Joe said as he picked his clubs up heading towards the 10th, teeth clenched.

When the two had gotten to the 10th tee box, Len said, "It looks like we're in good shape to make the cut."

"I guess," was all Joe said.

Both golfers played the back nine one under par. When they finished their round, they went to the starter to register their final scores.

"Simpson, 69."

"Campbell, 70."

"That's pretty good playing gentlemen. So far, you two are leading the way."

"What happened to Tommy Anderson?"

"Oh, he was disqualified. He hit a ball into the woods on eighteen and then was caught dropping a ball out of his bag when he couldn't find the first one he hit."

"You're kidding me," Len said.

"No, he'll have to enter another qualifier if he wants to play in the tournament," the starter said.

"See Joe, even Tommy can screw up."

"He'll be more careful on the next qualifier," Joe said.

"I don't know. I think he'll be even more aggressive."

"He's got two more shots at qualifying. He'll be in the tournament somehow," was all Joe said, shaking his head.

The two shook hands and decided to hang around for a while to see how the other golfers played. At 4 o'clock, the last group finished. Len had finished in first place, Joe in second. Both qualified for the tournament.

"Joe, I'll see you at Sundancers in a half hour for the recognition dinner."

"See you there."

After each qualifier, the tournament organizers had decided to hold a dinner and recognition ceremony at different places in the area to promote businesses. Sundancers was the first place.

Joe walked into Sundancers. A buffet had been set up on the stage for the golfers. Joe took up a stool at the bar.

"How'd you do Joe?" Dee said getting him a beer.

"Pretty good. I shot two under for a 70."

"Sounds good."

"Yeah. I took second place and my playing partner Len Simpson got first."

"You beat Tommy again?"

"Not really. He was disqualified."

"What?"

"Yeah, something about hitting his ball into the woods and then dropping another ball when he couldn't find the first one."

"Who caught him?"

"I don't know. But it happened on the last hole. Someone up near the green saw him do it and he ended up being disqualified."

"Good. He deserves it."

Len came into the bar and took up the stool next to Joe.

"Dee, give Len a beer, would you?"

"Sure."

Dee brought the beer back, "So Len, Joe said you took first place in the qualifier."

"Yes I did."

"Then you're the winner today."

"For what?"

"Didn't you read the rules?"

"Nah. I don't expect anything unless I actually win the tournament."

"Nope. You get something for winning the qualifier."

"Really. Like what?"

"I think you get a plaque and gift prizes put up by the merchants sponsoring the tournament."

"How about that."

"And Joe, you get something as well."

"What do I get for coming in second?"

Dee pointed to the door as Carol was coming in. "I think your prize has just arrived."

The three laughed as Carol approached.

"What's so funny?" she asked.

"Oh nothing," Dee said. "We were just talking about the qualifier. Len won and Joe came in second."

"Really? What happened to Tommy?"

"D-Qed."

"See Joe, things are looking up," Carol said.

Harry had come out of the kitchen as the food was being put into the buffet. He took a microphone from the DJ booth and spoke.

"Hi everyone. I just want to take a few minutes to thank everyone who participated in the first qualifier. Len Simpson posted the best score. He shot a 69."

Everyone clapped as Harry recognized Len for the day's lowest score.

Carol, seated next to Joe said, "That's my favorite number. What did you shoot Joe?"

"A 70."

"That's not bad either."

"He finished second," Dee added.

"Joe, after dinner, why don't we go to my place and work on your score?"

"I'd like that."

Harry had a plaque for Len and gift certificates from a number of merchants in the area. In all, he got about a $1,000 worth of stuff for winning the qualifier. It looked like it was a good night all around, except for Tommy Anderson.

Chapter 13

Carol took Joe to her place after the recognition ceremony had wrapped up. When they got to her house, she told Joe she wanted a drink and maybe something light to eat. Joe asked if she had any cold cuts in her refrigerator.

"There's honey ham, salami and cheese in the middle drawer."

"I'll make up a snack, you make the drinks."

"Martini ok for you Joe?"

"Sure."

He took the cold cuts and cheese out of the refrigerator. Then, he put a slice of ham on the cutting board, put a few slices of salami on the ham and a slice of cheese on the salami. Then, he rolled all three into a long roll. He stuck toothpicks every half-inch apart from one end to the other keeping the roll in tact. Then, he sliced in between the toothpicks creating pinwheel appetizers. He put them on a platter with some honey mustard, crackers, cheese and grapes. Then he brought them into the living room.

Carol had made both of them a martini. She had put olives in Joe's and onions in her's. What Joe didn't know was she put something else into Joe's. Carol looked at the appetizers, "These are so cute Joe. How did you learn to do that?"

"I don't know. I was just playing around with some cold cuts one day and came up with it."

She picked one up, dabbed a little mustard on the pinwheel and took a bite.

"These taste pretty good, too."

"They do, don't they?"

She picked up her martini.

"Here's to you Joe. You are a person of many talents."

Joe picked up his martini and joined the toast.

They ate all of the pinwheels and finished their martinis. Carol took the plates to the kitchen and cleaned up. She made them each another drink. When she came back into the room, she put the drinks on the table and sat close to Joe. She put her arms around him and gave him a passionate kiss. When she did, Joe started to get aroused. After a few minutes of foreplay, Carol reached down and undid Joe's belt and pants. Within a few minutes, they were both naked on the couch.

Within minutes, both had orgasms, and when they were finished, Carol asked Joe to join her in taking a shower. He did.

Joe spent the night at Carol's, and after the golf success, he felt this was a perfect ending to a great day. He had earned it.

When Joe got up, Carol had already showered and dressed. She was having coffee in her kitchen.

"Morning," Joe said retrieving a coffee cup.

"Good Morning Joe. Did you sleep well?"

"Sure did. Sex always does that to me."

"I've got to get going. I have an appointment at ten."

"What time is it now?"

"9:30. Joe, make yourself at home. I should be back around one."

"I'll take a shower and then get going. I've got a few things to do today myself."

"Ok. Maybe I'll see you later today at Sundancers."

"Maybe."

"See you then."

Carol picked up her purse and keys. She was conservatively dressed in navy pants with a matching navy jacket over a yellow blouse. She looked like she was going to a business meeting.

After she had left, Joe finished his coffee, showered, got dressed and cleaned up. When he was done, he went outside locking the door behind him. He got into his SUV. Checking his watch, it was 11:30. He decided to stop at Sundancers for lunch.

Coming into Sundancers, he saw Ron bartending. Joe took up a stool near the door.

"Hey Joe, what can I get you?"

"Where's Dee?"

"Oh, she's off today."

"Can I have a beer and a menu?"

"Sure."

Ron went poured a beer, grabbed a menu and placed both in front of Joe, "So I understand you did pretty good in yesterday's qualifier?"

"Yeah, I placed second."

"Looks like you're in the tournament?"

"Yeah."

"I heard about Tommy Anderson."

"Yeah, he did something wrong and got himself disqualified."

"So he'll have to enter one of the next two if he still wants to compete. I assume there are still slots open for him. If his luck holds out."

"Guess so. Say Ron, I'll have one of those Cheeseburgers in Paradise, medium."

"Sure. Fries?"

"Yup."

Ron entered the order into the computer.

"Should be out shortly."

"Thanks. So Dee's off today?"

"Yeah. She worked six days in a row. She needed a break."

"Oh. I wanted to talk to her about something."

"Anything I can help out with?"

"Probably not. I had showed her a software package I had written over the winter and she gave me some ideas. I wanted to tell her what I had come up with."

"She was telling me about your software. Said it has real potential."

"I think it does. Since I showed her the package, I've been able to sign up a few more businesses and I'm already seeing it put to use."

"That's great Joe. Maybe you'll strike it rich."

"Maybe. Anyhow, I just finished my first month where the software is running through my server when it's used. My cut for the month was just over ten thousand."

"As in dollars?"

"Yeah."

"How does that work?"

"It's the way everything is going these days, Cloud Computing. The applications are all housed on a server somewhere. The PCs or even smart phones for that matter access the system via the Internet. When that happens, I get a fee."

"No kidding?"

"Yeah. It's really neat."

95

"Sounds like it.

"In addition, I took Dee's advice and formed a limited liability corporation for my software."

"What's it called?"

"American Landscape Systems, LLC."

"Sounds good."

"And, I came up with a catchy name for the system, The Virtual Landscaper."

"Yeah. It has a ring to it that gives one a visual picture."

"That's what I thought."

"Too bad she isn't here. I know she would be real excited for you."

"I'll tell her about it when I see her."

"So Joe, have you celebrated the new company and name yet?" Harry said standing behind Joe.

Joe turned to Harry, "Not yet."

"I heard what you said to Ron. You need to mark this occasion properly," said Harry. "Set us up with a shot of Jack Daniels, Ron."

"Will do."

Ron set up three glasses. Harry held his up and made a toast. "Joe, to your successful business venture. And for coming in second in the qualifier."

Ron said, "I second that."

The three raised their classes, touched them and then drank the shot.

Harry said, "I'm looking forward to your continued success Joe in the tournament and remember us when your business interests take off."

"Don't worry Harry. How could I forget Sundancers?"

The phone rang behind the bar. Ron answered it. "Harry, it's for you."

"I'll take it in my office."

Joe was sitting by himself at the bar when Tommy Anderson came in. Tommy took up a stool two away from Joe.

After Tommy had ordered a beer, Joe had to ask him, "So, Tommy, what happened to you in the qualifier?"

"I hit a ball into the woods, and when I found it, the ball had a slice in it, so I took another ball out of my bag and replaced the one with a slice."

"And you were disqualified for that?"

"Someone reported seeing me take a ball out of my bag and then hit it from the wood line. I didn't get an official ruling on the sliced ball so I probably should have taken a stroke."

"Can you enter one of the remaining qualifiers?"

"Sure. As long as there's room and I pay another fifty bucks."

"Are you going to try again?"

"That's why I'm here." He took out a fifty and another entry form. "Ron, can you give this to Harry? I want to get into the next qualifier."

Ron picked up the form and money. "Sure Tommy. Harry's on the phone right now but I'll make sure he gets this as soon as he's done."

"Thanks."

Tommy finished his beer, threw a five on the bar and left. He passed Carol in the parking lot on his way out.

"Tommy, you leaving so soon?"

"Yeah. I just wanted to drop off another tournament entry form. I've got a date tonight."

"Really?"

"Yeah. I'm taking Tina to dinner in Hyannis."

"Why Tommy, you're becoming a real gentleman."

"It's just dinner Carol."

"And then what?"

"Oh, who knows."

97

"Tommy, this conduct is so not you."

"What do you mean?"

"You're usually so brash and cocky. Did getting disqualified affect you that much?"

"No. It had nothing to do with my demeanor."

"Well, have a nice time."

"Oh, I will. And so will Tina."

Carol walked in and sat next to Joe. She still had on the navy slacks and yellow blouse, but had taken off the jacket. Joe could see the blouse was fairly see-through, and the bra underneath was covered in lace.

"You look good. Did your meeting go well?"

"Yeah. I was meeting with my financial advisor. He's the best."

"If my business works out, you'll have to introduce me to him."

"Sure."

"Get you a drink?"

"Yes. I'll have a martini."

"Ron, can you get Carol a martini, onions, please?"

"You got it."

"I saw you talking to Tommy. What was that about?"

"Nothing really. I was just asking him why he was leaving."

"What did he say?"

"He said he has a date."

"Tommy?"

"Yes. He said he's taking Tina to dinner in Hyannis."

"We're talking Tommy Anderson here, aren't we?"

"I had the same reaction. Tommy has never been the gentleman type for as long as I've know him."

"Me either."

"I think his thinking is a little screwed up having been disqualified from the qualifier. But he said otherwise."

"That's so unlike him."

"It is. I'll have to talk with Tina tomorrow and see how it went."

"Will she tell you?"

"Sure. Girls tell each other everything."

"Kind of like what the guys do the next day. Gloat."

"Kind of."

"Since Tommy put in another entry form for next weekend's qualifier, he's going to get serious about the tournament. I think it's getting to him."

"That's what I said to him in the parking lot. But he denied being affected."

"I guess I'm going to have to bring my "A" game if he qualifies."

"Remember what I've told you Joe. You need to have an edge. Use everything available to you. Whether it's Tommy or anyone else. Tommy's already psyching himself out. He's doing you a favor."

"I know you told me Carol. But it's just not me. I'm not sure I could do some of the things you've suggested."

"Sure you can. Remember, physical distractions and mental distractions can both be your friend."

"When your opponent makes a mistake, you pounce on him? Is that what you're saying?"

"Joe, you just need to assess every situation and respond accordingly. It's just like my putting the Viagra in his drink. Minimize the downside. Hey, it worked for you when you, Tony and Harry played a round of golf with Tommy."

"So you said."

"And it worked for you the night you, me and Tina got together."

"I guess."

"No guessing about it. Do you think you could've performed that way with two women without help?"

"No."

"Damn right you couldn't. Joe, when the situation presents itself, take advantage of it, be discreet and don't get caught."

"Is that what you would do?"

"I do it all the time."

"I'll have to remember that."

Kevin Martin, the DJ from WCOD, had been at the DJ booth setting up for a while. While Carol and Joe were talking, Kevin started his live on-air show broadcasting from Sundancers. In the background, Carol could hear, "This is Kevin of WCOD broadcasting live from Sundancers. We're having a sign-up party down here for all those golfers who want to enter the Mid Cape Open. Come on down, grab a bite to eat, have a drink, listen to some good music and enter the tournament qualifier."

Then, Kevin started the music, and walked around the bar saying hello to everyone he knew. He stopped at Joe.

"Joe, how've you been?"

"Pretty good Kevin."

"Did you have a good winter?"

"Yea. I worked on a new business venture over the winter and it's just getting going."

"Want me to give it a plug on the radio?"

"Not just yet. I'll come by the station when I'm ready to begin an advertising program."

"Good."

Kevin turned to Carol.

"Carol Tindle. I haven't seen you in quite a while."

"I've been down south for a little."

"And now you've come back?"

"Yeah. I came back for Katherine Sterns's services, and decided to stay."

"That was too bad about Katherine."

"Did you know her?"

"We went out a few times."

"Well, I guess that means you knew her."

"I got to know her when she worked for Harry as a hostess."

"Ah, I see."

"Say, you seeing anybody these days?"

Joe turned to look at her to see what her response would be.

"I'm not committed to any one man, Kevin. What did you have in mind?"

"Interested in doing anything on the air?"

"Oh, I'm interested in doing it anywhere and everywhere."

Kevin looked at Joe who was rolling his eyes.

"Then how about we get together after I finish my show tonight?"

"If I'm still here, we could do that."

"Ok. Then let me get back to doing the show."

Kevin went back to the DJ booth. He had an extra bounce in his step along with a big smile.

When Kevin finished his show, he looked around for Carol. She was still there seated on the opposite of the bar.

"What did you think of the show, Carol?"

"Based on how crowded the place was tonight, I'd say you did a good job."

"That's what Harry wanted. I'm done here for the night. What are your plans?"

"I was thinking of going home and going to bed. Tomorrow's another day."

"I was thinking along the same line." Kevin said with a smile.

"Then why don't we get out of here and go to my place. We could go to bed at the same time."

"I like the way you think."

"Oh Kevin, you'll like a lot more about me come morning."

Carol paid her tab and they left.

Chapter 14

On Saturday, the second qualifying round was played at Dennis Pines Golf Course. Joe Campbell was already in so he decided to go and just watch. Tommy Anderson joined thirty-six other golfers for the qualifier. He was paired with Bill Johnson, another local golfer out of Hyannis. Joe and Tommy knew Bill having competed against him in high school. Joe approached Bill as he was practicing on the putting green.

"Bill."

"Joe Campbell. How the hell are ya?"

"Good."

"You in this qualifier?"

"Nah. I already qualified."

"Oh, you played Bayberry?"

"Yeah, last week."

"I thought Tommy played last week also? But I see him here today."

"He did. He got D-Qed."

"I heard something about that but didn't know what the details were."

"Tommy said it had something to do with a cut ball and taking another one out of his bag."

"Didn't he get a ruling?"

"Guess not."

"Well, I'm paired up with him today."

"Good luck."

"It isn't the first time. The last time I played against him was in the State sectionals in high school."

"Oh yeah. I remember. Didn't you beat him?"

"Sure did. By three strokes."

"As I remember, he wasn't very happy about it."

"He tried his best to distract me at every chance. He dropped clubs while I was putting, coughed when I was driving and even tried to bury my ball once in the sand."

"I know what you mean. He'll do whatever he has to do to win."

"Well, two can play that game."

"What're you gonna to do?"

"I don't know. But if the situation presents itself, I'll have to take advantage of it."

"Someone else told me something like that just recently."

"Hey Joe. When you're playing someone like Tommy, you have to be prepared."

"I guess. Good luck Bill."

"You gonna watch today's play?"

"Yeah. I think I'll hang around for a while and see how things go."

"I'm gonna get back to practicing Joe. Maybe I'll see you later."

"See you Bill."

Joe walked off the practice tee. He decided to go down to the 1st green and start watching the qualifier from there.

The weather for the second qualifier was perfect for golf. The sun was shining, no breeze and temperatures were already near 50 and expected to reach near 60 by mid-afternoon. Joe had brought a bag chair with him. He set it up just off the 1st green.

For the first two hours, half the golfers coming through had hit par on the 1st. The other half had shot bogey or worse. Only one golfer had a birdie. A little after ten, Joe could see Tommy Anderson and Bill Johnson coming down the fairway. Tommy had out drove Bill by 50 yards on the 373-yard par-4 from the blue tees. Bill's second shot was a 125 yard nine iron landing about eight feet from the hole. Tommy landed a wedge shot about two feet from the hole. Bill got par on the hole and Tommy recorded the second birdie of the day on his first hole.

Joe decided to follow the two for a few holes. He picked up his chair and started for hole two. He was ahead of Bill and Tommy by about five minutes and had just sat down when he saw Tommy walking into the woods on the left side of the 2nd fairway. Joe thought Tommy must have hit his drive too far on the 369-yard dogleg par-4 2nd. He could see Bill following Tommy.

A few minutes later, a ball came flying out of the woods not making much forward progress. Tommy must have been behind a tree or something. When Tommy emerged from the woods, Bill was right with him. The two golfers walked to the middle of the fairway where Bill hit his second shot. It landed at the edge of the green right in front of Joe's chair. Tommy hit his third shot landing it in the right side bunker. As the two golfers reached the green, Bill saw Joe sitting by his ball.

"Hey Bill."
"Joe."

"Bill, I saw you and Tommy coming out of the woods. What was that all about?"

"Tommy had hooked his drive into the woods. I wanted to make sure he didn't pull something getting back out."

"That's smart thinking."

"I know. I don't mind getting beat fair and square but I'm not going to let someone beat me unfairly."

"You'll have to watch him every step of the way."

"I plan to."

Tommy hit his ball out of the sand trap landing it fifteen feet from the hole. It took him two putts to get it in giving him a double bogey. Bill took two putts as well ending up with a par. Joe watched a few more holes. Tommy was playing pretty aggressively and shot par on the 471-yard par-5 3rd and 188-yard par-3 4th. He got a birdie on the short 476-yard par-5 5th and par on the 420-yard par-4 6th. Bill had shot par on holes three through six.

At the 176-yard par-3 7th, Tommy almost got a hole-in-one. His six-iron hit the stick on the fly. The ball stopped eight feet from the cup after the ricochet. Bill safely landed his tee shot eighteen feet from the cup. Bill's first putt fell short of the cup by six inches. He tapped in for par. Tommy's putt lipped out and he had to settle for a par, too.

Joe decided to skip the next few holes and take up viewing at the 357-yard par-4 11th. On his way to the 11th, he stopped by the clubhouse to see how the golfers were doing. To his surprise, Tommy was in ninth place with Bill in tenth.

"Tommy might not make the cut if he doesn't get it in gear. Now wouldn't that be a damn shame."

As he watched the golfers come onto the green on the 11th, it looked pretty clear to Joe the pressure of competing was affecting some of the golfers. They were amateurs after all. Three golfers hit their second shot into the water. Two hit their shots up on the side of the hill and very few golfers were figuring the green out on the 11th.

Joe had recognized the golfers just finishing putting as the group right in front of Tommy and Bill. He looked back up the fairway to see where the next group's balls had landed. To his surprise, he saw one ball about fifty yards from the green. The other ball was a little over a hundred yards from the hole back up the hill in the center of the fairway. Joe knew the long ball had to be Tommy. Sure enough, when the golfers went to their balls, Tommy's was the one just short of the green.

Bill's next shot landed on the green twenty-five feet from the hole. Tommy hit a lob shot just past the flag with enough backspin to bring the ball back to within three feet of the cup. Bill walked up to the green and set his bag down next to where Joe was sitting.

"Bill, was that Tommy's drive?"
"Yeah. He's unconscious right now. Really in a groove."
"I checked the scores when I came to eleven and he was in ninth place."
"Since then, he's birdied three holes and shot par on the rest."
"How are you doing?"
"I was in tenth at the turn and I think I'm holding my own."
"Well, good luck the rest of the way."
"Thanks Joe."

Bill shot par and Tommy got a birdie. Joe decided to move on to hole seventeen and watch the action on the final two finishing holes. Bill ended up shooting birdie on the 513-yard par-5 12th, Tommy a par. The both shot par on the 172-yard par-3 13th and 405-yard par-4 14th. On the 472-yard par-5 15th, Tommy shot a double bogey having put his tee shot

106

into the woods and having to drop a ball when he couldn't find it. Bill shot a par. They both shot par on the 344-yard par-4 16th.

When Joe saw the two on the tee box at the 186-yard par-3 17th, he thought Tommy must have kept playing aggressive and was sure to make the cut but Bill was the first to tee off, which meant he at least fared better on sixteen. He hit his 5-iron right on the green ending up nine feet from the cup. Tommy put his drive into the bunker on the left side of the green. As Joe watched, he could see Tommy slam his 6-iron into the ground on the tee box.

As the two came up to the green, Joe said to Bill, "Did things go wrong for Tommy?"

"Yeah. He dropped a few strokes over the last few holes. I think he thinks he might not make the cut."

"I checked again when I came to seventeen. There were only five groups left on the course at that time. The cut line was sitting at 81."

"Wow. I'm at 79 right now and Tommy's at 81."

"It could be tight for both of you."

"Plus, we don't know how the other four groups are playing."

"The group behind you didn't play the front nine very well. So you don't have to worry about them. The other groups were pretty close."

"Thanks Joe. I'm just going to have to play careful."

"What about Tommy?"

"I think he's just going to remain aggressive."

"I'll see you when you finish."

"See you then."

Tommy Anderson took his sand wedge out of his bag. He surveyed the shot from a number of different angles. Finally, he got into his stance. The lip of the trap in front of him was relatively flat, not presenting an obstacle. Tommy walked back to his bag and took out his 7-iron. He went back into the trap and hit a bump-and-run shot. The ball raced across the fifty feet of green between him and the hole stopping right on the edge of the cup. As Tommy walked out of the trap, his ball dropped into the cup.

"That's the way to do it," Tommy could be heard as he walked up to the hole, bent over and took his ball from the cup. A birdie.

Bill two putted getting par.

The two golfers went to the 18th a 405-yard par-4. Tommy was first to hit. He pounded his drive 300 yards down the center of the fairway. Bill did the same but was thirty yards behind him. Bill hit a wedge on to the green twenty feet from the cup. Tommy hit a wedge a little long ending up at the edge of the green thirty feet from the hole. Bill took two putts to get down ending up with par. Tommy hit his putt aggressively running it past the hole ten feet. His second putt stopped just short of the hole and he tapped in for a bogey.

Joe greeted Bill at the starter's shed where the golfers had to report their scores.

"How'd you finish Bill?"

"Par, Par. I ended up with a 79."

"Congratulations. You're in."

"I thought I'd need to get one birdie to get in or else be in a playoff."

"Nah, only one other golfer was in contention for the tenth spot and he doubled the 18th. All you had to do was shoot par."

"Great."

"How did Tommy finish?"

"You will not believe it. He birdied seventeen. Then he hit a monster drive on eighteen. His wedge approach was long. Then he got aggressive on the putt putting it well past the hole. The return putt ended up being short and he tapped in for a bogey."

"So he shot 81."

"Yeah."

"Then I think he's going to have to enter the last qualifier if he wants to compete. The starter said the cut line is 80."

"Guess so."

Tommy saw the two talking and walked over.

"Looks like you didn't make the cut Tommy."

"No kidding? I'll make it next time." He said in an arrogant tone.

Tommy reported his score with the officials and left.

"He doesn't seem too happy," commented Joe.

"His game was inconsistent today. I know he wasn't happy with the way eighteen ended."

"Let's see how he does next weekend."

"I'm sure he'll settle down."

"Unless he gets distracted again."

"I know what you mean."

"I'm going over to Sundancers for a beer Bill. Want to come?"

"Nah. I'm going to the recognition buffet at American Pub. Even though I wasn't low score, I'd like to talk to the other guys who made the cut."

"Ok Bill, see you soon."

"You too Joe."

Chapter 15

Joe arrived at Sundancers. The bar was pretty full so he took up a stool at the end of the bar by the DJ booth. Dee saw him come in, poured him a beer, and put it in front of him on a coaster.

"Hey Joe. How you doing?"

"Pretty good Dee. I just came from the Dennis Pines Course. They played the second qualifier there today."

She nodded her head across the bar to where Tommy Anderson was sitting. He had a beer and a shot in front of him.

"Yeah. I know. Tommy came in a little while ago. Guess he didn't play so well today."

"He just missed the cut. Didn't make a putt on eighteen he needed to make."

"I heard him say something about you being there and distracting him on one of the holes when you sneezed or something like that."

"Oh, so Tommy's putting the blame on me for not making the cut?"

"Something like that."

Just then, Joe felt a pair of arms come around him from behind. A woman's voice whispered in his ear, "So you took my advice."

Joe turned slightly to see Carol behind him. "I didn't do anything to make Tommy not make the cut."

"Joe, there's nothing wrong with leveling the field on Tommy."

"But I didn't do anything."

"That's not what Tommy said."

"I know. I don't remember doing anything to effect his game."

"But you do admit you watched him play today?"

"Yeah. I was there. I was following Bill Johnson."

"And Tommy?"

"Tommy was playing with Bill."

"So you were in a position to distract Tommy."

"Carol, why are you pressing me?"

"Just trying to get make sure you're in the right frame of mind to use everything you have at your disposal to win should you end up being in a close situation."

"If I sneezed or something, it was by accident."

"That's not the right way to look at it Joe. You need to be proactive if you want to be a winner."

"I don't know."

"Joe, you need to listen to Carol. She's right," Dee said as she turned to go wait on other people.

"Joe, if Tommy makes the cut next week and you end up in the tournament where it's just you and Tommy, God forbid, to determine the winner, you have to be prepared."

"That's weeks away right now. I'll worry about it if and when it gets to that point."

"You need to be preparing now mentally. Remember what I said. It's a mindset."

"Yeah. I know what you told me."

"Just think about it. Tommy's blaming you for a sneeze or something. He says he missed a putt because of it. His mindset was affected."

"I don't know."

"Even if it wasn't, perception can be a valuable tool."

"Yeah, Yeah. You want a drink Carol?"

"Go ahead Joe, change the subject."

"It's just not me Carol."

"It better become you if you want to win."

While they were talking, another woman came into the bar, Ann Benard. She walked around the bar not finding any open seats. When she got to the end where Carol and Joe were, Carol said, "Hi Ann. How you doing?"

"Good Carol. This place is pretty busy tonight."

"Sure is."

"Ann, do you know Joe Campbell?"

"Hi Joe. I know we've met before."

"Hi Ann. Yeah, I met you in here once before when you were talking to Katherine Sterns."

"That's right. I didn't remember when, but I did remember meeting you."

Joe continued, "Where have you been? I haven't seen you in here lately."

"I moved to Boston a little over a year ago. Just after Katherine died. My company promoted me. Along with the promotion, my new job required me to be in the home office in Boston. I couldn't take the daily two hour commute so I got an apartment up there in town."

"Have you moved back here now?"

"No, I'm only in town for a few days R&R."

Carol said, "Well you've come to the right place."

"I see a lot of the regulars I used to see when I lived here," she said looking around the bar.

"Yeah, there's a golf tournament going on sponsored by Sundancers and some of the other businesses around."

"Oh, I see. What's up with Tommy Anderson over there," Ann said looking across the bar watching Tommy down a shot.

"He didn't make the cut yet," said Joe.

112

"Yeah, he's sulking and pouting," added Carol.

"I think I'll go talk to him and see if I can cheer him up," said Ann.

Ann left them and walked around the bar to Tommy. When she got there, Tommy greeted her with a big hug and kiss.

Joe said, "Looks like she's just the thing Tommy needed to change his mood."

"That and a little romp in the sack," said Carol.

"You think?" asked Joe.

"They go back a long way Joe. Ann and Tommy hooked up quite a bit from what I remember."

"Well, looks like he might get lucky again tonight."

"It'll be good for him. Too bad it's not next Friday night."

"Why?"

"Because he'd have his play effected for the next qualifier next Saturday."

"Positively or negatively?"

"That remains to be seen. That gives me an idea."

"Of what?"

"Of what I think I'm doing next Friday night."

"What's that?"

"Tommy."

The two of them watched Ann and Tommy for a little while. Tommy was getting a little loud and could be overheard saying things about how his play had been affected by some of the spectators and officials at the first two qualifiers. Ann had tried to quiet him down but wasn't having too much success. At one point, she whispered something into his ear getting his attention. A few minutes later, he paid his tab and the two of them were seen leaving the bar.

Carol said, "Looks like Ann's taking Tommy home."

113

"And it's a good thing," said Dee as she brought Joe another beer.

"Yeah, he's getting a little out of control," Carol added.

"Inebriated?" Dee questioned. "He's totally out of it."

"What's Ann going to do with him in that condition?" Joe asked.

"Oh, she'll think of something," Carol responded.

"I bet she will," Dee added.

When Ann and Tommy had left, Carol said to Joe, "See Joe, Tommy is just like everyone else."

"I wouldn't go that far," said Dee. "He goes way overboard on some things."

"No. I mean in how things affect him."

"Like liquor?" Dee said.

"Liquor, sex, anger, golf. You name it. Right now, I could beat him in golf or anything else for that matter," Carol said confidently.

"She's got a point Joe," Dee said turning to survey the bar to see if anyone needed anything.

"I think I understand."

"You stick with me Joe and you'll benefit," Carol said.

The two talked for another hour. Then they paid the tab and left.

Chapter 16

Later in the week, Tommy Anderson stopped in to Sundancers to find out if there were any spots remaining open in the third qualifying round.

"Ron, is Harry in?"

"Sure, he's in his office."

"Can you give him a call and see if he'll talk with me for a few minutes?"

"Sure."

Ron picked up the phone pressing the intercom number one. He talked for a minute and then hung up.

"He'll be out in a minute. Can I get you a beer?"

"Sure."

Ron poured Tommy a Bud placing it in front of Tommy. Tommy took a few drinks. As he put the glass back down on the bar, from behind he heard, "Tommy, what can I do for you?"

Harry had come through the kitchen walking up behind Tommy.

"Harry, are there any openings left for this week's qualifier?"

"Yeah. We've got twenty-seven golfers entered so far leaving nine more slots to fill the field."

"I'd like to enter again."

"Have you filled out another entry form?"

"Not yet. Can't you use the same one I put in last time?"

"No. It's for a different course and there's another fifty dollar entry fee."

"Got any forms left?"

Ron went to the register and picked something up from behind it. He came back placing the form and a pen on the bar. "Here's one."

"Thanks Ron," said Harry. "Fill it out and give Ron the entry fee. I'll be back in a few minutes to pick it up."

Tommy filled out the form. He took two twenties and a ten out of his wallet handing the money and entry form to Ron.

Harry came back into the bar about ten minutes later, "I just got off the phone with one of the other tournament sponsors, and there's only one spot left."

Ron went to the register picking up Tommy's entry form and money. He handed it to Harry.

"Here's Tommy's completed entry," Ron said extending his hand to Harry.

"Looks like you're the last one in," Harry said to Tommy. "Think you can get your game together this time?"

"Not only am I going to keep my game together Harry, I'm gonna win the qualifier and then win the tournament."

"That's the attitude Tommy," Ron said.

Tommy finished his beer, paid his tab and left. After he had gone, Ron said to Harry, "You think he could win?"

"He's got the game but who knows."

"He just has to stay off the stuff and the women."

"That's not easily done when you have an ego the size of Tommy Anderson's," said Harry turning and walking back to the kitchen.

"Well, we'll see in a few days," Ron said, turning to unload the dishwasher.

The third qualifier was being held at Bass River Golf Course, and the thirty-six golfers all assembled at 7:30 am. The weather was a little cold for springtime, around fifty degrees and cloudy. A breeze had picked up overnight coming off Nantucket Sound right up the Bass River. Play would definitely be affected by the wind.

Tommy Anderson showed up a little after 7:30, took some time on the practice range and putting green and was ready to play. The starter began announcing the pairings. Tommy looked over the competition and to his surprise, saw Tony Davis in the group. He walked over to him.

"Tony, you playing?"

"Yeah. There was one spot left in the qualifier as of last night. Harry said I could have the day off if I wanted to give it a try."

"I thought I took the last spot."

"You did until someone called in yesterday and had to cancel. Harry wanted to have a full field so he asked me if I was interested."

"I know you play, but I didn't think you played competitively."

"I played in college many years ago. Used to be pretty good."

"No kidding?"

"I was a scratch golfer back then."

"Who would have known," Tommy said sarcastically.

"So we're playing together," Tony said.

"That's what the starter said."

"Oh Boy."

"What does that mean Tony?"

"Hey, I know you Tommy. You can be a hot head. I'm just here to have a good time and fill in. I don't want to hear any crap from you about my game when we start playing."

"Tony, what have I ever done to you?"

"Not to me personally, but I see you around the bar all the time and I won't put up with any BS."

Tony turned and walked away. He certainly said what was on his mind to Tommy. When he walked away, Tommy saw Tony walking towards Joe Campbell. Tommy went and picked up his bag and then went to the 1st tee. It would be forty-five minutes before he and Tony would tee off.

When Tony approached Joe, Joe said, "I see you had words with Tommy."

"I just put that prick in his place. I'll take none of his crap playing with me."

"Tony, you're taking this seriously."

"Not really. I just don't want him to try to get inside my head."

"Well, you told him."

"That I did. So Joe, you going to hang around and watch?"

"Yeah. You'll see me from time to time. I want to see what the competition looks like for the tournament."

"I'll be the one with the attitude," said Tony.

"That's the way to think," Joe said.

"I mean with the frown," Tony came back with.

"Why a frown?"

"I'm paired with Tommy Anderson. Any other way you think it could go?"

"I guess I see your point."

"I got to practice some putting Joe. I'll see you on the course."

"Good luck Tony."

"I'll need it," he said taking his putter out of his bag and heading towards the practice putting green.

A half hour later, the starter announced, "Anderson and Davis. You're on the tee in five."

Tony and Tommy picked up their golf bags and walked over to the 1st tee.

Chapter 17

Tommy was first to hit. He took out his club along with a new ProV1 golf ball. He put his ball on a long tee on the right side of the tee box. Tony was standing off to Tommy's right, "Remember how you played the last time you and I played this course Tommy?"

Tommy looked at him with a smirk on his face, "Yeah, I remember Tony. Don't worry about me. I plan on playing a lot better today."

"Tony, please. And you'd better. Didn't you shoot a 97 or something like that?"

"Something like that."

Tommy took out an 8-iron. He addressed his ball, took a smooth swing, and made contact. His ball flew straight landing eight feet from the cup. He put his club back into his bag, "You're up Tony."

Tony took out a 7-iron. He took a few practice swings. When he hit his ball, it flew straight to the green landing twenty feet from the cup.

When the two golfers walked up to the green, Tommy said, "Looks like I'll be one up after this one."

"We'll see. And you're not playing against just me. You're playing against thirty-four others, too," said Tony.

He lined up his putt. He hit his ball sending it just past the cup. Then he walked up to it and tapped it in for par. Tommy took little time to line up his put. He took one practice swing and addressed his ball. He dropped it into the center of the cup for a birdie.

"That's better than you did a few weeks ago Tommy."
"Like I told you. I'm focused."
"So you say."

They went to the 2nd hole, a straight away 310-yard par-4 from the blue tees. Both golfers played the hole conservatively making par.

At the tee for the 425-yard par-4 3rd, Tony said, "Didn't you bogey this one last time we played?"

"Yeah. Don't expect that to happen again."

"Then the tee is yours," Tony said stepping to the back of the tee box with driver in hand.

Tommy went through his routine. He had slowed his swing down somewhat from the last time they played. Maybe Tony's comments were having an effect on him. As Tommy made contact with his ball, he hit it high and straight down the middle of the fairway about 290 yards. He watched it land, and then turned to Tony,   "Your turn."

"Hey, I'm not the one who pretends to be king of the hill."

"That's because you're not and I am."

"Still, I'll just play my game."

"Hey Tony, you're not getting any shots this time."

"Don't need them. My game may be slow, but it's reliable."

Tony hit his ball 240 yards right down the center of the fairway.

They each hit their second shots. Tony landed a fairway wood on the fringe of the green. Tommy put a 9-iron shot on the green thirty feet from the cup. Tony used his putter even though he was a few feet off the putting surface and almost sunk the putt. He tapped in for par. Tommy two putted for par.

Tony said, "That's an improvement."

"Sure is. Hey, I was a few over last time we played this course. Now, I'm one under."

"You'll have to keep playing this way to make the cut Tommy. Another 97 and you'll be out."

"I'm not shooting a 97 today. I can feel it."

Tony shot par on the next four holes. Tommy continued to play well. He had birdies on number four and seven and par on five and six. The two golfers walked up to the tee box on the 8th hole, a 488-yard par-5.

"You should be able to make this green in two Tommy with that big swing of yours."

"I'm playing under control today Tony. I might have been a little more aggressive the last time we played but today, I'm doing what I have to do to make the cut."

Tony knew Tommy was right and his game definitely showed it. The last time they played, Tommy couldn't buy a par let alone a birdie. But on this day, Tommy was in a zone. He hadn't bogeyed a single hole.

Tommy was first to hit. He addressed his ball, took a slow swing, and struck his ball sending it down the center of the fairway.

"Nice shot. I guess you're right Tommy. You are playing better."

"Plus, we're not drinking this time."

When he had played with Tony, Harry and Joe, they had two coolers of beer in their golf carts. By the time they were on this hole the last time, Tommy had already drunk a six-pack.

Tony hit his usual 240 yard drive straight. As he put his club into his bag, Tommy said, "Usual boring game Tony."

"Yeah. And I'm playing at par."

"You'll have to do a little better if you want to make the cut."

"I don't know Tommy. If the other competitors play aggressive, par may just make the cut. This course doesn't suit aggressive players too well. It's more of a finesse course."

"Maybe so, but I think you'll have to get more aggressive if you want to be playing next week."

"I'll stick with my game just the same."

"Suit yourself."

They finished the hole with Tony making par and Tommy scoring a birdie.

On the 9th hole, Tommy started to get aggressive. He hit a 7-iron a little strong ending up past the hole and down hill on the severely sloping green. Tony conversely had used an 8-iron landing his tee shot short of the cup on the left side of the green. His ball rolled to within five feet of the cup. Tommy had a very difficult putt. The slope of the green required him to aim ten feet to the right of the cup. When he hit his putt, he missed the hole by three feet ending up seven feet from the cup. His return putt went past the cup by two feet. He had to settle for a bogey. Tony sunk his putt for a birdie.

Walking off the green, Tony said, "Now that's a change of pace, me getting birdie and you a bogey."

"Its only one hole."

"Yes, and nine more to go," Tony said with a smile on his face.

Both golfers shot par on the 10th hole. As they walked up to the 11th tee, a 406-yard par-4 number one handicap hole, Tony said, "Let's see how you play this one Tommy. Didn't you double this one the last time we played?"

"Maybe."

That was all Tommy said. He took out his driver and made a good shot. He was back in control. Tony continued to play his game. His drive was straight down the middle landing about 242 yards away. They both shot par.

Holes twelve and thirteen were both par-5s. Tommy used the opportunity to shave two strokes off his play by getting birdie on both. Tony shot par. The next two holes both cross a ravine. On fourteen, Tommy laid up on his first shot short of the ravine. He hit his second shot with a three wood easily clearing the ravine by fifty yards. His third shot was a short wedge shot landing twelve feet from the hole. Then he dropped a one putt for birdie. Tony, hit a full drive landing his ball right at the top of the beginning of the ravine. He hit a 5-wood over the ravine leaving him with a 100-yard wedge shot to the green. Then he two putted for par.

Tommy played the remaining holes at par and Tony played sixteen and seventeen at par and bogeyed eighteen. When they had finished, Tommy had played the course two under par, Tony was even par.

When they checked in at the starter's shed, Tommy was in first place. Tony was in ninth place with one group left in the field whose golfers were playing pretty good. The starter said to Tony, "You might make it if one of those two in the last group chokes."

"Don't count on it," Tommy said to Tony.

"There's nothing I can do about it now," said Tony.

They waited another half hour for the rest of the golfers to finish. When everyone had registered their scores with the starter, it was official. Tommy had finished first, Tony tenth. They were both in.

"Looks like you get the prizes Tommy," Tony said putting his glove, tees and balls into his bag, and putting the club covers back on.

"Looks like it," Tommy said.

Tony picked up his bag to go put it into his car. As he walked away, Tommy said, "See you at Riverside?"

"I didn't win anything Tommy. I'm going to Sundancers."

"I'll be over there later," Tommy said. Then he walked to his car and put his clubs in the trunk. He went to the Riverside restaurant for the reception after the final qualifier. He needed to collect his prizes and praises.

Chapter 18

Tommy walked into the bar side of Riverside Restaurant and Bar on Route 28 just west of the Bass River. The bar was full. He looked around and recognized some of the guys at the bar from the tournament. He took up a stool at the end of the bar. Martin Yates and his wife Helen owned Riverside. Helen greeted Tommy.

"Tommy Anderson. So you won the qualifier today?"
"Yeah. I had a good round."
Martin who was helping out with the bartending because they were so busy added, "What did you shoot Tommy?"
"Two under, seventy."
"That's pretty good."
"I had a few tough holes but mostly I managed my game."
"Think you can keep it going next week for the tournament?"
"I think so."
"I'll take a break in a few minutes to do the presentation Tommy. Don't go too far. We've got some good prizes today."

"I'll be right here Martin."

"And I'll keep an eye on him," said Helen.

Helen was an attractive woman. She stood five-foot eight, had shoulder length brunette hair, and was physically fit. Helen had on a pair of pink espadrilles, khaki capris and a top that was loose but low. It had the same shade of pink as her shoes, but was multi-colored and floral.

She had a pad and pen in front of her on the bar. When Martin had gone to assist one of the other patrons at the bar, she said, "Tommy, can you jot down who you were paired with today, what you scored and something we can say to the other competitors when we announce you as today's winner?"

"Sure."

Tommy picked up the pen. He wrote down that he was paired with Antonio Davis, the chef at Sundancers, shot a 70 and is ready to take on all challengers. He handed the pad back to Helen, she leaned over to read it and made sure Tommy was looking. Tommy could easily see down her blouse and smiled at being able to see everything she had to offer under the loose fitting clothing.

"Nice."

"Oh, you like what you saw?"

"Definitely."

"Maybe you'd like to see some more sometime."

"What did you have in mind?"

"Let's see how things play out."

"I'm game."

Martin came out from behind the bar with a microphone in hand.

"Everyone, can I get your attention for a few minutes."

It took a few minutes for everyone at the bar and in the adjoining room to quiet down. Martin walked over to the buffet set up in between the bar and table area and picked up a trophy. There were a number of other envelopes on the table and a few gift boxes. He held the microphone up again, "Helen, would you come up and do the honors."

Helen walked over. She took the microphone from Martin.

"As you all know, a number of merchants in the area have gotten together to put on The Mid-Cape Open. The final qualifying round was held today at Bass River Golf Course. This is the last qualifying reception before the tournament starts next weekend. There will be thirty golfers competing for the top prize. Good luck to all of you. At this time, I'd like to ask Tommy Anderson to come up."

Tommy drank his beer and a shot, stood up, and walked over to Helen.

"Ladies and gentleman, Tommy Anderson was the winner of the final qualifier. He shot a blistering two under par seventy today at Bass River. Tommy was partnered with Tony Davis who also made the cut. Tommy has indicated he's ready for the tournament so watch out."

Everyone clapped. Martin handed Tommy a trophy inscribed with the words 'Low Score – The Mid-Cape Open Qualifier Three'. Helen picked up the envelopes. She read each one out loud so everyone could hear what the prizes were for winning the qualifier. When she was done, everyone politely clapped again and Tommy held up the trophy.

"You're looking at a winner guys. The winner," Tommy boasted.

"I'm going to go back to the bar to help out," Martin said, as it was now two deep all around the bar and the two regular bartenders were working feverishly.

Tommy had been picking up the things he had been presented when Helen approached him.

"Want a hand?"

"Sure. I'm just going to put these things in my car."

"Where are you parked?"

"Out back over to the back of the lot."

Helen picked up two of the gifts and followed him out. It was already getting dark as they walked in between the packed parking lot to the back of the lot. Tommy opened the back of his SUV and put the stuff he had into the back. He turned and took the gifts from Helen and put them in as well. When he turned around the second time, Helen put her arms around him and kissed him.

"That's another reward for winning."

Tommy brought his arms up and pulled her to him. Then he returned the kiss passionately.

"Now, that's better," she said. "Why don't we get inside where we can get a little privacy?"

Tommy didn't have to be asked twice. He opened the back door to his SUV and they both got in. He had barely sat down and Helen went down. She took control. Tommy just sat there enjoying her attentions. While this was all going on, a vehicle pulled into the parking lot parking a few cars further out than Tommy's. Joe Campbell got out.

As Joe began to walk to the bar, he saw Tommy sitting in the back seat of his SUV, with his head tilted backwards, like he was passed out. Joe walked over and was about to tap on the window when he saw a head moving up and down in Tommy's lap. Just then, Tommy noticed Joe looking in the window. Tommy gave Joe a thumbs up and smiled. Joe turned and continued to the bar shaking his head. He didn't know who the person was with Tommy but he wasn't surprised.

Joe went into the bar side of Riverside. He worked his way through the crowd to the bar and ordered a beer. Martin waited on him.

"Martin, looks like business is good tonight."

"Sure is. The reception for the tournament qualifier is here tonight."

"Anderson won right?

129

"Tommy Anderson, right."

"I should have known."

"Were you in it?"

"No. I had already qualified, round one. I just like to know who my competition is next week."

Joe knew Martin and Helen well. He did their landscaping at Riverside and at their home. Martin got him a beer.

"Tommy's around here somewhere if you want to congratulate him on finishing first today."

"I saw him out in the parking lot. He was in the back seat of his SUV with someone working on him."

"Oh really?"

"Guess someone wanted to personally reward him."

"I guess you could call it that. Say, where's Helen? You give her the night off?"

"She's around her somewhere. She was helping Tommy, but I guess someone else distracted him."

Joe turned to see Tommy coming in the back door. Helen was right behind him. She was red in the face looking like she had just run a few miles in a workout. Tommy walked over to where Joe was standing, "Looks like we'll be competing again Joe."

"So you won the final qualifier."

"Sure did. Shot a 70."

Joe, looked at Helen trying to compose herself, "Looks like you shot something else along the way."

Tommy smiled, "Just another one of the perks of being a winner Joe. Perhaps someday you'll find out what it's like."

Martin saw Joe and Tommy talking. He walked over to that end of the bar.

"There you are Tommy. People been asking for ya. They wanna buy you a round. What'll it be?"

"Give me a shot and a beer. And get Helen the same."
Helen stepped out from behind Tommy, fussing with her hair
and blouse as she did.

Just then, Martin remembered what Joe had told him
and that she just might have been working outside the bar.
Martin didn't say anything. He just got the beers and shots.

Tommy picked up the shots and handed one to Helen.
He took the other one and downed it in one gulp. Helen did
the same. Joe looked at the two, "Helen, things look pretty
busy in here tonight."

She shook her head trying to clear out the effects of the
shot while drinking her beer. She looked at the bar seeing
Martin and the other bartenders working very hard, "Yeah. I
better get back to work. It's gonna be a crazy night."

"Already has been," Tommy said taking a drink of his
beer, as Helen finished her's and moved back behind the bar.

And like that, Helen was the worker bee again.
However, she might have to answer for her conduct later.

"Well, you go ahead and celebrate Tommy. You
earned it. I'm going to Sundancers where it's a little quieter
tonight."

"I'll probably be over in a little while. Got a few more
people to see in here. They want to buy a winner a drink"
Tommy slurred as he slid off his stool.

Chapter 19

Joe had gone to Sundancers. He saw Tony sitting at the end of the bar so he took up the empty stool next to him.

"I didn't see how you finished. How'd you do?"

"Believe it or not, I qualified. Got the last spot of the day."

"Good for you."

"Dee, give Tony and me a Jack and a beer. Dee poured a shot of Jack for both of them and two beers. When she put it in front of them, she said, "Joe, Tony was paired with Tommy Anderson today. He said Tommy finished first."

"Thanks for the drinks Dee. To us Tony." Joe and Tony toasted and threw back their shots.

"I heard Tommy won. I just came from Riverside. I stopped in to say hi to the Martins and see how things ended today. I ran into Tommy over there."

Tony drank his beer, "So Tommy's still celebrating?"

"He sure was. When I got there, he was out in the parking lot with a woman in his SUV. I think he was getting his first prize of the night."

"That's so like Tommy," said Dee. "He'll do anyone, anytime."

"I didn't go over there because I'd probably have had a run in with him after having to play eighteen holes with him." Tony said.

"I know what you mean," Joe said as he picked up his beer.

"But the guy did shoot a good score, didn't he?" Dee asked.

"Yeah. I guess he got out the kinks from the last time we played with him."

"He'll be really obnoxious next week in the tournament. Hey, Tony, maybe you'll be paired with him again."

"I sure hope not. I'll probably kill him if I am."

"Don't talk like that Tony. Tommy might be a little loud and flamboyant, but underneath he's really a nice guy."

"Dee, how can you say that?" Joe asked.

"I think she's been out with him once or twice," Tony snickered. "It's not a sound person talking Joe; it's the sound of Tommy's penis."

Dee didn't like where the conversation was going so she turned and went to the other end of the bar. When she did, Tony said, "All the women who go out with Tommy want to defend him. I don't get it."

"I'm with you Tony. The guy's a real dick."

"Well, what do you know, here he comes now."

The two turned and looked at the door. Tommy Anderson was walking in, or rather tripping in the door.

Tommy worked his way around the bar by the windows talking to a few guys who were seated there. He was rather loud, talking about his finishing first in the final qualifier. As he came to the section where Tony and Joe were sitting, he stood back, "So here you are Tony. I didn't see you at Riverside."

"I had other things to do."

133

Tommy motioned to Dee to come over. "Give everyone at the bar a drink on me Dee. I got the $1,000 first place money for winning."

"You sure you want to do that Tommy?" came a voice from behind him. Harry was standing there.

"Harry, you should have seen my play today."

"Tony already told me. He said you shot the lights out."

"Sure did," Tommy garbled.

Harry motioned to Dee to cancel the 'buy everyone a drink' order. Dee moved away pretending to be doing something for someone else at the other end of the bar.

"So you're in Tommy," Harry said.

"And I'm going to win."

"What about the other thirty golfers?"

"I've got my 'A' game back now. It'll be hard to beat me."

Tony turned to Joe, "If he keeps drinking like this, any one of us will beat him."

"You think so?" Joe responded.

"Look at him Joe. He can hardly stand up. Imagine him trying to hit a golf ball in that condition next weekend."

"Good point. Carol was telling me the same thing last week. She said competition can be greatly affected by physical and mental things."

"She's right. And that prick doesn't deserve to win anything. We should make sure his physical and mental things are in disorder."

"You planning on doing something Tony?"

"Nah. It's just the booze talking."

"I hear ya."

"You know Joe, it wasn't only a few weeks ago where Tommy shot a 97 at Bass River. Now he shoots a 70. The guy's all over the place."

"When he shot the 97, Carol said he had been with her the whole night before and his play had been affected by the night's activities."

"So we know Tommy has weaknesses. What's it mean?"

"And what can we do about it next weekend?"

"Let's see how the tournament goes. If it boils down to one of us or Tommy in the end, we might have to get creative Joe."

"I don't know Tony."

"I do."

Harry talked with Tommy for a few minutes and eventually got him to go and sit at a table to talk with Tina Fletcher. Harry brought Tina a drink and gave Tommy a coffee. Tommy wouldn't drink the coffee and instead drank Tina's drink. She had to order another one for herself.

Then Tommy started to get out of control and he was all over Tina. She tried to push him back but Tommy wouldn't be denied. Finally, Harry came out of the kitchen and saw what was going on.

"I'm sorry Tina, I thought he would settle down once I got him to talk to you."

"He didn't drink the coffee you got him. Instead, he drank my drink."

"Tommy, it's time to go home," Harry said in a firm voice.

"But I want to celebrate. I came in first today."

"You've already celebrated enough for one day. Why don't you go home and sleep it off?" Harry turned to Tony, "Can you give him a ride home?"

"Hell no. I'm not letting that prick in my car."

Harry knew Joe wasn't going to do it either. "Guess I'll have to take you home Tommy."

"Let's stop in at Riverside on the way Harry," Tommy said as Harry helped him up.

"I don't think so," Harry responded.

"I want to say something to Helen."

"It's not a good idea for us to stop anywhere Tommy. I'm just going to take you home."

Harry got Tommy out the door and into his car Harry could be heard saying as they walked out, "You can get your vehicle tomorrow Tommy."

After they left, Joe said, "Yeah, he wanted to stop in at Riverside and see Helen. I think that's who he was out in his SUV with when I got there. I didn't want to say that earlier while people could hear."

"He better hope Martin Yates doesn't find out."

"Oh, I think Martin knows. I was there when Tommy and Helen came back into the bar. Martin knows."

At that point, Dee came over. That girl had awesome hearing skills. "You know, Joe, Martin has a temper, and this wouldn't be the first time. He put a guy in the hospital once for touching Helen's breast," Dee said as she set down another beer in front of Tony and Joe.

"I didn't know that," said Tony.

"This guy had been drinking at Riverside one night. Helen tried to get him to leave. When she helped him up from his stool, the guy put his hand right on her breast. Martin went nuts and knocked the guy out. The guy ended up falling and cutting himself pretty badly. Helen had to call 911 and get an ambulance to take the guy to the hospital."

"Maybe I should have taken Tommy home," Tony said. "I could have stopped at Riverside with him. Maybe I'll have a talk with Martin just to make sure he knows about Tommy and Helen out in the parking lot."

"Tony, would you do that?" Joe asked.

"Sure he would," Dee responded.

"Hey, I can be a real prick if you get on my bad side. And Tommy Anderson is on my bad side.

"I don't know if I'd bring up the Helen and Tommy thing with Martin, Tony. Listening to what Dee said, Martin might take it out on you."

"You mean he might think I'm making it up?"

"Yeah."

"Then, you should tell him. After all you were there. He'd believe you if you told him you saw the two of them out in Tommy's car in the parking lot and she was doing him."

"Maybe so, but I didn't see her."

"I thought you said you did?"

"I only saw the top of a woman's head out in the parking lot. She was going at it in Tommy's lap."

"You said it was Helen."

"When Tommy came into the bar, Helen was right behind him. Her face was red and she was winded. You didn't have to be a genius to draw the conclusion I did."

"So, you should tell Martin."

"He saw them also. Tommy ordered a beer and a shot for both of them. It was Helen. Martin didn't say or do anything at the time. It was pretty busy in the bar. Saying something might embarrass him, too."

"Oh, Tommy's screwed," said Tony. "Martin's going to have his ass. You watch and see. We might not have to worry about young Tommy after all," Tony said finishing his beer.

"Well, I'm calling it a night," Joe said as he took two twenties out of his pocket to pay his tab. "See you Dee, keep the change. See you next weekend Tony. Get plenty of rest. We're gonna need it."

"What, you're not coming back in for the rest of the week?"

"I might. But just in case, I'll see you at the tournament."

"Have a good one Joe."

Joe got into his car and left. Tony still seated at the bar said, "What a day Dee."

"Want another beer Tony."

"Sure."

When she had put the beer in front of Tony, he said, "I can't believe that prick Tommy doing Helen."

"I don't think that's what Joe said."

"Yes he did. You heard him."

"No, he said Helen did Tommy."

"So, there's a difference?"

"Kind of."

"I don't think Martin is going to see it that way."

"Tommy better watch his back either way," Dee said as she started to clean up the bar as the night wound down.

"Oh, yeah. Tommy's screwed royally," Tony said as he picked up his beer.

Chapter 20

A few days later, Tommy Anderson was seated at the bar in Sundancers still gloating about his performance from the prior Saturday.

"I was really on my game last Saturday," Tommy said to Dee as she put a beer and shot in front of him.

"Are you talking about your golf game, Helen Yates or something else?" Dee asked him.

Tommy thought about it for a few seconds, "All of the above."

"Tony says Helen's husband Martin isn't the kind of person to look the other way and your indiscretion with her isn't something he's gonna forget."

"So what? What's he going to do?"

"From what I gather, Martin has a pretty bad temper."

"He didn't say anything to me Saturday."

Harry came out of the kitchen. He saw Tommy seated at the bar and walked over.

"Tommy, how's it going?"

"I was just telling Tommy what Tony told us about Martin Yates," said Dee.

"What did Tony say?"

"He said Martin has a bad temper and if he knows about what Tommy did with his wife in the parking lot last Saturday, Tommy had better watch out."

"Hey, Hey. I didn't do anything. She did it to me."

"Tommy. I heard you talking to some of the guys about getting lucky in the parking lot after you won the qualifier. You haven't been very discreet about it," said Harry.

"So?"

"So, Joe Campbell told us Martin saw you hand a shot and beer to Helen when you had come in from your encounter with her last Saturday. He knows you were with his wife," Dee added.

"There's nothing I can do about it now," Tommy said.

"I'd avoid Martin at all costs if I were you Tommy," warned Harry.

"Sounds like good advice to me," Dee added.

"You need to know a few things about Martin, Tommy." Harry said. "Martin has had his share of run-ins with some of the toughest guys around this area. From what I can recall, he came out on top in every situation. He doesn't have a bouncer at Riverside. He's the bouncer. He knows how to handle himself."

"So what am I supposed to do?"

"I'd stay clear of him. But if you do end up being confronted by Martin, try to apologize."

"You think that might help?"

"Probably not, but at least you tried."

"I think I'll just avoid him for a while."

Tony stuck his head out of the kitchen. "Harry, can you come in here for a minute?"

"Sure."

Harry turned and left the bar area. When he had gone, Dee said, "Tommy, I think you want to lay low for a while. It doesn't sound good for you."

"I'm not doing that. I've got the tournament in three days."

"Keep in mind Martin is one of the sponsors. He's bound to be around."

"Yeah, I'll keep it in mind."

When Harry went back into the kitchen, Tony said, "I saw you talking to Tommy out there about Martin Yates. I was over Martin's place last night and he's really ticked off at Tommy. He wanted to go out, find Tommy and put a real hurt on him but was shorthanded at the bar so he had to stay and work. I'm sure he'll be looking for Tommy real soon."

"You let me know if you see Martin coming in here. I don't want any problems."

"Maybe you want to ask Tommy to stay away until after the tournament?"

"Might not be a bad idea. If they're gonna have it out, it doesn't have to be here. Thanks Tony."

"No problem, not that I'm trying to protect Tommy Anderson. I still think he's a piece of garbage and deserves to get his ass kicked. I just don't want it to be here either."

"I'll have a few words with Tommy."

Harry walked back out of the kitchen and right up to Tommy. "I was thinking about it Tommy. It might not be a bad idea for you to hang out somewhere else the next few days so you don't create any trouble for me."

"Harry, you kicking me out?"

"Not for good. Just until the tournament's over."

"You worried about Martin Yates?"

"Not Martin, just the impact it might have on my business. Think of how it would look if there were some kind of brawl or fight at Sundancers just when I'm trying to promote the business and golf tournament. People might get

141

the wrong idea about the kind of place we are. If that were the case, the whole idea of this tournament would be for nothing."

"I guess I see your point. But I don't agree with it."

"Plus, Martin is one of the other merchants sponsoring the tournament. I'm sure he'll be here for the tournament kickoff meeting tomorrow night."

"I planned on attending the meeting as well. After all I won the last qualifier. Shouldn't I attend?"

Harry thought about it for a few minutes. "Yeah, I guess you have to be here if you want to play. But please, come late, sit in the back of the room and don't make yourself very visible."

"You asking me or telling me Harry?"

"Right now, I'm asking. But if you become a problem, I'll be telling."

"I get it. I'll play a low profile."

"Ok. Now if you don't mind, why not go somewhere else in case Martin happens to come in to talk with me about the tournament or something."

Harry turned and walked back into the kitchen.

Tommy saw Tina Fletcher leaving the bar. He walked to the door.

"Tina, you leaving?"

"Yeah. I was going to go down to Hyannis tonight. There's a good band playing at the Merchant and I wanted to see them."

"Whose playing?"

"The Brothers."

"Are you going with anyone?"

"No. If you're willing to behave tonight, are you interested in going with me?"

"Sure. Let me pay my tab and I'll be right with you."

Tommy asked Dee for his tab, paid it and left. When Harry came out of the kitchen again, Dee said, "Tommy's gone. He went to Hyannis with Tina."

142

"Great."

"You think he might run into Martin in Hyannis?"

"For Tommy's sake, I hope not."

"Well, if he does, he deserves anything he gets."

"That's for sure."

Dee and Harry went about their business for the rest of the night without incident.

Chapter 21

The night before the tournament a meeting was held at Sundancers for the participants, officials and merchants sponsoring the tournament. Harry Adams had been the primary businessman organizing the tournament, and as such, he took over as the meeting began.

"First, I want to thank all the other merchants who are participating in putting this event together. I think it will go a long way in jump starting our season."

He went around the room, mentioning all of the merchants by name, their business and what each one had contributed.

There was a round of applause for the merchants.

"Next, I'd like to recognize the thirty golfers who qualified for the tournament by competing in the three qualifying rounds held at Bayberry, Dennis Pines and Bass River golf courses. Each course did a great job running the qualifying rounds. Would each of the qualifying golfers please stand up to be recognized?"

Another round of applause was given for the golfers.

"After each round, a reception was held, one here at Sundancers, one at American Pub and the last one at Riverside. One player from each qualifier finishing with the lowest score received a number of gifts and a cash prize of $1,000. I'm sure everyone had a good time at the receptions."

Again, another round of applause was given.

"The first qualifier was won by Len Simpson who shot a 69 at Bayberry."
Len stood and waved to everyone. He was greeted with a loud applause.

Harry continued, "The second qualifier, held at Dennis Pines, was won by Russ Ford. Russ shot a 70."
Russ stood and waved. He got another round of applause.

"The final qualifier was won by Tommy Anderson. He also shot a 70 on the Bass River course. Tommy, are you here?"
Harry was looking around the room to see if Tommy was in the room. Someone stood up from behind the fake flowers separating the bar from the rear dinning room and raised a hand.
"Oh, there you are Tommy." Harry pointed to him. Everyone clapped except Martin Yates.

Tony had been seated near the kitchen. When he saw Tommy stand, he immediately looked at Martin. Tony leaned over and said to Dee, "Oh crap. Martin Yates looks like he's about to take Tommy out. I can't believe Harry had the winning guys stand up knowing Tommy was one."

Dee looked over at Martin and then at Harry. She nodded to Harry so he would look and see Martin, which he did. Harry acted quickly.

"Martin, why don't you say a few words to the competitors?"

Martin Yates composed himself quickly. He stood, and took the microphone from Harry, "Thank all of you for coming down and supporting this effort. Your participation has made the event a success already. Our businesses are already up ten percent over last year and I'm sure it's partly to do with it. Thank you and good luck tomorrow."

Martin looked back to where Tommy Anderson had been standing. Tommy wasn't there. Martin scanned the room, and then the bar. He saw Tommy heading for the door.

Harry noticed Tommy leaving as well. Before Martin could do anything, Harry said, "I'd like to go over the tournament format, rules and courses. Martin, would you hold up the posters for me? This should only take a few minutes."

Harry knew Tommy would be long gone by the time the meeting adjourned so he kept going.

Martin held up the first poster indicating the courses to be played.

"The tournament will consist of four rounds of golf to be played on four different courses over two weekends. You'll play Dennis Highlands, Bayberry, Bass River and Blue Rock Golf Course. Low score composite will be the winner. Standard golf rules will apply. We'll be using the back tees on three of the four courses. In case of a tie, a sudden-death tiebreaker will be played on holes 18, then 17 and 16, if needed, on the Bass River course until a winner emerges. Any questions?"

Russ Ford stood.

"What's the deal with Blue Rock? It's a par-3 course, not really challenging."

Harry was getting the next poster so Martin stood to address the question. Harry handed him the microphone and then picked up the second poster.

"Blue Rock is one of the top Executive Courses in the country. While it isn't long, it can be challenging. You have to bring your best short game. Some of the holes require the golfer to hit a long way over water. Some of the holes are narrow and some very easy. It isn't always just about hitting a long ball. Plus, Red Jacket Resorts, who owns Blue Rock, had been a key merchant in putting this whole thing together. We strategically placed it third in the rounds, so it's not the course that will directly dictate a winner. I think all of you golfers will have a good time playing there. It should be interesting."

Russ sat down. Then Tony raised his hand. Harry acknowledged him. Harry handed the second poster to Martin and he held it up. It contained a complete list of the pairings for the first round.

"Yes, Tony. You have a question?"

"Yes. Are the pairings the same for all four days?"

"Not necessarily. The pairings will be made daily based on composite score. To begin the tournament, the lowest scores attained by each golfer during the qualifying rounds have been used to determine pairings. You can find your names on the poster Martin is holding up. Golfers with the highest qualifying scores will tee off first with the lowest scoring golfers going last."

Tony leaned over to Joe who had been seated next to him, "Good. I don't have to worry about being paired with Tommy."

"I don't either."

"Well, not yet anyway."

"Good point."

147

"Looks like Tommy will be paired with Russ and Len. That should be interesting."

"Tony, you ever played a round with either of them?"

"Nah. But from what I hear, Russ is a real good golfer. He was one of the tops in this area coming out of high school a few years ago."

"Yeah, and Len is no slouch. He has been one of the best amateurs around here for some time."

"It should be interesting."

Harry looked to Tony, "And by the way Tony, you're in the first group to tee off tomorrow."

"Exactly what time do I need to be there?"

"7:30 am."

"Let's see. That means I have to wake up at 6. The last time I saw 6:00 am was on an all-nighter."

Everyone in the room laughed.

Harry said, "Just don't be late or you'll be disqualified."

"I'll be there."

Harry asked if there were any more questions. There were none. "Ok, then the meeting's over. The bar's open. Good luck everyone."

All the golfers went around talking with those they knew, everyone except Tommy Anderson. He was nowhere to be found.

Harry walked over to Martin Yates, "Buy you a drink Martin?"

"Sure Harry."

The two stepped up to the bar right next to where Joe and Tony were sitting.

"Dee, can I have a beer and get Martin whatever he likes."

"Sure."

"Can I have a beer and Jack, Dee?"

"Got it."

"So Martin, I think everything went well, don't you?"

"Pretty much. Looks like this event will turn out to do all we expected."

"And then some," Joe added.

Harry saw the expression change on Martin's face from a smile to a frown. It was pretty clear Martin was thinking about the Tommy and Helen incident. Harry quickly changed the subject.

"You're going to be one of the officials at Blue Rock aren't you Martin?"

"Yeah."

"Me too. Think we'll have to do anything out of the ordinary?"

"Nah. It should be pretty much settled down by then. If there are any issues, they'll surface during the first two rounds."

"I hope so."

Tony leaned into Joe, "Looks like round one will be real interesting. I'll bet Martin does something to get Tommy back."

"Like what?"

"I have no idea. But I can't wait."

Chapter 22

On Saturday morning, the thirty golfers along with most of the merchants sponsoring the tournament were at Dennis Highlands Golf Course. The practice green was a buzz of activity as was the driving range. The restaurant at the course was open for breakfast sandwiches and doughnuts, with coffee, soda, tee and energy drinks available. Harry, Martin and a few other merchants were sitting at a table having coffee and talking.

"Harry, who do you think has the best chance to win?" asked Martin.

"I don't know. I think Russ Ford might surprise everyone. And then again there's Tommy Anderson. But he can be very erratic."

"I still have a beef with that guy. I don't want him to win anything."

"I heard about Tommy and Helen."

"She said he asked her to help him put his stuff in his car after the recognition buffet held at my place. Then, when he got her outside, he put the move on her. I just don't know why she didn't walk away."

"Tommy tells a different story Martin. I'm not sure you'll like his version."

"What did you hear Harry?"

"Well, Tommy said he told Helen he was going to put the stuff he won in his car but she insisted on helping him. He says she came on to him when they were out in the parking lot. In fact, he said it was her idea to get into his car."

"Why would she do something like that?"

"I don't know, but then Tommy said she took over once they were in the car and she told him to put his head back and just enjoy it."

"I can't believe she would do something like that."

"Joe Campbell said he saw Tommy with a woman in his car that night and she was definitely giving it to him. Joe's a pretty upstanding guy. He wouldn't lie."

"How could he be sure it was Helen?"

"Joe said he saw Tommy and Helen come into the bar together a short time later and she looked like she had been overheating. Joe thought you saw them as well."

"I don't remember seeing her with Tommy."

"Joe said you gave Tommy two beers and two shots and he gave one of each of them to Helen who was standing behind him."

"I couldn't see who he gave the drinks to but I did see Helen come out from behind the group a minute or two later. I just assumed she had come from the other room."

"I'm sorry I'm the one who confirmed your doubts Martin."

"It's not your fault Harry. Helen and I have had our differences from time to time and I know she likes the attentions of the younger guys. But that Tommy Anderson didn't have to rub it in my face at my own place after I gave him the trophy and other things that night. My wife wasn't on the gift list."

"Martin, you're letting it upset you. Why don't you go outside for a few minutes and cool off?"

"You're right Harry. I'll be back in a few minutes."

151

Martin got up and went outside. When he did, he saw Tommy Anderson taking his golf bag to the driving range. Martin went to his car and took out two older golf clubs, one a lob wedge and another being a chipper/putter. He walked over to the practice range and when Tommy wasn't looking, he put the two clubs into Tommy's bag.

At 7:45 am, the starter called Antonio Davis and two other golfers to the 1st tee. The tournament was about to begin. Joe Campbell was standing by the starter's shed when Tony walked up.

"You look like crap Tony," Joe said to him.
"Yeah. I haven't gotten up this early in years."
Then Tony took out one of those five-hour energy drinks, popped it open and drank it. Then he took out a second one and did it again.
"You might want to go a little slow with those things Tony."
"I do these all the time. Helps get me going."
"Well, good luck."
"Yeah, Yeah. I'm here to play a round of golf. I don't expect to be competing for anything other than not having to play any rounds with Tommy Anderson."
"You despise him that much?"
"I just don't want to have to listen to his crap for five hours while I'm trying to play golf."
"I know what you mean."

"Davis, you're on the tee," came the command from the starter.
Tony picked up his bag and walked with his two playing partners to the 1st tee. He was the first one to hit. He put his ball on a rather high tee. Then he took one practice shot. His next swing made contact and he hit his ball 245 yards right down the center of the fairway on the par-4 324-

yard 1st hole. They were playing from the blue tees for the competition.

Ben Peters, who had been paired with Tony said, "Nice shot Tony."
"Thanks. It's the energy drink doing all the work."

The other two golfers both hit their first shots and the tournament was underway.

Over the next hour, six other groups of three started out their first round of the tournament. Finally, at 9 am, the starter announced, "Campbell, Connors, Williams, you're next on number one."
Joe Campbell was a little nervous. He picked up his bag and headed to the first tee box. Williams was first to hit followed by Connors. Both golfers hit their drives safely down the center of the fairway over 250 yards out. Joe was next.
He put a brand new Pro-V1 on his tee. Then, he took a few practice swings. Finally, he stood behind his ball looking down the fairway. Taking a big breath, he stepped up to the ball. His take back was slow and he followed through with grace. As his driver struck the ball, it exploded forward ending up 280 yards down the right center of the fairway. Joe had started out in good shape.

The golfers in groups eight and nine began their tournament following Joe Campbell's group. At 9:30, it was time for the last group to be called up.

Tommy had stayed on the practice range for an hour and twenty minutes hitting practice balls. He only used his driver and 5-iron. When he was ready, he put the clubs back into his bag, picked it up and walked back to the starter's shed. He took out his putter and went to the putting green next to the starter's shed. Tommy had practiced putting for another fifteen minutes when he heard the starter call his name. It was time for the last group to go to the 1ˢᵗ tee.

Tommy joined Len Simpson and Russ Ford for the walk to the tee box. As they started to walk away from the starter's shed, Martin went over and said something to the official for the tournament. The official called to the three golfers, "Gentlemen, I forgot to check your bags."

Tommy turned, "For what?"
"The application specified the number of clubs and supplies each golfer can start with. We just need to make sure the rules are being followed so everyone starts and ends with the same advantage."
"Or what?" said Tommy.
The official said, "Any rules violations will result in penalties or possible disqualification, depending on the violation."
"Ok, so let's get this over with," said Len as he walked back to the official. "I want to play golf while the sun shines."

The official counted at Len's clubs, and checked his balls, tees, ball markers and assorted supplies in his bag and hanging on his bag. "You're all set Mr. Simpson."
Russ Ford followed Len. The official looked through Russ Ford's bag, "You're all set Mr. Ford."

Then the official had to walk over to Tommy Anderson who was sitting on a bench while all of this was happening.
"Your bag Mr. Anderson?"
"It's that one next to the fence," said Tommy.
The official looked through the bag. "You're all set Mr. Anderson."

Martin was standing back by the starter's shed with a smile on his face. When the official gave Tommy the OK,

Martin said, "How can that be? I thought a golfer can only have fourteen clubs in his bag."

"He only has fourteen clubs."

Martin watched as Tommy picked up his bag. When he did, Martin saw the two clubs he had put into Tommy's bag laying on the ground next to the practice green behind where Tommy had been sitting.

Tommy, Len and Russ went to the 1st tee.

Chapter 23

Tony had a pitching wedge shot of 80 yards to reach the green. He had a smooth swing, making contact with his ball and then took a 4-inch divot out of the ground. His ball went very high landing just past the flag. It had enough backspin on it drawing the ball to within three feet of the cup.

"What a shot Tony," Adam Crane, the third golfer in Tony's group, said.

"I don't ever remember putting backspin on my ball, ever."

"Still, that was a great shot," added Ben Peters.

Ben hit his second shot on the green as well, about twenty feet from the cup. Adam hit his second shot over the green and had to chip back on. When the hole was done, Tony had a birdie, Ben a par and Adam a bogey.

The group went to the 2nd hole. Tony was first to hit. He put his drive, again, about 250 yards right down the center of the fairway on the par-5 524-yard hole.

"You're in a zone," said Ben.

"Not really. I'm just trying to play within my game."

"We'll see," Ben added.

The three played the front nine pretty much the same as the first hole. Tony shot par on the 2nd, 3rd, 5th, 6th and 8th holes. He got birdies on the 4th, 7th and 9th holes. At the turn, he was four under par. Ben was at one over par and Adam was eight over par.

Harry was standing at the starter's shed when the first group made the turn. Ben Peters walked up to the tournament official, "Peters, 36."

"Nice playing Ben."

"If you think my score was nice, Tony's four under."

"You're kidding me?"

"No, the guy's unconscious. He said it's the energy drinks he had before we started, but he's playing great."

Tony and Adam were now registering their scores with the official at the starter's shed. The first scores were being put up on the leader board. Harry looked up and sure enough, Tony was four under.

"Tony," Harry called out to him.

"Yeah?"

"Where did you find that golf game?"

"Don't know. Things are just clicking today."

"Keep it up. You're the leader."

"Oh boy. Just what I wanted to hear."

"You don't sound happy."

"Oh, I am. It's just that my game will probably go down hill from here."

"Think positive. You'll do ok."

Tony, Ben and Adam walked off ready to start their back nine. Over the next hour, groups came in registering their scores with the tournament official.

Joe Campbell was having a pretty good round as well. He shot par on 1st, 3rd, 4th, 5th and 9th holes. He got an eagle on the 2nd, and birdies on the 6th, 7th and 8th holes. As Joe walked up to the tournament official, Harry was standing there.

"How'd you do Joe?"

"Pretty good. I'm at 30, five under par."

"Pretty good? That's excellent."

"The course is playing pretty easy today. The greens are putting true and there isn't much wind."

"Anyway you look at it, you're playing great."

"I see Tony's doing pretty good, too."

"Yeah. He made the turn four under."

"Really?"

"That's what I said. Ben Peters is playing with him and said Tony's been playing really well."

"Ben would know."

"Well, keep it up Joe. You and Tony could end up in the final group tomorrow if you both continue to play as you did on the front."

"See you later Harry."

Joe picked up his clubs walking towards the 10th tee box with his playing partners Tom Connors and Sean Williams.

Tommy Anderson had been able to control his emotions as he played the front nine. He got a birdie on the 1st hole to kick things off.   On the 2nd, Tommy hit his drive over 300 yards and almost went out-of–bounds on the left side of the fairway. He was able to place his second shot, a 5-wood, on the fringe of the green and then two putted for a birdie. On the 177-yard par-3 3rd, Tommy almost got a hole in one. His ball landed two inches from the cup and stopped eight feet away. He made the putt for a second birdie. Tommy shot par on the 4th, 5th and 6th holes. On the 187-yard par-3 7th, his ball hit the flag and dropped straight down. He tapped in the six-inch putt for birdie. He made par on the 8th and 9th holes.

Making the turn, Tommy approached the tournament official.

"Anderson, 32."

"Nice front," the official said to Tommy.

"So, by how much am I leading the field?"

"You're not leading Mr. Anderson. Joe Campbell posted a 30 and Antonio Davis a 31. You're in third place."

"You have got to be kidding me. Campbell and Davis?"

"Yes. And from what I've heard so far, they continue to play well."

"We'll see if that's good enough. I'm on fire."

Tommy joined his playing partners Len Simpson and Russ Ford on the 10th tee. He was determined to do well on the back. He didn't want to come in second to Joe, let alone Tony. Russ Ford had registered a 34, one under par for the front and Len Simpson was at even par.

On the back nine, Tony continued to play well. He shot par on the 10th, 12th, 13th and 14th; he got a birdie on the 11th. When he arrived at the long 563-yard par-5 15th, Ben Peters said, "You've been playing great Tony. Let's see how you handle this long one."

Tony took out another five-hour energy drink. He downed it, took out his driver, and hit his tee shot. It sailed 290 yards down the left side of the fairway ending up just into the rough. He hit his second shot with a 3-wood 240 yards back to the center of the fairway and then did a bump and run shot to within ten feet of the cup. He made the putt for a birdie.

"Guess you still have it going," Ben said to Tony.

"I'm sure it'll be gone soon."

"I don't know," Ben said.

Tony had made birdie, Ben and Adam both got a par.

Tony again made par on each of the remaining holes to finish the back nine with a 35. He was five under for the first round. When he registered his score with the starter, he noticed he had been in second place on the leader board. Joe Campbell was one ahead of him. But what annoyed him was Tommy Anderson was one behind.

The tournament official posted Tony's score. For a little while, he was leading the tournament.

Joe Campbell had continued his blistering pace on the back nine. He shot a birdie on the 390-yard 10th, par on the 11th and 12th and was standing in the middle of the fairway on the 13th 300 yards from his tee shot. He took out his pitching wedge for the hundred yards or so shot. To make sure he didn't over hit, he only took a three-quarter back swing. His ball didn't have much height on it and landed in the trap on the right side of the green. Joe thought to himself this was ok and he could manage a decent sand shot being that his ball had a good lie in the sand. As Joe took his sand wedge back, someone coughed and Joe flopped his shot. It didn't make it out of the trap.

Joe was a little annoyed at himself. He hit the next shot onto the green but it ended up about twenty-five feet from the cup. He two putted for a double. He was now one over on the back, but still four under for the round.
"Don't let it get to you," Sean Williams said to Joe.
"I just need to settle down."

Joe did settle down. He shot par on the 14th, birdie on the 15th and par on the 16th and 17th. Standing on the 18th tee, Tom Connors said, "Joe, if you can birdie this one, you'll set the course record."
"You're kidding me?"

"No. The course record for an amateur has been 66. You're on course to match that and if you can get a birdie here, you'll have the record."

"Nothing like a little extra pressure," Joe said out loud. Then he thought to himself. This is just what Carol had been saying. It's a mindset.

The 18th hole was a 541-yard par-5. The hole plays straight away and is fairly open. Joe took out his driver. When he hit his ball, it went 310 yards right down the center of the fairway. His second shot found the green and he two putted for a birdie. He had done it. He set the course record with a 65 for an amateur.

Joe Campbell walked up to the tournament official. "Campbell, 65."
"What a round Campbell."
"I played well today. Plus, the conditions were pretty good."

Tony had been standing around watching the other golfers come in. When Joe's score was put up on the board, Tony said, "Holy crap."
Joe came out of the starter's shed and walked over to Tony.
"Nice round Joe."
"You too Tony."
"I guess we might be in the final group tomorrow."
"Looks that way. Who else is playing good?"
Tony had a frown on his face. "Who do you think?"

Joe looked up at the leader board. He quickly found Tommy Anderson's name and looked at his score through the front nine. He was in third place.

"Maybe Tommy didn't have a good back nine," Joe said to Tony.

"We'll know in a soon enough," Tony said as he looked over to the 18th green. Tommy Anderson's group should be on it in about an hour or so.

Tommy Anderson had played the back getting pars on all the par-4 holes. He got a birdie on the par-5 15th and a bogey on the 16th. As Tommy took his putt on the 18the, he let out a big cheer.

Tony looked to Joe, "Wonder what that was all about?"
"He must have made the putt."

Tommy walked up to the starter's shed. He went inside and registered his score. When he came out and started to put things in his bag, the tournament official put up his score. He had shot a 6 under par, 65. Tommy and Joe were tied for first place.

"Isn't that nice," Tony said sarcastically.
"Hey, he had a good round," Joe commented.
"And now we have to play with him tomorrow. Won't that be fun?"
"Don't get yourself upset Tony. You had a great round."
"Yeah, Yeah, Yeah. I'm going to Sundancers to get a drink.
"Me too. I'll see you over there in a little while."
"I just hope we don't have to see Tommy over there again today. I've had all I can take from him for one day."
"Don't worry about it Tony. You played well. Let's meet over there and have a few drinks."
"Ok. I'll see you there."

Round one ended. Tommy and Joe were tied for first. Tony, to everyone's surprise, including his own, was in third place. Russ Ford was in fourth at even par. Six golfers were at one over, seven golfers at two over par, and everyone else was not having as good a day.

Chapter 24

Most of the golfers went to Sundancers after the first round. Harry had arranged for WCOD to do a live broadcast from the bar on a Saturday. Kevin Martin set up around 4:00 pm for the broadcast. Harry had also scheduled the band M-Sound to play at 10:00 pm. By 5:00 pm, the place was packed.

Joe Campbell couldn't get a parking spot in the lot and had to resort to parking across the street. He had to wait for a few minutes for traffic to let him cross when Carol Tindle stopped in the middle of Route 28 and tooted her horn at Joe. She waved him across the street. Joe crossed and waited by the edge of the street as Carol realized there were no parking spots left in Sundancers' lot so she parked next to Joe's car.

Carol didn't have half the trouble crossing Joe did as she was dressed in a short, tight dress, with an eye-catching peacock blue Coach bag. The first pickup that came around the bend stopped and waved her on to cross. The guys in the pickup rolled down their window and whistled at Carol. She waved back, "Thank you."

Joe and Carol walked down the hill and into Sundancers together. There were no stools open at the bar and all the tables were full as well. Joe asked Carol what she wanted, went to the corner of the bar and ordered himself a beer and a martini for Carol. The two stood by the windows with their drinks.

"So Joe, how did you do today?" Carol asked.
"Pretty good. I'm tied for first place."
"Who are you tied with?"
"Tommy."
"No kidding?"
"Yeah. And Tony's in third place."
"Really? I didn't think Tony was supposed to be that good a golfer."
"He had it going today."

Just then, Tony came out of the kitchen, still in his golf clothing. He saw Joe by the door talking with Carol, so he walked over.

"Tony, I understand you're in behind Joe."
"Yeah. Joe and Tommy. Now I'm going to have to play in the same group with Tommy tomorrow."
"Is that a problem?"
"He's just so annoying."
"Well, Joe will be in that same group as well, won't he?"
"Yeah, you and me, Joe. We both get to play a competitive round with Tommy."
"If we only had Harry playing with us, it'd be just like the round we played a few weeks ago."
"Not really Joe. We were drinking beers last time. This time, the beer is out."
"So?"
"So, we don't have anything to dull our senses from Tommy. We'll have to listen to all his crap and nonsense."

165

"Why don't you do something about it?" Carol asked.

"Like what?" Tony asked.

"I don't know. Do something that will make Tommy focus on something else."

"Tell me more," Tony continued.

"Well, you could put something in his coffee before you start that would affect his play."

"Hmm." Tony thought. "How about a laxative?"

"Yeah, something like that," Carol responded.

Joe chimed in, "That would take Tommy's mind off golf."

"Yeah, if he could get out of the crapper enough to play," Tony said, and began to laugh. "And nothing gentle either, we want to really knock the crap out of him." The three laughed heartily at the joke.

"Why don't the two of you work together to get to Tommy?" Carol said to the two.

"What could I do?" asked Joe.

"You distract Tommy and Tony can poison the well or vice-versa."

"Yeah, that would work," Tony, quipped.

"If he's still a thorn in your side, you might work together next week and see what else you can do."

"Why not?" Tony said. "I'll bring the poison Joe. You buy the coffee and play nice to Tommy. When the time is right, we'll drop the stuff in his coffee."

"I don't know," Joe sounded a little wimpy.

"You want to be in this thing or not, Joe?" Tony asked.

"Yeah. But I'd rather win the clean way."

"You think Tommy is playing straight? He'll use everything he can think of to beat you. You watch. Right now, you're tied with him. I'll bet he tries to get into your head before the night is out."

"Tonight?"

"Yeah, tonight. There he is over there at the end of the bar. Go say something to him and I'll bet you he has something to say to humiliate you or make you feel inferior as a golfer. He'll be trying to get inside your head as much as he can."

"Let's see."

Joe walked over to where Tommy was seated. Tommy was talking with another golfer Joe didn't know.

"Hey Tommy. Looks like I'll be playing with you tomorrow. We're tied for the lead after today's round."

"You just got lucky Joe and I didn't finish the way I'm capable of finishing."

"And Tony will be joining us in the final group tomorrow."

"Tony, how the hell did he play that good? When we played a few weeks ago, we had to give him strokes. The guy's a cook, not a golfer."

"You know Tony's game. He might not be the longest hitter, but he keeps the ball in play. Today, he was pretty good with the short game as well."

"So, just about any duffer can have a good round. Come to think of it, look at your play today Joe. You tied me."

Joe couldn't believe what he was hearing. Tony was right. Tommy was belittling his play and was suggesting, no saying, it wouldn't continue.

"Well, see you tomorrow Tommy."

"Tomorrow you'll get to see a good golfer in action Joe. Why don't you bring the coffee and doughnuts?"

"How do you like your coffee Tommy?"

"Cream and sugar. And Joe, tomorrow, I'll show you some things on the course that might help your game.

"Sure Tommy, sure. Don't stay up too late. See you tomorrow."

Joe walked back to Tony.

"I'm bringing the coffee and doughnuts Tony. You bring the laxative."

Kevin did an on-air interview with Tommy Anderson. Everyone at the bar was quiet during the couple minutes where the interview was taking place.

"I'm speaking with Tommy Anderson live from Sundancers on Route 28 in West Dennis. Tommy, I understand you're leading in the Mid-Cape Golf Tournament after the first round held today."

"Yes I am Kevin. I played pretty good today."

"You're tied with Joe Campbell, aren't you?"

"Well, yes, for today anyway. I plan on taking sole command of the lead after tomorrow's round."

"What about the other golfers?"

"There are a few pretty good golfers in the field, but they didn't play that well today."

"What about Joe?"

"Joe and I have competed for years. He has never beat me and I don't expect this will be the first time."

"That's kind of cocky, isn't it Tommy?"

"There's a difference between skill and luck Kevin. Joe was lucky today."

"Well, good luck tomorrow Tommy."

"It's not luck Kevin, it's skill."

"Whatever you say Tommy. Well, there you have it folks. More to come after tomorrow's round."

Kevin started the music at the DJ booth. Tommy walked back to his seat at the bar.

Tony said to Joe, "That guy's really a piece of garbage. You heard him Joe. He put you down right here in front of everyone. In fact, he put you down on live radio, all over Cape Cod. You really shouldn't be taking that crap."

"Tommy is just being Tommy. I'm used to it."

"Don't you ever get tired of his humiliating you?" Carol said to Joe.

"I don't think he really means it," Joe responded.

"Oh, he means it Joe," Tony said. "Now, let's do what we can to put him in his place."

"Like I said, I'll bring the coffee and doughnuts."

"Good for you Joe. Get into the game," Carol said and smiled. "Why don't we get out of here Joe? I think a reward is in order."

"You two have a nice time," Tony said as he turned and walked away.

Joe and Carol left together. Joe followed Carol out and crossed the street from Sundancers to get their vehicles. They were going to her house.

Chapter 25

On Sunday morning, the golfers began arriving at Bayberry Hills Golf Course at 7:30 am. Joe Campbell met up with Tom Connors in the parking lot at the bottom of the hill from the clubhouse.

"Tom, know who you're playing with today yet?"

"No. I had to get home right after playing golf yesterday so I didn't get a chance to look at the pairings yet."

"I think you're playing with Russ Ford."

"Who's the other player?"

"I'm not sure. Tony said Ben Peters played pretty well yesterday. It might be him."

"Just so long as I don't have to play with Tommy Anderson I'll be fine."

"You have a problem with Tommy?"

"Yeah. He was hitting on my girlfriend last week. I wanted to punch the guy out but I didn't."

"Tommy seems to be on everyone's list these days."

"He on yours also?"

"He's been on mine since High School."

"That's a long time to carry a grudge Joe."

"I think everyone who has ever competed with Tommy has something against him."

"And everyone who has had a run-in with him for other reasons has it in for him as well."

Martin Yates was walking around with a clipboard checking the golfers in for the second round. He walked up to Joe and Tom.

"Ready for round two Joe?" Martin asked Joe as he shook his hand.

"Yeah, we're ready."

"How about you Tom?"

"I'm ready to go as well."

"Joe, you're in the last group with Davis and Anderson. Tom, you're playing with Russ Ford and Ben Peters."

Joe said, "That's what I thought."

Martin leaned over to Joe, "Kick the crap out of Tommy Anderson today Joe, will you?"

"I'm going to do my best to win."

"Let me know if you need any help."

Martin turned as he saw a couple of other golfers walking down to the practice green. When he walked away, Tom said, "What's up with Martin? What's his beef with Tommy?"

"Something to do with Tommy and Martin's wife, Helen."

"Are you kidding me? Tommy and Martin's wife. Is he crazy or something?"

"Tommy always thinks with his dick, Tom. Everyone knows that."

"Yeah, but Martin's got a reputation. I don't think anyone I know would screw with his woman."

"Well, Tommy did."

171

Tony came walking down the hill to the putting green. Martin stopped him and checked him in. Then, Tony walked over to where Joe and Tom were practicing putting.

"Hey Connors," Tony said.
"Tony."
"Morning Tony," Joe added.
"Looks like its you and me against Anderson," Tony said.
"And everyone else," Tom said.
"You got a beef with Tommy too?"
"Doesn't everyone?"
Joe looked up from his putt, "I think so."

Tony took a couple of balls from his pocket and began to practice putting. The conditions seemed pretty good for the second round. The sun was rising in the east. Only a few scattered clouds were visible in the sky. A slight breeze was blowing out of the west and temperatures were already in the mid-50s.

Two guys were arguing by the starter's shed when Tony was finishing practicing his putts and he looked up to see what the commotion was about. Tony walked to the edge of the practice tee to see who it was. There on the other side, Martin Yates had Tommy Anderson by the shirt looking like he was going to punch him. Harry Adams had just come out of the snack bar. He ran down to get in-between Martin and Tommy. Harry couldn't contain Martin by himself. He called Russ Ford over to help him. After a brief struggle, they were able to separate Martin and Tommy.

"That prick. He screwed with the wrong guy," Martin said as Harry and Russ held him back.
"Martin, get a hold of yourself. This isn't the time or the place."

172

"I overheard that piece of garbage talking trash about my wife. He was telling some of the other golfers they might be able to get a good blowjob at my place after playing today if they could win. He said it worked out for him after the qualifier when the reception was held at my place. I know what he was talking about."

Tommy Anderson had a little blood in the corner of his mouth. Martin had connected.

"I don't know what he's talking about."

Harry said, "Tommy, go practice or something and stay away from Martin if you know what's good for you. Martin, just check him in and walk away. Deal with this later."

"Ok, Ok Harry. I've got it under control," Martin said, as he re-tucked his shirt in and fixed his hair. Then Martin walked away looking for other golfers to check-in.

Tommy walked up to the practice putting green and began to practice. Tony kept practicing and eventually, the two were right next to each other.

"Same old Tommy," Tony chided him.

"I didn't do anything to him," Tommy responded.

"But you did his wife and he knows."

"No, actually, she did me."

"And how is that better?"

"He should be after her, not me."

"I don't think that's how Martin sees it Tommy. You must have done or said something to trigger his reaction."

"He's just a hothead."

"And you're not?"

"Screw you Tony."

Tommy picked up his balls and walked away. Joe had observed the whole thing from a little ways away. He said to Tony, "What was that all about?"

"Just getting under Tommy's skin."

"You still want to do this?"

"Absolutely. Did you bring the coffee?"

"I'll go into the restaurant and get three."

"Only bring two, one for you and Tommy. I've got my Red Bull with me. But bring a few donuts, too."

"Ok."

Joe left to get the coffee. Tony continued to practice for a few more minutes. When he was done, he went to his golf bag checking to make sure he had the laxative. Fifteen minutes later, Joe came out with two large coffee cups in his hands and a small bag. He walked over just past the starter's shed setting everything down on the bench. Tony finished up his practicing and joined him. He took a capsule out of his bag, opened it and put the contents into one of the coffees.

When he put the cap back on the cup, he picked up the other cup and made a mark on the side of the Styrofoam cup with his fingernail.

"Yours is the one with the J on the side Joe," Tony said as he handed Joe the cup of coffee. The two stood there talking for a few minutes waiting for their group to be announced for the second round. Tommy Anderson came walking up the path from the driving range setting his bag next to Joe's.

"Here's your coffee Tommy. Should still be hot, and I have a few doughnuts in the bag if you want one. Just as I promised."

Joe held up his coffee cup and pointed to the other cup on the bench.

"How did you get it?"

174

"Black. Cream and sugar are in the bag."

Tommy picked up the bag. He took out two sugars and two creamers. He opened the coffee cup putting the sugar in along with the creamers. He stirred the coffee and took a sip.

"That's still hot," Tommy said blowing into the opening in the cap on the cup.

Tony mumbled to Joe, "He has no idea how hot that cup is."

Tommy thought he heard Tony, "I'm not stupid Tony. I know the coffee's hot. I already tasted it."

"Yeah, Yeah, Yeah, Blah, Blah, Blah," Tony said turning and picking up his bag and a doughnut. He walked away from Joe and Tommy, opting instead to stop and talk with Russ Ford for a few minutes.

Chapter 26

All the golfers had been checked in for the second round. Martin Yates handed the clipboard over to the starter, Dave Golden. At 8:00 am, Dave walked up to the practice green asking everyone to gather by the starter's shed. The putting green is right next to the shed and is a few feet higher than the shed and adjacent pavement. Dave used the elevation difference as a stage to be able to speak with the golfers.

"Gentlemen, we are about to begin round two of the Mid Cape Open."

"Yesterday, we had some good scores posted. There are a few golfers under par and most of you are within a few strokes of the leaders. We expect another good round today although there is a chance of thunderstorms around mid-day. If you hear this horn go off, take shelter and stop play." He pressed the button on the air-horn releasing a very loud shriek.

"Same rules today as yesterday. Good luck out there."

Then, the first group of golfers was summoned to the 1st tee. Round two was underway.

Tommy, Joe and Tony knew they would have an hour or so to continue to practice before their tee time. Joe and Tony went back to the putting green. Tommy went to the driving range.

Tony said to Joe, "How long before that stuff kicks in?"

"I don't know. Maybe an hour or so?"

"Good. It should be hitting him just as we tee off."

"What if he didn't drink the whole cup of coffee?"

"You saw him. He had a few sips."

"Yeah, but he said it was too hot to drink."

"Did he take it with him to the driving range?

"I think so.

"Let's hope he finished it. But even if he didn't drink it all, it'll just take a little longer to kick in."

"I've never done anything like this before Tony."

"Don't feel guilty Joe. Tommy deserves everything he gets."

"Well, that prick is going to get the runs."

"Fitting isn't it?"

After about an hour of putting and chipping, they saw Tommy coming back up the hill from the driving range. Tommy put his bag by the fence and walked into the clubhouse.

"Must be working," Tony said.

"I don't think so," Joe said as he looked at the clubhouse. Tommy was coming back out. He had only been in there a minute or two and when he came back out he had a bottle of water in his hand.

"Anderson, Campbell, Davis. You're next on number one," came the call from the starter.

The three picked up their bags and walked to the 1st tee box. There, the starter said Davis would be first, followed by Anderson and Campbell.

"We've made a change for today and we're using the white tees today gentlemen," the starter said motioning to Tony to move from the blue tees to the white tees.

Tony took his driver out of his bag. Then, he walked up to the white tees placing his ball on the right side of the tee box. He took a few practice swings. As he had done in past rounds, Tony hit his drive right down the center of the fairway about 240 yards out on the 395-yard par-4 1st hole.

Tommy Anderson was next to hit. He took his driver out of his bag and walked up to the tee box. He put a Pro-V1 ball on a tee, then stepped back to take a few practice swings. He addressed his ball. Then he took a swing as hard as he could, hitting his ball down the right side of the fairway over 300 yards out.

Tommy turned to Tony and Joe, "That's how it's done."

Tony had already put his driver back into his bag and just turned, "Blah, Blah, Blah."

Joe Campbell was last to hit. He also had elected to use his driver. Joe put his Pro-V1 ball on a tee and took a couple of practice swings. When he hit his drive, his ball had a curve to the right landing in a sand trap on the right side of the fairway.

"Not how you want to begin Joe," Tommy teased him.
"Don't worry about me Tommy. I'll be alright."

The three picked up their golf bags walking off the tee box down the fairway. Joe was first to hit his second shot. He decided to hit a 5-wood out of the trap hoping to be able to cover the remaining 200 yards to the green. He picked his ball clean of the sand sending it high and straight. His shot landed on the front of the green running up about ten feet short of the cup.

Joe said out loud, "Yeah, now that's how it's done."
He wasn't speaking to anyone directly, just talking out loud.

Tony hit next. He sent a 6-iron sailing past the cup ending up on the fringe behind the hole. Tony and Joe walked down the fairway together stopping about thirty feet behind Tommy to watch his second shot. Tommy took out a wedge and then took a few practice swings. On his third practice swing, he stopped and put his left hand to his stomach.

Tony took notice. "It's starting to work."
"You think?"
"Look at him."
Joe looked at Tommy. Tommy had a wince on his face while he was holding his side.
Tony said, "Problem Tommy?"
"Just a little indigestion."
"I have some Tums in my bag if you need it."

"Thanks anyway, but I'll pass. Probably just the coffee. Not used to getting up this early or having coffee this early."
Then, Tommy hit his wedge shot. His ball landed on the green a few feet from the cup leaving a ball divot on the green.
"Give it time," Tony said to Joe.

The three walked up to the green. Tony was first to hit. He selected his putter. He lined it up and then hit his putt just short of the cup. He tapped in for a par.

Joe lined up his putt. He stood over the ball for a minute and then sank it for a birdie.

Tommy was last to putt. He only had a few feet to go. As he stood over his ball, Joe and Tony could hear Tommy's stomach growl. Tommy sank the putt for a birdie.

They played the 2nd hole, a 485-yard par-5 cautiously. The hole made two slight turns to the left with a pretty significant drop-off on the left side of the fairway for any golfer who became too aggressive. All three golfers had been over there before so they knew what to do.

Tony played his usual game, under control, straight and down the middle. Joe opted to use a fairway wood twice and then a wedge to get to the green in two. Tommy used his 3-wood, and two 8-iron shots to navigate the hole. All three golfers two putted for par.

As they walked off the second green, they heard a loud clap of thunder followed by a rumble.

"Joe looked up to the now cloudy sky, "Looks like we might be in for a storm"

"Or Tommy's stomach has kicked in," Tony said and laughed.

Tommy was already on the next tee box so he didn't hear the comments. He had put his bag down and was now running for a port-a-potty next to the wood line. He went inside closing the door behind him.

Joe and Tony stood on the tee box waiting for Tommy to return. When he didn't right away, Tony said, "Looks like Tommy isn't going to be able to continue. Go ahead and hit, Joe."

"Isn't Tommy up?"

"Hit anyway. If he can't continue, he'll be disqualified."

Joe teed his ball and hit. He hit a soft 9-iron onto the center of the green leaving a 6-footer. Tony took out an 8-iron and hit. His ball ended up on the green as well, about fifteen feet from the cup. Now it was Tommy's turn. But he was still in the outhouse.

"You're up Tommy," Joe yelled out.

They waited another five minutes. When Tommy didn't come out, Tony said, "If you can't continue Anderson, guess you'll have to drop out."

The door to the outhouse cracked open.

"Give me a few more minutes," Tommy requested.

"If you can't play, you're out," Tony insisted.

Just then, they all heard the stop play horn sound.

"Looks like we're stopping play Tony."

"Yeah. I can't believe Tommy's luck."

"Should we take his clubs with us?"

"Hell no. Let them sit there. If it rains and we resume play, his clubs will be soaked."

"Should we tell him we are going?"

"Nah. He'll figure it out."

The two picked up their bags and walked quickly back to the clubhouse. On the way back, they stopped in the cart barn and dropped off their clubs so they would remain dry. They were just getting there when the heavens opened up. It came down real hard. There were a few lightening strikes around followed by long rumbles. Harry was standing inside the clubhouse when they came in.

"Where's Tommy?"

"When we left him, he was in a port-a-potty out by number three."

"Keeping himself dry?" Harry asked.

"I think he had the runs," Tony said.

181

"How long do we expect play will be delayed?" asked Joe.

"About an hour or two," Harry said.

Joe turned to Tony, "You think Tommy will be able to compose himself by then?"

"Who the hell knows. We'll have to check and see if he's still in that port-a-potty when play resumes," Tony said. "Is the bar open yet?"

"Tony, you going to drink and then try to continue to compete?"

"Hey, this weather might not let up until tonight. We might be done already."

"No. I watched the weather channel a little while ago and they said this will clear in an hour or two," Harry responded.

"Then we better not go to the bar," Joe said.

"Ok. Let's wait in the restaurant and get a breakfast sandwich or something," Tony said.

An hour later, the rain stopped and the weather front had moved through. The sun came back out. It was announced the second round would pick back up in another half hour. Joe and Tony hadn't seen anything of Tommy Anderson during the stoppage.

Chapter 27

Joe and Tony retrieved their bags from the cart barn. They had left them in there when play had been stopped. They started to walk back towards the clubhouse when Joe said, "I'll be right back."

Joe left his bag just outside the cart barn and ran to his car. He came back with a zip-lock bag in his hand.

"What's in the bag?" Tony asked.

"Carol gave me some ideas she said I might consider using against Tommy. If the opportunity presents itself, and if Tommy returns to play, I might give this one a try."

"So, what's in the bag?"

"Poison ivy."

"Really?"

"Yeah. She told me to rub it on his putter. He'll hardly notice it and then he'll start to feel the effects a short time later. Like before next weekend's round."

"What if he isn't allergic to poison ivy?"

"He had it a couple of times in high school from what I remember."

"Well, if he returns, it's worth a try. You're becoming pretty devious Joe. I'm going to have to keep an eye on you. Carol give you any more tips?"

"Yeah. But the ivy's all I've got with me today."

"You've got my interest. I can't wait to see what else you have up your sleeve."

They walked back to the 3rd tee ready to resume play. To their surprise, Tommy Anderson was standing on the tee box practicing his swing.

"We've already hit," Joe said as he and Tony walked up.

"I can see your balls on the green," said Tommy solemnly.

Tommy hit his 9-iron on to the very soft and wet green. The ball died right where it had landed, three feet from the cup. They all started to walk to the green.

Tony had to ask, "We didn't see you inside Tommy. Where did you go during the storm?"

"I stayed right in the port-a-potty."

"You're kidding me?"

"No. I was able to get my clubs before the rain came down and took them in with me."

"What did you do for the hour and a half, sit around on the crapper?" Tony joked.

"I had an upset stomach. So it worked out for me."

"Our luck," Tony remarked.

The three walked up to the green. Joe was first to putt. He missed and tapped in for a par. Tony hit next sinking his putt for a birdie. Tommy tapped in for a birdie as well.

On the 4th hole, Joe and Tony got a birdie, Tommy a par. All three golfers shot par on the 5th. Tommy and Joe got par on the 6th while Tony shot a bogey. They walked up to the par-5 505-yard 7th but Tommy kept stopping and resting every time they had a long distance to walk.

"Joe, look at Tommy. It's still working."

Tommy was sweating and drinking water frequently. He would fill up his water bottle at every canteen by each tee box.

"He's dehydrated."

"Good. He's being affected both mentally and physically then."

"Carol was saying something about being in the right frame of mind to play well. I guess she was right."

"She's a smart girl," Tony said. "What else did she say?"

"She told me she had lots of ideas I could use on Tommy."

"I'll bet she did. Hold off on the ivy Joe until we see how Tommy's playing."

"Sure."

Tommy was first to hit. He took out his driver blasting his drive over 300 yards down the right side of the fairway. Joe hit next. He hit his drive about 280 yards down the center of the fairway. Tony hit last. He hit his drive about 250 yards down the left side of the fairway. The three left the tee box, Joe and Tony leading, Tommy following a good distance behind.

Tony hit a 3-wood for his second shot right down the center of the fairway. Joe hit a 3-wood as well, a little over 220 yards landing just short of the green. Tommy took out a 4-iron landing his second shot on the green. He was in position to be shooting for an eagle. He didn't get the eagle and settled for birdie. Joe and Tony both shot par.

185

All three golfers shot par on the 8th and 9th holes. Making the turn, they stopped at the starter's shed to register their scores for the front nine.

Martin Yates was standing next to Dave as the three approached. Joe looked at Tony, "I don't have a good feeling about this."

"Hey, we might not have to do anything else to Tommy. Leave it up to Martin."

Harry had seen the three coming off the 9th green, then he saw them approaching the starter's shed with Martin standing near it. He ran out of the restaurant down to where Martin was standing. Martin saw him coming just as Tommy peeled off to hit the restroom in the clubhouse.

"How'd you guys do?" Harry asked the three as they reached the starter's shed.

Tony was first to speak. "I shot a 35."

"Wow. That's a first, isn't it Tony?"

"Yeah. I can't believe I'm actually under par in a competition."

"He's playing pretty good," Joe added.

"I'm sure my game will turn south very soon," remarked Tony.

"How'd you do Joe?" Harry asked him.

"34."

"That's pretty good Joe."

"Tommy got a 33."

"You guys are tearing the course up," commented Harry. "Where'd Tommy go?"

"Another pit stop," Tony giggled.

Martin stood there with his arms crossed and didn't say anything. After Joe had announced Tommy's score, Martin just let out a "humph." He turned and walked away. Tommy trotted back down to the shed, grabbed his bag, and the three headed to the 10th.

Harry walked over to Martin. "Glad you didn't overreact back there Martin."

"I'm not going to create another scene right here Harry. I want this thing to be as much a success as you do. But sooner or later, I'm going to get even with Tommy Anderson."

"Just deal with it outside of here if you have to Martin."

"Oh, I will."

The two went back inside the restaurant. It was time for a morning cocktail. As Joe and Tony walked, they looked at the leader board. Their scores were just being entered. Tommy was tied for first place with Russ Ford. Joe, along with three other golfers, was in second followed by a group of nine golfers at even par.

On the 10th tee, Tommy was first to hit. The par-4 hole was playing 372 yards from the white tees. Tommy placed his Pro-V1 high on his tee. He took a few practice swings and then addressed his ball. He hit it as hard as he could. The ball traveled along the right side of the fairway and just over an outcropping of trees on the right side. His ball disappeared around the corner.

Joe hit next. His drive went right down the middle of the fairway right to the place where the fairway bends to the right. Tony hit last. His drive went 245 yards down the left center of the fairway. The three golfers picked up their bags in silence and walked down the fairway.

Tony was first to hit his second shot. He selected an 8-iron. As he hit his ball, it began to curve to the left.

"Crap. I didn't want that much movement," Tony said in disgust.

"What're you afraid of Tony?" Joe asked.

"Every time I play this hole, I end up in one of those traps up by the green. So I closed the face down on my club a little hoping to keep the ball to the left."

"Well, it worked. Your ball definitely went left."

"Yeah, but twenty yards left of the green."

"You'll get it back Tony. Just be careful."

"Yeah."

Joe hit next. His 9-iron shot landed just on the green and ran forward another twenty feet. He was about ten feet from the cup.

Tommy's ball had rounded the bend in the fairway nicely. He narrowly missed the trees on the right side and was able to find the down slope when the ball landed giving him an extra twenty yards on his drive. The short 50 yard approach shot remaining proved no match for his lob wedge. Tommy ended up two feet from the cup.

Tony decided to use a 7-iron and run his ball on to the green. He addressed his ball but hit the grass first dubbing the shot. His ball fell short of the green by five feet. He used the same club again and this time successfully got on the green running the ball twenty feet past the cup. Tony was definitely annoyed now.

"That was for par," he said in disgust.

Tommy and Joe marked their balls. Tony was first to putt. He spent extra time lining the putt up. Then he hit the ball. It missed by a few inches. He tapped in for a double.

Joe missed his ten foot putt by six inches, and then tapped in. Tommy made his short putt for a birdie.

"That's not how I wanted to start the back nine," Tony said angrily.

"You just need to settle down," Joe remarked. "Remember how I started this round? It gets better."

"Back to your old self, I see," Tommy said.

"Screw you Tommy," Tony struck back.

"Let's get to eleven," Joe said trying to get things back on track.

The three golfers walked to number eleven. It was a straight away 384-yard par-4. Again, Tommy was first to hit. This time, he didn't blast away. Instead, he took a smooth swing, made contact and sent his ball about 280 yards down the center of the fairway.

Joe hit next. He tried to make up some ground and hit his ball about as hard as he could. He got some extra distance, but his ball ended up a few feet into the tree line on the left side of the fairway, right behind a big pine tree. Tony, having watched Joe's shot said, "You'll never beat him that way Joe."

"I can't let his play get to me. I just need to calm down."

"Isn't that what you told me last hole?"

"Yeah."

"You need to listen to your own advice."

Tony walked up to the tee with his driver. He took a practice swing and then hit his ball. It went 240 yards right down the center of the fairway.

"That's the way," he said as he turned and walked back.

They walked down the fairway. Tony hit a 5-wood for his next shot sending it straight down the fairway. It landed a few feet short of the green. Then, Tony and Joe walked to Joe's ball. It was right up against the pine tree.

"You're going to have to lay it out to the right," Tony said.

"That'll cost me a stroke," was Joe's response.

"What other choice do you have?" Tony said.

Joe knew he just had to do the right thing. He took out a 7-iron and hit his ball back to the center of the fairway.

189

Then, he put his wedge shot right on the green five feet from the cup.

Tony said, "See? You were rewarded for playing smart. Now, tap it in for a par and move on."

"You're right," Joe responded.

Tommy hit his second shot nearly hitting Joe's ball on the green. It stopped a few feet away. They walked up to the green. Tony used his putter even though he was a few feet off the green. His ball ended up inches from the cup. He tapped in for par. Joe made his putt for par as well. Tommy made another birdie.

On the 12th tee, Tommy had to use the port-a-potty again. He was in there for about five minutes. While he was there, Joe and Tony were standing on the tee box. A dark set of clouds could be seen coming in from the west. Then, all of a sudden, a streak of lightening followed by a crack of thunder a second later.

"That one's close," Tony remarked.

"Yeah. Must be moving real fast," Joe said.

They heard the horn blow signifying bad weather.

"We better get going or we'll get stuck out here," Tony said picking up his bag. The two hurried off seeking shelter.

As Tommy came out of the port-a-potty, he could see Tony and Joe hurrying off to the clubhouse. They were about as far from the clubhouse as they could be. He got his clubs and decided to ride another one out in the port-a-potty.

Chapter 28

Joe and Tony had to run the last few hundred feet to the cart barn. The rain started to come down very heavy. They made it, but not before getting pretty soaked. They decided to just stay there along with a dozen other golfers who were escaping the weather as well.

Fifteen minutes later, they could hear the rumble of weather off in the distance well past the golf course. The rain stopped, too. They picked up their golf bags and walked over to the starter's shed.

"Giving any thought to continuing this round on another day?" Tony asked Martin Yates.

"That was supposed to be the last one," Harry remarked.

"We think we can finish the round now," Martin said as he spoke to the group of golfers getting ready to retake the course. He looked over at Joe and Tony but didn't see Tommy Anderson. Dave, the starter, came out of the shed, "Ok. We can resume play."

Martin said, "Let's get this round in guys."

Everyone started to go back to the course. Martin walked over to Joe and Tony.

"What happened to Anderson?"

"He was in the crapper when we heard the horn," Tony said.

"How's he playing?" Martin asked.

"Pretty good," remarked Joe.

"Figures," Martin said.

"But don't worry Martin. Joe's got a few things going as well."

Martin was glad to hear Joe was having a good round too, and perhaps giving Tommy a run for his money.

Tony and Joe got back to the 12th. Tommy was waiting for them.

"Sat another one out, did you?" Tony sarcastically said to Tommy.

"I saw you two running down the fairway. Then I could see the rain coming. I wouldn't have made it before getting wet and my game would have made a turn for the worse had my clubs gotten wet," Tommy said matter-of-factly.

"Just as well," said Tony. "You must've been right at home right where you stayed."

"You're up Tommy," Joe said getting their minds back into the game.

Tommy decided not to use a tee on the 130-yard par-3 12th. He selected a spot on the tee box containing smooth grass and carefully placed his Pro-V1. He hit a soft 9-iron. His shot didn't gain too much height and landed softly on the green twenty feet from the cup. He had another chance at birdie.

Joe used a 9-iron as well. But he put his ball on a tee. When he hit it, it went very high. It landed on the green ten feet from the cup rolling only inches. Tony, not being the same kind of ball striker as the other two, selected an 8-iron. He hit his shot a little long staying on the green about thirty feet from the cup. The three of them walked up to the green.

Tony was first to putt. He hit his ball pretty hard running it five feet past the cup. He walked up and marked his ball. Tommy took extra time to line up the twenty foot putt. When he hit his ball, it looked like it would drop into the cup. It went 270 degrees around the cup and lipped out. Tommy putted in for a par. Joe was able to drop his putt for a birdie. Tony put his ball down and picked up his marker. He made the putt for a par.

Walking to the 13th tee, Tony said, "Tommy's in a zone Joe. You might want to think about the ivy."
"If the opportunity's right, I'll consider it."

The 13th hole is a fairly straight away 320-yard par-4. As the guys walked out on to the tee box, a breeze came up from behind them. Joe was first to hit. He took his driver out and after feeling the breeze pick up, he took a few big practice swings.

Tony said to Joe, "I don't know if I'd try to reach the green in one if I were you."
"I'd have to hit a great shot to reach. I'm just going to try to place the ball in front of the green."

Joe then addressed his ball. He took his club back and rotated further than he usually did. When he followed through, he hit his ball and then extended way past his normal follow through. He had put everything he had into the shot. His ball started out heading for the right side of the green. It hit on the fringe just short of the green about 305 yards out. The ball must have hit a sprinkler head or something as it took a very big bounce ending up over the green past the sand traps.

Joe looking down the fairway at his shot said, "Did you see that? My ball definitely hit something."

"Sure did," Tony said.

"It should have ended up on the green," Joe complained.

Tommy was next to hit. He took out his driver. Unlike Joe's swing, Tommy could hit the ball 300 yards without having to exaggerate his swing. He took a few practice swings and then hit his shot. His ball was heading right for the center of the green. It landed just past the cup and continued on until it came to rest in the sand trap on the right side of the back of the green.

"I should have taken something off my swing to compensate for the breeze," Tommy said throwing his club on the ground.

"Still, that was a nice drive Tommy," Joe said.

Tony took his driver out of his golf bag. He put his ball on an oversize tee. After a few practice swings, he drove his ball about 240 yards down the center of the fairway. They picked up their golf bags and began to walk down the fairway. Tony took out a wedge and placed his second shot on the green fifteen feet from the cup.

Walking past the green, Joe could see his shot had landed on the fringe past the green and not in the sand trap. He used his wedge to put his ball four feet from the cup. Tommy had dropped his bag on the side of the green. He took out his sand wedge and putter. He walked back to the trap. The lip on the trap in front of his ball was almost non-existent and Joe thought Tommy was going to consider putting out of the trap. But, the sand was still wet from the recent shower so Tommy decided to use the sand wedge. He put his putter down on the sand rake next to the back of the trap to keep the grip out of the wet grass. Stepping into the sand trap,

Tommy's putter resting on the rake was behind him and in front of Joe. Joe saw this as an opportunity. While Tommy stood over his ball in the trap, Joe took a zip-lock out of his pocket, opened it and carefully using the zip-lock as a glove from the outside in and rubbed the contents in the bag on Tommy's putter grip. Joe quickly closed the zip-lock and stuffed it back into his pocket before Tommy had hit.

When Tommy turned around to get the rake, Joe picked it up allowing Tommy's putter to drop on the wet grass. Tommy picked up his putter, "I was trying to keep it dry Joe."
"Sorry Tommy, I was just trying to help."

Tommy raked the trap with the rake in one hand and the putter in the other. His shot out of the trap had been successful with his ball lying about eight feet from the cup.
Tony two putted for a par. Joe two putted as well. Tommy dropped his putt in the cup for a birdie.

"Yes."
Joe added, "Nice recovery Tommy. You're shooting all three's so far on the back nine aren't you?"
"Yes I have."
Tony said laughing.
"What's so funny Tony? You know I'm a scratch golfer."
"You could say that," Tony said laughing even harder.

Joe picked up his bag and started walking to the 14th hole. Tony and Tommy followed. All three golfers shot par on the par-4 352-yard hole. As they walked up to the 15th tee box, Tony said, "This is the number two handicap hole Joe. We need to do well here."
"I agree."
"Stop trying to play like me," Tommy said to the two trying to distract them. Then, he did something that made

Tony laugh. Tommy walked over to the edge of the woods by a stand of trees to relieve himself. When he did, Tony motioned to Joe to look. They both knew what was happening, and what it could mean.

On the tee box, Tommy hit his drive 300 yards down the center of the fairway. Joe hit his drive about 280 yards down the left side of the fairway. Tony, feeling the breeze behind him, hit his drive 250 yards down the center of the fairway.

Tony hit his second shot, a 3-wood about 210 yards down the center of the fairway leaving a short sixty yard wedge shot to the green. Joe tried to use a 5-wood for his second shot but topped the ball gaining only about 125 yards in distance. Tommy hit his 5-wood 210 yards landing on the green. He would have another chance at eagle. Joe hit his third shot, an 8-iron on to the green leaving a sixty foot putt.

The three walked up to the green. Tommy took his putter out of his bag. The grip looked wet. He tried to dry it off somewhat and then walked on to the green to putt.

Joe was first to putt. The sixty foot putt had two breaks in it. Joe navigated the first break all right but that was because he had to hit the ball so hard to cover the distance. He didn't judge the second break very well and the ball broke right of the cup by seven feet. Then, he left the seven foot putt short. He tapped in for a bogey. Tony took two putts to get in for a par. Tommy lined up his putt. This one was for eagle. He hit his ball. It rolled true for ten feet and then just as it reached the cup, it hung up on the edge.
Tommy turned from the putt, looking up to the sky, "Just a little more?"
As he turned to tap it in, his ball dropped into the cup. He had the eagle.

On the 16th hole, Joe shot a par, Tony shot a bogey and Tommy shot another birdie. The 17th hole wasn't as nice to Tommy. He pulled his 7-iron tee shot left landing in the sand. He muffed the sand shot the first time and had to take a second sand shot. He two putted for a bogey. Joe and Tony both shot par on the 17th.

Walking up to the 18th tee, Tommy said, "What the hell did I get on my hands? It's like I burned them, or I'm having an allergic reaction to something."

He was looking at the blisters that were forming in between the fingers. Joe walked over to look at them, "Looks like poison ivy to me."

"What did you do with your club when you took that leak back there by the woods Tommy? Lay it in a patch of ivy?"

Tommy thought back. He had set his club up against a tree that did have some brush around the base and when he went to pick it up, it had fallen over. He didn't give it any more thought. "Guess I must have," he said taking his driver out of the bag.

Joe was first to hit. He took a little off the drive ending up 270 yards down the left side of the fairway. Tony did his usual. His drive ended up 240 yards down the center of the fairway. Tommy placed his ball on a tee. He took a few practice swings and then hit the ball pretty hard. It had a pretty significant curve to the flight ending up just inside the wood line on the right side of the fairway.

As they walked down the fairway for their second shots, Tony said, "Watch out for the ivy Tommy."

Tommy made a sour facial expression in Tony's direction but didn't say anything.

Tony hit his 3-wood straight another 200 yards, leaving him with a thirty-yard chip shot on the short par-5 hole. Joe laid up short with a 5-wood to within ten yards of the green. Tommy had to chip out of the woods. Then he hit a 5-wood right on to the green. Tony chipped on and then made a one putt for a birdie. Joe took two putts to finish ending up with a par. Tommy, clearly agitated, missed his putt but followed it with a second putt that found the cup. He ended up with a par.

They stopped at the starter's shed on the way back in to record their scores. Joe had shot a 71, Tony a 75 and Tommy a blistering 67.

After entering their scores, Joe said, "Anyone interested in going to Riverside for a drink?"

Tony said, "Sure, I need one."

"How about you Tommy?" Joe asked him.

"I don't know. Martin's a little ticked at me."

"You should be ok. After all, everyone will probably be there and I think you're in the lead."

"Why not then. I'll just blend in with the crowd."

The three put their clubs into their vehicles and left to go to Riverside.

Chapter 29

Joe and Tony arrived at Riverside at the same time. They went inside. Martin greeted the golfers as they came in through the back door to the bar. He offered each golfer a complimentary beer or wine of their choice. Most of the golfers came in with friends and family. Within a half hour of the second round ending, the bar and adjacent restaurant was full. Tony and Joe were standing at the corner of the bar talking with Russ Ford.

"So Russ, how did you play today?" Joe asked.

"Ok. I shot three under par."

"Then, you're right up there for next weekend?"

"Yeah."

"What did you shoot for the first round?"

"I shot five under. If I can get my short game going at Blue Rock, I should be able to be in contention for the final on Sunday."

"Didn't you play in the PGA event last year up in Norwood? I didn't think you could participate in this tournament if you played pro," Tony questioned with a frown on his face.

"I played as an amateur."

"We'll have to look into that Joe," Tony said as if Russ had done something wrong.

"The rules just stated a golfer has to be an amateur. I'm in that category," Russ explained.

"You're good enough to be on tour Russ. Who you kidding?" Tony remarked.

"Glad you think so Tony, but I'd have to quit my job up in Boston to play professionally and I'm not sure I want to."

"You could make millions playing golf," Tony said.

"I already make a nice income. Plus, if things go right, I'll be in the big money in a few years."

Joe jumped into the conversation. "Hey Tony, Russ works for one of those hedge fund companies up in Boston. He's right. If he can stick with it and be successful, he'll make millions and not have to worry about winning one or two tournaments a year. Although playing golf's not a bad way to spend a day."

"Plus, golfers are like any other athletes," Russ came back. "They might be good for a dozen years or so and then someone else comes along. There are only a few golfers who actually build an empire and make the big bucks year in and year out."

"Oh, you mean like Woods or Norman?" Tony said.

"Like them. At the hedge fund, I can minimize the downside making intelligent moves and the rewards can be huge."

"I've read about some of those guys. Hey, it's your life. But, I'd give it a try if I had your game," Tony said.

"Thanks for the thought Tony. But I think I'll keep things the way they are."

The three had another beer. Joe picked up the tab. As they continued to talk, Tommy Anderson came in. Martin was at the other end of the bar. Another bartender, Paul Jackson, was working the end of the bar where Tony and Joe were talking with Russ.

"What can I get you Tommy?" Paul asked.

"How about Helen?" Tony spoke out hoping Martin would hear him.

Tommy looked at Tony with an annoyed look.

"I'll have a Bud," Tommy said to Paul.

Paul poured a bud and handed it to Tommy.

"Nice round today Tommy," Joe said to him.

"Thanks. How did you do today Russ?" Tommy asked.

"Par."

"Maybe you two could be paired up next weekend," said Tony. "Then you'd have some competition Tommy."

Tony definitely rubbed Tommy the wrong way, all the time. It was just the way Tony would talk to him. It was always with a snicker and tone of intimidation. He was always trying to get under Tommy's skin.

"I'm going to get something to eat," Tommy said.

He turned and walked to the buffet. As Tommy filled his plate, Helen came out of the kitchen with a new batch of wings. She put them in the buffet tray.

"Tommy, I see you're in first place," she said as she pointed at the leader board easel.

"Yeah. I played well today."

"So you think you can win the whole thing?" she asked.

"That's my plan."

"Too bad we don't have any prizes for winning the second round. I could have helped you put them in your car."

Tommy thought he knew what she was referring to. He said, "I'm going to go out and have a smoke in a few minutes. Care to join me?"

"I'd like that. I'll watch to see when you go out the back door, then, I'll come out. Where are you parked?"

"I'm in pretty much the same spot as the last time."

She knew where he meant.

Tommy ate his meal, got up, and walked out the back door. Joe saw him going out, "Leaving already Tommy?"

"Just having a smoke."

"Let me buy you a drink."

"When I come back in."

Tommy continued out the door. Tony said, "Joe, what the hell are you doing. You're playing nice with him. We don't want to be nice to Tommy."

"I'm remembering what Carol said. She told me to keep myself under control and look for opportunities. I think the best way for me to find opportunities is to stay close to the competition so I can recognize an opportunity when it shows itself. Haven't you heard the saying, keep your friends close and your enemies closer?"

"Even still, you don't have to buy the guy drinks."

"Tony, if I can keep Tommy's guard down, I might be able to catch him off guard come the end of the week."

"That's good thinking Joe. Why didn't I think of it?"

Joe could see the door to the kitchen open as he was talking to Tony. Helen had come out and walked to the back door. She went outside. Joe walked over to the door just in time to see Helen getting into the back seat of Tommy's SUV across the parking lot. He went back to the bar.

Out in the parking lot, Helen could see Tommy sitting in the back seat of his SUV with the window half down and smoke coming out. She walked over and opened the door and got in.

"You should get something for coming in first today, Tommy," Helen said as she put her hand on his zipper. Then she leaned over. Tommy sat back and enjoyed the moment. While Helen was busy, Tommy reached under her blouse unhooking her bra. Then he reached around and caressed her breasts. When Helen finished, Tommy reached down and undid her pants. He slid his hand down. He was starting to push her pants off when he looked up and could see Martin at the back door of the bar, looking around the parking lot. Tommy stopped, "I think we should go back inside."
"But I want you, now."
"Maybe next time."
"I can bring you around again."
"It's not that. I just think I'd rather wait."

They both composed themselves. "You should go in first Helen. Use the front door and I'll come in the back door in a few minutes."
"Ok."

Helen entered the front door and walked back to the kitchen. Since the front door has a lobby and a set of doors that open to the bar, Martin didn't see her come in, but Joe did see her come through the lobby doors to the bar and enter the kitchen. He thought it strange she left through the back and then came back in the front.

Tommy came back into the bar a few minutes later through the back door. When he did, Helen walked over to him and making sure Martin and anyone else around could hear said, "There you are Tommy Anderson. Congratulations on being in first place," she kissed him on the cheek.

"Thanks," was all Tommy could say.

"Martin, give Tommy a beer on the house," Helen said motioning to Martin.

He poured a draft and put it on the bar.

Tony leaned over to Joe, and in a low voice said, "Martin probably wants to rip Tommy's head off and here his wife is buying the guy a beer."

"It's called damage control, Tony."

"What do you mean?"

"I saw her getting into Tommy's SUV in the parking lot. She's just deflecting any ill thoughts Martin might be happening. She'd be stupid to be screwing around with Tommy and then buying him a drink right? So obviously she's not screwing around. That's what she wants him to think."

"And Tommy gets the rewards." Tony said taking a big sigh.

"Doesn't he always?" Joe said picking up his beer.

"I'm heading over to Sundancers. I don't think I can take any more of this," Tony said finishing his beer and placing the glass on the bar.

"I'll be right behind you," said Joe.

Chapter 30

Joe and Tony walked into Sundancers about fifteen minutes later. The place was kind of quiet. There were a few people at the bar and a few having dinner in the restaurant side. The parking lot was about half full. Joe took up a seat at the corner of the bar by the door.

"Dee, can I have a beer and a shot of Jack?"

"Sure."

"Me too," Tony said as he took up the stool next to Joe.

"I thought you guys would be celebrating at Riverside tonight?" Dee asked as she put the shots and beers in front of the guys.

"We were there. Just couldn't stand the drama anymore," Tony responded.

"What happened?"

"Tommy Anderson," Tony replied.

"What did Tommy do now?"

"Everything. He's leading the tournament. He's out in the parking lot with women in his car. Everyone's buying the guy drinks," Tony looked at Joe with a frown on his face. "And I just can't stand the guy's attitude."

"Tony, you should take things more in stride, like Joe here."

"Yeah, he's taking things in stride," Tony said taking a drink of his beer. "Even the stuff we tried to do to make him play bad didn't work."

"What did you do?" Dee asked.

"Tommy had gotten the craps during the round of golf. Wouldn't you know it, mother nature got him off the hook by providing a thunder storm where they stopped the tournament so Tommy could take as long as he needed," Tony was getting on a roll now. "Then, the guy got poison ivy on his golf clubs and it started to affect his play. But somehow he finished the round and ended up in first place."

"So what did you do to affect his play? Those things all sound like Tommy's just lucky."

"Oh, he's lucky, he gets lucky and he's cocky about it," Tony said in a loud voice.

The door to the bar opened and Carol Tindal came in. She walked over to the other side of Joe, "What's all the noise about Tony?"

"Nothing, I'm just letting off some steam."

"About what?"

"Tommy Anderson."

"What did Tommy do now?"

"Everything and everyone."

"Tell me more."

"You tell her Joe. I'm out of here."

Tony threw back his shot, chugged his beer, paid his tab and left. Carol ordered a martini. When Dee put it in front of her, she said to Carol, "They just came in a little while ago from Riverside. Tommy's in first place and these two aren't happy about it."

"Oh really?"

"Yeah."

A customer on the other side of the bar was waving a Keno ticket, signaling Dee she was ready to place a bet. Dee headed over, took the cash and ticket, and went to the Keno machine.

"So Joe, what was Tony so excited about?"

"I remembered what you had said about looking for opportunities to get ahead if a situation arose. Two did come up today. I put laxatives into Tommy's coffee before the start of today's tournament round trying to impact his play. It worked, but there were two stoppages of play for thunderstorms at exactly the right time when Tommy was in the john and he was able to get by."

"You said there were two things you did?"

"Yeah. On one of the holes on the back nine, I had an opportunity to put some poison ivy on Tommy's putter. He used the club on every hole after I rubbed the ivy leaves on the club. It didn't take long and he was itching like crazy."

"So, didn't those things work?"

"The guy still found a way to be in first place."

"Joe, if you had put the poison ivy on him on Saturday, it might have had an effect on his game on Sunday. Putting it on the club on the back nine didn't allow sufficient time to bring his game down."

"But I didn't play in his group on Saturday."

"Then you should have come up with something else."

"Like what?"

"Remember what I told you about the night before you, Harry and Tony played a round with Tommy?"

"Yeah."

"You could have gotten him out on Friday night and made sure he had too much to drink or tried to put something in his drink that would carry over to Saturday."

"Oh."

"Like I did with the Viagra."

"Yeah, that, the liquor and keeping him up most of the night."

"It worked didn't it?"

"I guess."

"Guess nothing. He was affected."

"Do you think I should do some of those things to Tommy at the end of this week?"

"Well, I don't think he'll take to you trying to sleep with him."

"Not that, but the other things?"

"Can't hurt. You might even want to try to come up with a few other ideas.

"I'll think about it."

"Don't just think. Be prepared and act."

"I will."

"Joe, why don't we get out of here and go to my place."

"Sounds good to me."

Chapter 31

On Wednesday night, Helen Yates stopped into Sundancers. She walked up to the bar with an envelope in her hands.

"Dee, is Harry in?"

"He's here somewhere."

"Martin wanted me to give this to him," she held up the envelope.

"He should be in here in a few minutes, can I get you something?"

"Sure. I'll have a cosmo."

Dee made the drink and put it in front of Helen. When she did, she noticed a rash on Helen's face and around her lips.

"Looks like you got a case of poison ivy."

"Yeah. Itches like hell."

Helen scratched at her breast as she responded.

"Got it in other places as well?" Dee asked.

"You don't even want to know," was all Helen said.

"I see him in the kitchen," Dee said and walked to the kitchen door. "Harry, Helen Yates is here to see you."

Harry came out of the kitchen. He walked over to where Helen was seated.

"Hi Harry. Martin asked me to drop off the official paperwork for the golf tournament from last weekend."

"Oh, thanks. I'll see to it that Mary over at American Pub gets it for this weekend."

"Thanks."

"I'm going to put this in my office for now so it doesn't get lost."

Harry walked back into the kitchen with the envelope. Dee said to Helen, "Where did you get the poison ivy?"

"Someone must have passed it along to me at the bar. I haven't been working around the yard or anyplace else recently so I really don't know."

"How long do you think it'll take to clear up?"

"I hope only a few days."

"It looks uncomfortable," Dee said as she turned to wait on another patron.

As Helen finished her drink, Tommy Anderson came into the bar. He took up a stool next to Helen.

"Hey Helen, what's up?"

She looked down at his pants, "Nothing I guess."

"No really, why are you over here?"

"Martin asked me to drop something off for Harry. I thinks its something for the tournament."

"Oh, I thought you might be looking for me."

Tommy scratched his crotch and then began itching his hands. Dee came over.

"Tommy, want a beer?"

"Sure."

Dee poured a beer and put it in front of Tommy. He was itching his hands as he reached for the beer and Dee said, "You have poison ivy too?"

"Yeah."

He held his hands up for her to see. His fingers were all red and swollen with the rash. Then Dee looked at Helen remembering what she had said to her just minutes before.

"Well, I've got to be going," Helen said placing a ten on the bar.

"But I just got here," Tommy said.

"Then enjoy your drink Tommy."

Helen got up and left.

Tommy finished his beer and then he left. As he was walking out the door, Joe Campbell was just getting out of his car. Tommy walked the other way in the parking lot and got into his car. Joe went in and sat at the end of the bar.

"Beer?"

"Yeah, and a shot of Jack."

"Got it."

As she was getting the drinks, she said, "So what's up with your software business?"

"You're not going to believe this, but it's brought in over $50,000 in three months in commission overrides. They're generated by other landscapers using the software with some of the merchants around here."

"No kidding? That sounds great."

Joe drank his shot. "I made $50,000 on $600,000 worth of business run through my software."

"So it's a win-win for you, the merchants and other landscapers?"

"Looks that way. In fact, I've been contacted by one of the big home improvement companies wanting to license my software for all their outlets across the country."

"Wow, Joe! That could be big."

"Sure could. The interested company has over seven hundred stores across the country. We're talking about leasing the software to each store at a price of $3,000 per month per store."

"Joe, that's millions in just one year."

"I know. But it hasn't happened yet."

"Keep your fingers crossed. I hope it works out for your sake."

"Me too. Say, Dee, can I have another shot of Jack?"

While Dee was pouring the shot, Joe said, "What's up with Tommy? He left early, for him."

"Helen Yates."

"What do you mean?"

"She was just in here a little while ago also."

"With him?"

"Not at first. But when she left, Tommy left shortly after."

"You know, I saw them together Sunday night in the parking lot again at Riverside after the tournament."

"You think they have a thing going?"

"Definitely. They were going at it pretty heavily in Tommy's SUV when I saw them."

"That explains the poison ivy."

"What do you mean?"

"She has it on her face and private parts. So does he."

"I never intended for her to get it."

"What are you talking about Joe?"

"Oh, nothing."

"That Tommy better be careful who he's getting involved with. Martin Yates isn't someone Tommy wants to mess with. The ivy could be the least of his problems."

"I hear you."

Carol Tindle came into the bar. She took up the stool next to Joe.

"Martini, Carol?" Dee asked.

"Yes, and extra onions please."

"Sure."

"Did you think about what we talked about a few days ago Joe?" Carol said while Dee was making the martini.

"Yeah. But right now, I'm in second place in the tournament. I might be able to beat Tommy without having to do anything else."

"Joe, Joe, Joe. Haven't you been listening?"

"I have. But I might be able to beat him heads up."

"Ok. You might want to have a few cards in your back pocket if things fall apart."

"I know that's what you think, but it's just not me."

"You need to make it you. Remember, it might not even be Tommy you have to prepare for. Didn't you say there were some other golfers who could win?"

"Yeah. But what can I do to any of them?"

"Hey, they're all guys, aren't they? Well, you're all alike. Just think of the kinds of things that distract all guys."

"Like what?"

Carol put her hands under her breasts and lifted them up. "Like these."

"So if I show my chest, it's doing to distract them somehow?"

Carol laughed.

"Not yours, but if I showed mine, I'll bet I'd get a reaction."

"Yeah. But you're not competing."

"Are spectators allowed?"

"Yeah."

"Then I'll come watch on Saturday and if you need me to flash one of the other golfers, I'll do it."

"You're kidding?"

"No. You just need to point out the golfer you want me to distract and I'll do it."

"Huh?"

"Joe, you tell me when you make the turn at number nine on Saturday and I'll go find the golfer in question if you're still concerned. Don't worry, it'll work."

213

"What if there is more than one golfer who I'm in contention with?"

"Hell, I'll just take my top off and stand by the greens jumping up and down. That should do the trick."

"You know what I mean."

"Joe, you need to think out a few more possibilities."

"I guess."

"Think about it and let's get together on Friday night and see what you have come up with."

"Ok."

The two drank for another hour. Then Joe paid the tab and they left, together.

After they had left, Martin Yates stopped in.

"Dee, is Harry around?"

"Yeah. He's in his office going over those papers with Mary that Helen dropped off. Do you want to join them?"

"No. I can wait until he's done talking to her."

"Mary went into his office some time ago. They're probably just about done. Let me find out for you."

Dee called Harry on the phone. "Hey Harry. Martin's here to see you." "OK, I'll tell him."

"Harry said they'll be out in a few minutes. They're just finishing up."

"Thanks. Say, when did Helen leave?"

"Maybe three hours ago."

"Oh, she didn't come back to the restaurant."

"Maybe she went to the pharmacy to get something for that poison ivy. Seems to be a lot of going around."

"Who else has it?"

"Tommy Anderson."

"Was he in here also?"

"Yeah. He left a little while after she did."

Martin was getting a little pissed off. His whole body language was changing. Finally, Harry came out of the kitchen followed by Mary.

"Martin, thanks for sending these papers over for me," Mary said.

"No problem. You should have everything you need."

"I'm the official Saturday at Blue Rock, so I'll bring the updated scores with me to The American after play concludes, Mary," Harry added.

"Then I should be all set," Mary responded. "I think I'll get back to my place. I've got a lot to do. See ya."

"See you Mary," Martin Said.

"If you need anything else," Harry said, "just call."

"I will."

Mary left. Martin looked at Harry, "I've got to get going as well Harry. I've got something to attend to."

"Thanks again Martin for getting that stuff over to us. Was there something else you wanted? Dee had said you needed to talk to me."

"No, nothing. It can wait. No problem."

Then Martin left in a hurry.

"Dee, did I miss something? Why does Martin seem angry?"

"It has nothing to do with you Harry."

She went on to tell Harry about the conversations she had with Helen and Tommy. She told him about the poison ivy and Martin said she didn't come back to work. Then she said Tommy had left right after Helen did.

Harry said, "Tommy better watch his back."

Chapter 32

On Friday night, Joe and Carol went to Sundancers together for a light dinner and a few drinks. Arriving at Carol's at six, she was already waiting in the front yard. She was wearing a very tight black pair of skinny jeans under a lacy, off shoulder, over-sized shirt. Under that she wore a honey-gold tank top, but from a distance you'd never know it was there. The shirt seductively fell off one shoulder, revealing her neck, collarbone and left shoulder. The shoes were flat and simple, with gold, copper and silver trim. Carol locked the door to her place when Joe pulled into her driveway.

"Hey Joe."
"Wow, Carol, you look great."
"I don't look any different today than I did a few days ago."
"Yes. You've done something different."
"I did get my hair cut. Remember it used to be down to the middle of my back. Now, it's shoulder length."
"Maybe that's it."
"Or maybe you're just horny."

"Could be that too. Actually, I think the colors you have on are just real flattering. You wear gold well."

"You seem to be gaining some confidence lately Joe. Good for you."

"You've had something to do with it Carol. I used to be pretty shy. I probably still am with other woman, but I feel at ease around you."

"Lots of guys feel that way around me."

"Oh? You sleeping with lots of guys these days?"

"No. I'm just saying guys tend to be at ease around me."

"I don't know about others Carol, but I definitely am."

"I'm glad. Let's get going to Sundancers."

They drove down Route 28 and turned into the parking lot at Sundancers. As they were about to get out of Joe's car, Carol said, "There's Tommy. What the hell happened to him?"

"I don't know."

The two looked at Tommy as he crossed in front of Joe's car. Tommy had his arm in a sling and a black and blue right eye.

Carol said, "He must have crossed someone the wrong way."

"Tommy's done that quite a bit lately."

"Yeah, I heard about him and Helen. I wonder if he and Martin tangled?"

"He'd probably be in the hospital or worse if Martin went after him."

"You're probably right. Let's get inside and see what he has to say."

Joe parked at the end of the nearly full parking lot. They went inside. The bar was pretty full. It was very loud with people talking and Harry had WCOD doing another live show in anticipation of a good turnout for the golf tournament.

They couldn't find a seat at the bar but did find a table over by the DJ booth. They sat down.

Dee saw them come in. She came around from behind the bar walking up to Joe and Carol at the table they had taken.

"Pretty busy tonight," Joe said to Dee.

"Sure is. Harry's running a special for dinner and drinks tonight and it looks like its bringing them in."

"Say Dee, do you know what happened to Tommy?"

Dee looked back at the bar. Tommy was seated on the opposite side of the bar next to a few women.

"He said someone jumped him Wednesday night when he got home."

"Anyone we know?"

"Tommy said he didn't see who jumped him. He was hit from behind and went down. The next thing he knew, he woke up lying in his driveway with a black eye, a lump on the head and a sprained ligament in his elbow."

Carol said, "Does that mean he isn't going to play tomorrow?"

"He hasn't said," Dee responded.

"I wonder who got to Tommy?" Joe thought out loud.

"I know Martin Yates was after him. Helen was in here on Wednesday and so was Tommy. Martin had come in a little while later looking for Helen and I told him she had left some time earlier. Martin asked if Tommy had been in here when Helen was here and I said yes, he was here also. Then I said, come to think of it, Tommy left right after Helen did. Martin became noticeably angry and left right away. He peeled out when he left the parking lot."

"You think he went after Tommy?" Joe asked.

"Maybe. He seemed like he was really pissed and has good cause to be after Tommy. Did you know both Helen and Tommy have poison ivy, and in relatable areas?"

218

"I didn't know that for sure, but I'm not surprised. I knew Tommy did, and if they were together, well, it goes without saying, right?"

"Martin isn't stupid. Right Carol? I'm sure he figured it out. And now he's after Tommy."

Joe stood, "I'm going to find out if Tommy's still playing tomorrow or not."

He walked away from the women. Tommy was sitting next to a young woman probably in her mid-20s. Joe didn't know her. He approached Tommy from his other side.

"Hey Tommy. What happened to you?"

"Someone jumped me when I got home on Wednesday night. I ended up getting knocked out. When I awoke, who ever did this was gone."

He held up his arm with the sling and pointed to his eye.

"Looks pretty bad. You think you'll be able to play tomorrow?" Joe asked.

"I'm going to give it a try. Sharon is going to take care of me and help me get better," Tommy said, putting his arm around the woman next to him. "Joe, do you know Sharon Larson?"

Joe leaned around Tommy and shook Sharon's hand.

"No, I don't think I've had the pleasure before."

"Oh, you'd know Joe. She's all pleasure."

Sharon laughed. She leaned back, "Nice to meet you Joe, didn't you go to high school with Tommy?"

"Yes."

"I first met Tommy when I was a freshman in high school. D-Y was playing baseball against our team. I was one of the cheerleaders for my school."

"What school was that?"

"Falmouth."

"I remember that game. I was on the team as well."

"Then you probably saw me there. I was the cute blond with the tight ass."

Tommy turned, "She's still the cute blond with the tight ass."

Then he put his hand on her butt and pinched her.

"Not here Tommy. I'll take good care of you later."

"Nice to meet you Sharon."

"You too Joe."

Tommy turned to Joe, "Don't get any ideas Joe. Sharon only goes for the winners."

Joe turned and walked back to Carol.

"What did he say?" Carol asked.

"He said he's going to give it a try tomorrow."

"Do you think he'll be able to compete?"

"With Tommy, you never know if he has an actual injury or if he's using the situation to get laid."

"I didn't think he had any trouble in that area."

"He probably doesn't but he's working on an old friend over there. Maybe he thinks he needs the sympathy thing to get her in the sack tonight."

"Well, if he gets her in the sack tonight, that will take some of his stamina away from tomorrow. Plus, if there is anything to those injuries, he might not be able to perform."

"Not perform isn't in Tommy's dictionary."

"I don't mean that way, I mean on the course."

"I'm sure he'll come up with something. He'll take one of those energy drinks or some other kind of stimulant "

"That gives me an idea. Remind me to give you something when we get to my house later. I think I have just the thing that will help his game tomorrow."

"I'm not trying to help his game. I want him to play lousy."

"I'm kidding Joe. If its stimulants Tommy wants, I have just the thing."

"Ok. I'll remind you when we get to your place.

Tommy stayed at the bar for another hour or so. He and Sharon had a number of drinks and periodically got up and danced to the music Kevin was playing. After a while, the liquor started to kick in. Tommy had a little trouble maintaining his balance and at one point, tripped over a chair and fell to his knees. Sharon helped him up.

"Tommy baby, I think it's time for us to leave."

"Sure Sharon. Let's get out of here so you can take care of me."

Sharon put her arm around Tommy and led him to the door. They got into her car and left.

"Looks like Tommy can add inebriation to the list of things that might affect his play tomorrow," said Carol.

"Maybe I'll have a chance to win the tournament," Joe said raising his glass.

Carol picked her drink up and clinked his glass. "I think you're well on your way to finishing on top Joe. Just stick with me."

"Sounds good to me."

"Then why don't we get out of here and go to my place?"

"I'm ready."

Joe paid their tab and they left.

Out in the parking lot, Joe saw Tommy's car at the top of the hill next to the brush. They must have taken Sharon's car home. Joe then went to his trunk, opened it and took out a cooler. He walked over to Tommy's vehicle and tried the door. It was open. He opened the driver's side door and pressed the trunk release. Then, he closed the door, went to the back of the vehicle and opened the trunk. Tommy's golf clubs were in there along with a few other things. Joe took a zip-lock bag out of the cooler, opened it and put the contents inside Tommy's golf bag. It stunk. He closed the trunk and walked back to his car and drove away.

Harry came into the bar area, and walked over to Dee, "What happened to the golfers?"

"If you mean Tommy and Joe, they both left with the woman du jour."

"Pre-celebratory thing huh?"

"I guess."

"Well, I hope they show up on time in the morning. I don't want to have to disqualify either of them."

"You the official tomorrow Harry?"

"Yep. Me and Martin. And I follow all the rules."

"Yeah, Yeah, Yeah." Dee said. She went back to bartending.

Chapter 33

As Joe and Carol were leaving Sundancers, Carol said, "So what was that all about Joe?"

"I had something I wanted to leave with Tommy."

"And you put it in his trunk?"

"Actually, I put it in his golf bag, but yeah. He's gonna be pretty mad tomorrow."

"What did you put in there?"

"A dead mouse."

"A what?"

"A dead mouse. His clubs are gonna stink tomorrow. He'll think a mouse got into his trunk and died in his golf bag."

"And how does this help you tomorrow?"

"I got a whiff when I put it in his bag. It's nasty."

"So, you think it'll have an effect on his play tomorrow?"

"Yup. Whenever he's carrying his bag, that's all he'll smell. And every time he pulls a club, that's all he'll smell. That's gotta be distracting, don't ya think?"

"Good thinking Joe. I'm proud of you."

"You got me thinking a few weeks ago. Then one day, I found a mouse in one of the traps I had set down in my cellar. I decided to put it in a zip-lock and save it for an occasion just like this."

"I guess you are thinking ahead. You've come a long way Joe Campbell."

Carol moved over closer to Joe and gave him a big kiss. She ran her hand up his leg, "What other surprises do you have?"

"Oh, there's no more surprises there Carol. You've already discovered everything there is in there."

"Really?"

"Really."

She unzipped his fly and went to work. Joe had all he could do to keep the SUV on the road. Carol was successful in her endeavor after a few minutes.

"See, now there's another surprise," she said.

"I see."

They pulled into Carol's driveway and got out. Joe zipped his fly up and walked around to open her door.

"What a gentleman."

"I try."

"Let's get inside so you can try again."

"You'll probably have to wait until morning for me to be ready again," Joe said sheepishly.

"I doubt it," Carol said opening her front door.

As they walked inside, Carol turned to Joe, kissed him, "Joe, would you put some music on? I'll get us a drink. What'll you have?"

"Have any beer?"

"Yes. Coors Light or Bud?"

"I'll have a Bud."

"I even have frosted mugs as well."

"Perfect. You said you have something you want me to have for tomorrow?"

Carol went into her bathroom and opened the closet. She took out a pill bottle. She came back into the room and handed the bottle to Joe. He looked at it.

"It doesn't say what's in the bottle?"
"I took the label off."
"Why?"
"Don't ask. Just suffice it to say that when Tommy gets one of these, he'll be on overdrive."
"And how will that help me win?"
"He'll be so fidgety, he probably won't be able to play well."
"What do you mean probably?"
"Well, so long as he doesn't take a sedative to counteract these pills, he'll be on overdrive."
"How do I give one to Tommy?"

"If he has coffee, water, soda or anything to drink, just drop it in. The pill will dissolve quickly. It doesn't have any taste so he won't even know he took it."
"Ok, if you say so."
"I do."
"This isn't like, really dangerous, is it Carol? I don't want to hurt anyone."
"Nope. Your conscience should be clear."

Joe put the pills in his pocket.

"Let me get the drinks and then let's work on your game a little. I want you to be on top."

Carol went to her kitchen, opened the freezer door and took out two frosted mugs. She poured a Bud and a Coors Light. In the icy glass, she made a B on one and a C on the other one. Then, she took a jar of pills out of a drawer, taking one blue pill out. She crushed the blue pill to a powder and put it into the mug with the B on it. She slowly stirred it until the powder dissolved. Then, she picked both mugs up and walked back into the living room. Joe was using phone, didn't talk to anyone. He pressed a few keys and then put it away.

"What's up?"
"I was just checking my voice mail."
"Anything interesting?"
"Yeah. You know that landscaping software I've been working on?"
"Yeah."
"Well, I had a message from my attorney saying I've got an offer from a big company to buy out my software business."
"Really?"
"Yeah. Mark Goldstein, my attorney, left me a message saying one of the companies I had been trying to pitch my software to is interested in buying it."
"What company is it?"
"USA Landscaping Supply Company. They're out of Atlanta. He said they've been trying to contact me all day and when they couldn't, they called him."
"What're you gonna to do?"
"I don't know. Mark said I should call him as soon as I get this message no matter what time of the day it is."
"You gonna to call him now?"
"I guess I should."

Joe pressed the keys to look up Mark's phone number in his contacts list. The phone rang at the other end of the call.
"Joe, I've been waiting for your call."
"Sorry Mark. I'm playing in a golf tournament this weekend and I had a mandatory meeting I had to attend to tonight."

"Listen, USA Landscaping is really interested. They said they tried to contact you all day but couldn't get through."

"That's probably because I gave them my business phone at home and I haven't been there since this morning."

"Well, they don't want to lose this deal so they called me."

"What deal?"

"They told me when you talked to them a few weeks ago, you gave them your pricing and when their representative said it sounded a little steep, you told her they should just buy your company. Apparently, they took you seriously and want to make an offer."

"What kind of offer?"

"You'll have to confirm this, but I think they are talking around eight million to buy you out."

"Wow, eight million."

"That's the range their counsel was talking about when I talked to him on the phone this afternoon."

"Do you think I should accept it?"

"You'll have to make that call Joe. Eight million is quite a bit of money."

"It sure is. Can I think about it?"

"Sure. You don't have to accept it. And if you don't, they might up the offer."

"Really?"

"This company thinks you're on to something Joe. You might want to play coy."

"Ok Mark. Let me think about it. I'll call you tomorrow after I play golf."

"Talk to you tomorrow."

Joe hung up the phone. Carol looked at him with a puzzled look on her face.

"What was that all about? And eight million?"

"One of the companies I had been pitching my software to wants to buy the whole thing."

227

"Yeah?"

"Yeah, and Mark says they're talking in the range of eight million dollars."

"Joe, that's great. You'll be wealthy."

"It'll put me in your class."

"Joe, you're already in with me. What do you have to do next?"

"Mark thinks I should play hard to get. He thinks they'll offer more."

"Do you have any other companies offering to buy your company?"

"I never even thought about selling it."

"Maybe you want to see if there's any other interested parties?"

"I don't know. Mark said USA Landscaping wants to move fast. They might retract their offer if they think I'm trying to put them into a bidding war."

"Well, put it out of your mind for the rest of tonight and see what tomorrow brings."

Carol handed Joe a mug. Joe picked it up, "What's with the B?"

Carol held hers up so he could see the C. "I'm having Coors Light, you're having Bud."

"Good idea marking the mugs."

"Have to keep things straight."

"Don't you like Bud?"

"Not really. It has a different taste to it sometimes. Plus, Coors is the diet beer isn't it? Women are always looking to shave calories out their day."

Joe took a drink, "I know what you mean about the taste sometimes. This one's OK though. The frozen mug is a real winner."

"Normally, I'd have a martini or a glass of wine but since you're having a beer, I though I'd do the same."

"You know, now that you mention it, I don't think I've ever seen you have a beer."

"Hey Joe, I'm always flexible. Speaking of flexible, what do you think?"

"I don't know."

"Let's go to bed and see what comes up."

"Ok. I have to be up early anyway."

"Then we better get to it."

A half hour later, Joe was ready to perform.

Chapter 34

The golfers had pretty much all left Sundancers by 10 pm. The live broadcast by WCOD turned out to be a big hit. The place was still packed as the band M-Sound was about to take the stage. Harry had them play Saturday last weekend, and he figured he'd try them Friday this weekend, mostly because the crowds can be very different. This would give him a better idea who to book when as the busy summer season kicked in. Kevin from WCOD was just packing up his equipment.

"Good job tonight Kevin. I think we've been able to get a great jump start for the season," Harry said as he helped Kevin clean things up at the DJ booth.

"Glad to help out Harry. None of the other sponsors asked us to participate and I know our management was glad you asked us to do the live shows."

"The whole idea of the golf tournament has worked out real well. My business is already ahead of last year by thirty percent. And the other merchants have all indicated their business is up as well."

"Glad to be a part of that."

"Thanks again Kevin."

"No problem."

"Do you need a hand getting anything to your car?"

"Already done. I'm going to hang around for a little while if you don't mind."

"Stay as long as you want. Can I have Dee get you anything?"

"She already has. Thanks Harry."

"See you later."

"Later."

Kevin walked to the dark corner of the bar and took up a stool that had been leaning against the bar reserved for someone. A guy standing against the window said, "I think they're saving that seat for someone."

Tina turned to see Kevin sitting, "And here he is."

"Thanks Tina."

"Dee, get Kevin a beer and a shot and give me another shot please," asked Tina.

"I already ordered a beer, and I don't really do shots Tina. They kick my ass."

"Kevin, you're off duty now. Time to kick back and relax."

She ran her hand up his thigh under the cover of the bar. Kevin sighed. She took his hand and put it at the bottom edge of her skirt.

Tina picked up her shot glass and downed the shot. With her head leaning back, she said, "I like that warm feeling."

Then, she turned towards Kevin forcing his hand up and under her skirt. Kevin did not withdraw the hand.

"What do we have here Kevin?"

She had her hand at the top of his thigh. "Not another roll of quarters I hope?"

She gently rubbed him. He returned the favor.

231

Dee saw the action-taking place. She printed a check and put it in front of Kevin. Kevin turned back to the bar, "I didn't ask for a check."

Tina looked at him, "Yes you did. Now, let's get out of here."

Kevin got the message. He paid Tina's tab and they left.

As they were walking out, Ron said to Dee, "I thought Kevin was going to hang around for a while?"

"He thought so as well. Tina had other ideas."

"So she convinced him to leave?"

"I don't think he needed much convincing. She just cornered him."

"I saw Tommy leaving with a young woman, Sharon, I think."

"Yeah, I overheard him talking to her. They apparently go back to high school."

"Where did they go?"

"I think they're rekindling their past friendship."

"Oh, Tommy's going to put it to her."

"I didn't get that impression. I think she was going to be the one in control. He was tripping all over the place, so he may not be much good to her. Although he did offer to let her take care of his aches and pains. "

"Really? He used that line on her?"

"No, actually, she used it on him."

"I think I'd like to get to know her."

"Ron, you're all talk."

"So, that ace bandage and sling were for show?"

"I don't know. I heard Tommy telling Joe about being attacked Wednesday night at his house. He might have a real injury."

"I'm sure the golfers would all like that. Especially Joe and Tony."

232

"Why would Tony care?"

"He's in contention as of the end of the second round just behind Joe and Tommy."

"I always thought Tony was just a casual golfer."

"He is. He said he just had a couple of real good rounds."

"Doesn't he think he will do well at Blue Rock?"

"Actually, he might. He plays a pretty good short game. Straight and accurate with most shots plus he's a pretty good putter."

"Wouldn't it be funny if Tony were in the lead come Sunday?"

"Yeah. All that posturing by Tommy and Joe and Tony steals the show."

"It would be hilarious."

They both laughed. Tony had finished closing up the kitchen for the night. He wanted to have a beer and relax before going home to get a good night sleep. He wanted to be rested for golf.

"Dee, can I have a beer please."

"Sure Tony. Everything shut down in the kitchen?"

"All the food stuff. We don't get any orders after the band starts anyway."

"You hanging around for a while?"

"Nah. I have to be up by six to make it to the meeting at seven-thirty over at the Blue Rock Restaurant tomorrow morning. I'm playing in the last group so I can rest for an hour after the meeting and before my tee time."

"Well, good luck."

"Thanks. The only stressful thing I can think of tomorrow is I'm playing with Tommy again."

"Tommy a problem for you?"

"He never shuts up. He's an expert on everything and tells you what to shoot, where, how hard, and on and on."

"Gets on your nerves?"

233

"If it's not his expert opinion on golf, we have to listen to his escapades of the past couple of nights. He's always showing off about who he did, how they did it and for how long."

"I guess that could be annoying."

"Sometimes, I just wish someone would shut him up."

"From the looks of it, someone tried."

"I didn't see him today, what happened?"

"He said someone attacked him the other night when he was getting home. He had his arm wrapped and a sling on when he was in here before."

"He was probably faking it."

"He had a real good shiner on his right eye as well."

"Maybe he gave it to himself?"

"I don't know. It looked real to me."

"Well, I'll find out in the morning. I'm going home. I'll stop in tomorrow night. See you then."

"Good luck again Tony."

Later on in the night, the band had just played their last number for the night. They were packing up their equipment and loading it into a van outside the bar. Ron and Dee were cleaning up as most of the patrons had left. There were a few diehards still at the bar but most of them had already had too much to drink.

As the last patron paid and left, Dee said to Ron, "Tomorrow is going to be a very interesting day."

"Why do you say that?"

"Some of the guys still here are in the third round of the Mid-Cape Open tomorrow at Blue Rock. Tony is playing with Joe and Tommy. The bumps and bruises he sustained in the attack on him on Wednesday might physically affect Tommy. I overheard Carol talking to Joe about doing something to distract anyone who might be in contention with Joe on the back nine if Joe is positioned to win."

"What kind of distraction?"

"Carol said something about flashing."

"They'd distract me."

"Any skin would distract you Ron. Even the suggestion of skin would distract you."

"Dee, what are you saying?"

"You're easy."

"Plus, Tommy went home with that young woman Sharon earlier. If I know Tommy, he'll be up with her all night. He should be totally exhausted by the time they tee off."

Harry walked up to the bar. He sat at a stool by the entrance, "That was a good night."

"I'll say so," said Dee.

"I don't ever remember us being busy this early in the season," added Ron.

"This tournament was a good idea," Harry said.

"We'll see how things turn out tomorrow," Ron said.

"Everyone talking about it?" Harry asked.

"That and the talk by and about the golfers."

"What kind of talk?" Harry asked.

"Everyone was talking about Tommy and Tommy picked up a young woman for the night and left with her."

"So? There's nothing unusual about that."

"Maybe so, but he is supposedly hurting from that attack on him."

"Yeah, right."

"Tommy has some good points, doesn't he?"

"No he doesn't, at least none I'm aware of. Dee, have you been out with Tommy?"

"Why do you want to know?"

"No reason," Harry got up and went back to his office.

Dee opened the cash register and counted out the money. She put it in a canvas bag zipping it closed.

"I'm going to put this in the safe. I'll be right back."

235

Ron continued to clean up. When she came back in, she said, "Ron, make me a raspberry vodka and sprite, please."

"Sure."

"And get yourself a beer."

The two sat at the bar for a few minutes drinking their drinks and talking about how busy the place was that night. Then, they finished cleaning up and closed up for the night.

Chapter 35

At 7:00 am, Carol woke up to find Joe missing from her bed. She walked into her kitchen, and Joe was on the phone.

"Ok Mark. I'll call them in a few minutes."

"Who you talking to this early?"

"My attorney."

"Didn't you talk to him last night?"

"Yeah. I got up about an hour ago so I called in to my business phone for messages. There were eight in there from USA Landscaping."

"You already knew they called you and left messages."

"I know. But the last one was from after my call to Mark last night. They asked me to call first thing this morning."

"Even on Saturday?"

"The message said right away, any time of the day or night."

"They must really be interested."

"I think so."

"So, what did they say?"

"I guess Mark called them back last night after my call. He told them I was thinking about it and would get back to them."

"And?"

"And the message they left after I had talked to Mark increased their offer to ten million and if I agree, they would convene their Board of Directors over the weekend and approve the deal."

"Boy, that sounds like they're really trying to lock you up."

"That's what Mark said."

"What are you gonna do?"

"I gotta think for a few minutes. I'll call Mark before I go to the tournament."

"Listen Joe, why don't you ask for an exclusive retainer? Ask for a million, non-refundable. You won't shop the software, and risk a bidding war, if they'll lock you up with the retainer."

"Why a million?"

"It'll flush them out right away. Not too small, not too big. You can even say it has to be in writing with Mark by end of the day today. Tell them you'll give them an exclusive for one week."

"A week?"

"Sure, why not. If they're serious, you can wrap this whole thing up in a few days and you'll be set for the rest of your life."

"I like the sounds of that."

"Wouldn't it be nice to live a life that allows you to do whatever and whenever you want?"

"Like you Carol?"

"Like me. You could come with me when I travel. We could become friends with benefits."

"Sounds fascinating."

"It is. Think about last night. That was a nice benefit wasn't it?"

"Sure was."

Joe picked up his phone and called his attorney back again. He talked with Mark about his ideas, and after a few minutes, he hung up.

"What did he say?"

"He liked the idea. He's going to call them right away. He said he'll call me as soon as he has an answer."

"Good for you Joe Campbell."

"Thanks for the advice Carol. You may have just made me a millionaire."

"You're welcome."

"Well, I've got to get going. There's a meeting at 7:30 at the restaurant at Blue Rock for all competitors."

"I'll see you there later this morning. I'll be the one flashing the golfers."

Joe laughed. He kissed her and left.

Tommy was up and dressed at 6:00 am. He walked into Sharon's bedroom at 6:45 and gave her a kiss. Sharon was half under a sheet and half exposed. She was completely naked. She opened her eyes, "Tommy, what're you doing?"

"I've got to be to Blue Rock by 7:30 babe, and my car is still at Sundancers. Can you get up and take me there?"

"Take my car. I'll get it later."

"Want me to leave the keys somewhere for you?"

"Lock them in the car. I have another set."

"Ok. See you later."

He kissed her again and left. Driving down Route 28, Tommy had forgotten about the arm and sling, and had a smile on his face until he looked in the rear view mirror and saw the black eye again. It brought him back to reality.

He pulled into Sundancers parking lot. The only car there was his as he stopped in front of it pulling into one of the many open parking spaces. He got out, threw the keys on the floor on the driver's side and locked the door of Sharon's car.

He jumped into his car, started it up and put it in gear. He was on his way for the ten-minute drive to Blue Rock.

"What the hell is that smell?" he thought to himself. He turned at the light, went up the street and turned right again. He drove past Bass River Golf Course and made a left turn into the Red Jacket Resort where Blue Rock Golf course was located. He parked in the lot by the driving range.

Tommy got out of his car and opened the back door. The smell was a little stronger. He didn't find anything so he went to the trunk. He opened it. The smell almost knocked him over. If he had had a big breakfast, it probably would have come back up right there on the spot.

Tony Davis pulled into the parking lot and parked next to Tommy. He got out of his car and opened his trunk. As Tony was taking his clubs out of the trunk, he said, "Anderson, what the hell is that smell?"

Tommy pretended not to hear Tony. He took his golf bag out of the car and closed the trunk. The smell was still strong. Tommy began taking the clubs out of the bag. When he had all of them out, he turned the bag upside down. A dead mouse fell out.

Tony laughed and covered his nose.

"You better do something about that smell Anderson if you want to play in my group today."

"I don't think we're playing together today anyway. I thought the final group was going to be me, Joe Campbell and Russ Ford."

Tommy took his bag and walked over to the cart barn. As Tony walked up to the practice range, he could see Tommy hosing his golf bag down over at the barn. Tony put his bag down and walked in the direction of the restaurant for the meeting.

Tony entered the restaurant and seeing Joe Campbell, walked over taking a seat at the same table.

"Mornin' Tony."

"Hey Joe."

"Ready to play?"

"Yep."

"Seen Tommy yet?"

"As a matter of fact I did. He's over by the cart barn washing his golf bag as we speak."

"Washing it?"

"Yeah. When I parked next to him and was getting my clubs out of my car, Tommy was taking all the clubs out of his bag. Then he turned his bag over and a dead mouse fell out. The thing stunk."

"So, you think he's going to be able to play?"

"He's cleaning the bag probably hoping to get rid of that smell."

"Maybe it got on his clubs as well."

"Like the ivy?"

"Yeah."

"We can only hope. I told him if he didn't get rid of that smell, he wasn't playing in my group. He said you and Russ Ford are the ones he's playing with today. Maybe you want to check out the smell from his bag and tell him you won't stand for it."

"I don't think Tommy will cave to any threats we make."

"Maybe so, but we can complain to the officials and get him to play by himself or someone else."

"Isn't Harry the official today?"

"Oh, yeah."

"Do you think he'll come down on Tommy?"

"Probably not, unless he thinks it'll be bad press for the tournament. Harry has been real big behind this whole thing and I know he wants it to be successful."

"Let's see what Tommy does." Joe said as Tommy walked in to the meeting.

Chapter 36

Harry Adams stood in front of the group of golfers inside the restaurant at Blue Rock Golf Course. He had the leader scoreboard mounted on an easel. He began the meeting.

"Gentlemen, today we start the final weekend for the Mid-Cape Open. Blue Rock was selected in order to provide some diversity and challenge in the tournament. We expect there to be some very low scores on this par-54 course. If you have a great short game, you can do well here. If you hit left or right, you're in trouble. We expect a good crowd on hand around the golf course, as its more accessible than the bigger courses. There will be some vendor booths set up throughout the course for spectator benefit. Please be courteous of everyone today. It's important to the sponsors the tournament be perceived as a positive event. After play today, we will have a get together here starting at 5 pm. We'll hold a meeting at 4:30 to discuss tomorrow's round and answer any questions. Good Luck everyone."

Harry went through and read off the pairings for Saturday's round. For the ninth group, he said, "Antonio Davis, Len Simpson and Ben Peters."

Tony said out loud, "Thank God."

Then he looked at Tommy Anderson and smiled.

Harry announced the last pairing, "Joe Campbell, Tommy Anderson and Russ Ford."

Joe stood up, "Harry, I think Tommy has a problem with his equipment."

Everyone laughed.

"No, I'm serious. I understand his clubs and bag smell really bad."

"I've cleaned my stuff up," Tommy replied.

"I just don't want any unnecessary distractions out there today," Joe said.

"Don't worry Joe. My clubs are the last thing you need to worry about. Try thinking about your own equipment," Tommy laughed.

"Ok guys, let's get out there."

The meeting broke up. Joe said to Tony, "I hope he's right. I don't want to be around something nauseating."

"Oh, just being around Tommy is nauseating, Joe," Tony said with a snicker. "I'm just glad it's you and not me that has to play with him. You're going to have to withstand his bull all day. It should be interesting to see if you don't want to whack him with a club before the round's over."

"He's not that bad."

"Ok. Don't say I didn't warn you."

They walked out of the restaurant and down to the driving range. They had about an hour before their tee time would come up. Joe took out his 8-iron and pitching wedge. He hit a bucket of balls in preparation for the round. Tony took out a 7-iron, 6-iron and wedge. He also hit a bucket of balls.

243

As the two finished up, Tommy Anderson came over to the range with his clubs. The foul dead mouse scent was gone. It had been replaced with the distinct smell of gas.

"What did you do Tommy, pour a can of gasoline over your golf bag?" Tony said.

"I had to use something to overcome the smell. You wouldn't have had to worry about me using my clubs if they still had that smell. I would have voluntarily used another set of clubs."

"That's nice to know Tommy. But your clubs still stink."

"Give them a half hour and the gas smell will evaporate."

"He's probably right Tony," Joe said. "Let's go practice putting."

Joe and Tony walked under the arbor and up the path to the putting green. They practiced for fifteen minutes and then decided it was time to go to the clubhouse.

Tony recognized Ben Peters waiting by the starter and went over to them.

"Hey Ben."

"Hey Tony," Ben said. "Looks like we're playing together again."

"Yeah. It's you, me and Len Simpson."

"That should be a good group."

"Hey, anything's better than having to play with Tommy Anderson."

"I hear you."

Len Simpson came out of the clubhouse. He walked over to Tony and Ben.

"How's it going Len?" Tony said.

"Good. Starter says we're up in ten. You ready Tony?"

"Yeah. I was just telling Ben I'm just glad I don't have to play with Tommy."

"I know. He can get under your skin. Especially if he's behind and you're playing good."

"It's his way of getting under your skin to effect you mentally."

"Well, thankfully I don't have to put up with him today."

Len saw Tommy walking up to the clubhouse. "He's playing with Joe and Russ Ford, isn't he?"

"Yeah," Tony said.

"Joe's playing pretty good. I think he might give Tommy a run for his money," Ben said.

"I don't think Tommy's play will matter at all to Russ Ford," Tony said. "He's pretty good and he's played against Tommy before and beat him."

"Hey, we're in this thing too guys. Anything can happen especially playing a course like this one."

"I agree," Len said. "It should be interesting seeing who comes out on top after today."

The starter announced, "Davis, Simpson, Peters. You're on deck."

The three all took out pitching wedges and walked up just off the 1st tee.

Joe Campbell went to his golf bag and took out his cell phone. He remembered he had to make a call to his attorney before play started.

"Mark, it's Joe."

"Morning Joe."

"Did you hear from USA Landscaping?"

"Sure did. They agreed to our proposal. I have a signed letter in front of me right now indicating we have an exclusive deal with them on the table with a non-refundable one million dollar down payment for the next week. They only added one stipulation to our proposal. We can't say anything to anyone about the deal until the contracts are signed. USA is a public company and their stock could be affected by any premature disclosure. They are going to try to get their Board together later today to approve the deal. I hope to hear from them later on. So, don't say anything to anyone until we sign."

"Wow," was all Joe could say.

"I agree. Listen Joe, you'll have to come to my office to sign the papers. Then, you can work out the details for getting the software and documentation to USA. It shouldn't take very long since there aren't any employees or facilities to deal with. Can you stop by later today?"

"I'll come by after I finish playing in the tournament. I'm at Blue Rock."

"Good. I'm only a few minutes from there. It shouldn't take long."

"I should be there around 4 pm."

"Joe, you have a good round. I'll call if anything comes up. Congratulations. You're now going to be a millionaire."

"Thanks Mark. I'll see you later."

Joe hung up the phone and walked over by the 1st tee. He had a big smile on his face. Tony was waiting to tee off and noticed Joe walking over with the smile. He walked back to Joe, "What are you so happy about? You haven't won yet."

"Oh, nothing. I just hit a homerun with that software program I developed over the winter."

Tony had talked with Dee about what Joe had told her of his business so he had a vague idea what Joe was talking about.

"Just go out there and beat Tommy Anderson," was all Tony said to Joe.

"I'll do my best."

246

"Just do it, Joe."

Joe had the adrenaline going now. He'd have to get it under control before the 1st tee.

Tony turned and walked back to the tee.

Chapter 37

The first few groups of golfers teed off on the 1st hole by the clubhouse. Harry and Martin stood behind the tee watching. Adam Crane, one of the golfers in the fourth group to go off, shot a hole-in-one on the 1st hole. Many of the other golfers in the early groups had birdies.

Martin said to Harry, "Looks like we'll see some real low scores if this kind of play keeps up?"

"Yeah," Harry said. "We might see a shakeup in the leader board as well."

"Don't you think the leaders will play just as well?"

"Some of these guys are long ball hitters. That's what got them to where they are. This course requires accuracy and a great short game. We'll see some good chipping and putting today."

"I'm glad the weather's holding up. Seems to have brought out a good crowd to watch," Martin said looking up at the clear blue sky.

Harry saw Tommy Anderson walking up to the clubhouse from the practice green. He didn't want a confrontation between Martin and Tommy.

"Martin, why don't you take a cart and go out and see how things are going with the first groups that went out. Make sure they're keeping a ten minute per hole pace."

"Sure Harry."

"I'll keep things going here."

Martin took a golf cart and drove down the hill past the 9th green, across the bridge on the pond and up the hill on the other side. Within a minute, he was out of sight.

Tommy walked up to where Harry was standing and put his bag against the fence. Joe Campbell and Russ Ford were sitting on a bench outside the door to the clubhouse. Tony and his group were standing just off the right side of the tee waiting for their turn.

Tommy spoke to Harry, "What's it look like so far Harry?"

"Crane got a hole in one. Probably half the golfers shot birdie. Looks like we'll see some real low scores today."

"So, the course is playing pretty easy?" Tommy asked.

"I don't know about easy Tommy, I think some of these guys have a pretty good short game."

"I plan on continuing to be the leader after today. My short game is pretty good."

"Tommy, I know your short game. It's fair. I think you'll find some of these guys are better."

"We'll see."

Tony's group was called to the tee. Ben Peters was first to hit. He didn't use a tee. He took a few practice swings with his pitching wedge and then hit his ball. It went very high landing two feet from the cup.

"Nice shot Ben," Len Simpson said.

Len hit next. His wedge shot was a little long leaving a putt of around twelve feet. Then it was Tony's turn. As

Tony bent over to tee his ball, Tommy said, "You should do well here Tony. It's a short course. Kind of fits your game."

Tony looked back at him, "Screw you Tommy."

Harry walked up on the tee box to say something to Tony.

"Tony, try to keep it clean today. We've got a lot of spectators here and we're trying to promote this event."

"Ok Harry. I get it."

Then Tony took a few practice swings. He hit his ball. It didn't go very high. As everyone watched, the shot landed short of the green and ran up right towards the cup. It looked like the ball would fall short of the cup but at the last second, it dropped in.

"Tony, a hole in one! Nice shot!" Harry said from behind the tee.

The spectators watching clapped and cheered. Tony turned around and bowed. Then everyone laughed as he smiled, "Now that's how it's done."

The golfers picked up their bags and walked to the green. Tony walked up to the flag, pulled it out and bent down retrieving his ball. Len was first to putt. He made it for a birdie. Ben also made his putt for a birdie.

Joe and Russ had watched the group from the tee box.

"Russ, looks like the competition is going to be tough today."

"Yeah. Can you believe Tony got a hole-in-one?"

"He plays a control game. Straight, not real long but he has a deadly short game."

"Then he should score pretty low on this course."

Tommy had been sitting on the bench by the clubhouse drinking an iced coffee. At one point, he went inside to use the restroom. When he did, Joe took the opportunity to drop the upper Carol had given him into Tommy's coffee.

250

The starter announced, "In the final group we have Tommy Anderson, Joe Campbell and Russ Ford."

Tommy joined Joe and Russ on the tee.

Tommy was first to hit. He stood behind his ball for a pretty long time. Then, he took two practice swings. When he hit his ball, he hit it similar to Tony's shot. The ball didn't have much height on it and it was headed right at the stick. It looked like it would hit the flag but just missed. The low flight and not hitting anything, his ball ran all the way to the back of the green. He'd have a difficult putt from where the ball stopped.

Joe was next to hit. He put his tee shot ten feet from the cup. Russ Ford used a tee placing his ball very close to the ground. When he hit his shot, the ball went very high landing three feet from the cup. Both Joe and Russ shot birdie. Tommy had to settle for a par, as his putt required a pretty significant break in it to navigate the green. He missed the cup by a foot and then tapped in.

On the 2nd hole, 131 yards from tee to cup, the golfers had to be careful not to over shoot the green. On the right side, the slope led to the water. On the backside was a hill leading down to the 3rd tee. Joe was first to hit.

Joe took out a 9-iron. He hit his shot high and left. When the ball landed, it landed on the side of the hill to the left of the green. His ball then rolled down the hill and on to the green coming to rest five feet from the cup.

Russ was next to hit. He placed his wedge shot right on the green fifteen feet from the cup. Tommy wanted to show his strength and selected his pitching wedge for the tee shot. He reached back for a little extra when he hit his ball. It went very high landing on the backside of the green thirty-five feet from the cup.

The golfers walked up to the green. Russ and Joe marked their balls. Tommy went to the back of the green for the long putt. He surveyed the shot and then addressed the ball. It was a long putt and like the first hole, he ran the ball past the cup. He was able to sink the return five-footer for par.
Russ and Joe both tapped in for birdie.

At the 119-yard 3rd, all three golfers pulled out their pitching wedges. The 3rd requires hitting over water up onto an elevated green. The ground left of the green and behind the green pitches back towards the green. The terrain to the right drops off quickly eventually leading back to the water. The elevated green is faced with sand traps all along the front.

Joe placed his tee shot ten feet from the cup. Russ did a little better, leaving his ball about six feet from the cup. Tommy again, tried too hard and ended up off the back of the green. Fortunately, the upslope behind the green stopped his ball.

Joe missed his putt and tapped in for par. Russ continued on a good pace making another birdie. Tommy had to settle for another par.

Walking up the hill to the 4th tee, the golfers came up to Martin Yates seated in a golf cart by the 9th tee box.
"How you playing Joe," Martin said.
"Pretty good. I'm two under."
"Not bad. How about the other guys?"
"Russ is tearing the course up. He's three under. How's everyone ahead of us playing?"
"Pretty well. Adam Crane is six under through eleven."
"How about Tony?"

"He was four under when I last saw him."

"He had to be pretty happy."

"Yeah, I think he's satisfied with his play."

Tommy and Russ were now approaching Martin's cart.

"Well, I'll catch you later," Martin said as he started his cart up and drove back towards the 4th tee and beyond.

"Did you find out how everyone's playing?" Russ asked Joe.

"Yeah. Martin said some guys are playing real well. Adam Crane is six under. Looks like you might be playing with another group come tomorrow," Joe said as they continued on to the 4th tee.

"Tommy's going to have to get his game under control if he wants to be in it," Russ said to Joe.

"Let's just hope he continues to play the way he has so far," Joe said as they reached the tee box.

Tommy had been walking behind them talking to himself.

Chapter 38

The 4th hole is a straight away 130-yard par-3. What makes this hole a challenge is the overgrowth of the trees on both sides of the fairway and the trap in front of the green. Golfers hitting too long will find their ball resting around a stand of tall pine trees backing the green.

Russ was first to hit. He took out his pitching wedge. After a few practice shots, he hit his shot long. It landed at the back edge of the green. Fortunately, it had backspin on it allowing the ball to come back twenty feet ending up a few feet from the cup.

Joe hit next. His wedge shot caught one of the overhanging tree limbs on the right side of the fairway, dropping it straight down. He ended up 30 yards short of the green.

Tommy took out his pitching wedge. He took one practice swing and then placed his tee shot right in the center of the green ten feet from the cup.

"Nice shot Tommy," Russ complimented him.

"You too Russ.   Too bad Joe couldn't control his shot," Tommy said as they walked down the fairway.   "Joe's always trying to beat me at everything," Tommy said as he and Russ stopped to wait for Joe to hit his second shot.

Joe took out a lob wedge and dropped his shot a few feet from the cup.

"That's the way to come back," Russ said.

"Too bad you're only shooting for par," Tommy said to Joe.

Joe didn't respond.   He just picked up his bag and walked up to the green.

Tommy was furthest from the cup so he putted first. He made his putt for a birdie. Russ made his putt also. Joe only had a few feet to make par but he missed his putt and had to settle for a bogey.

Tommy said to Russ as they walked off the green, "See, Joe gets rattled when you say something to him. He gets quiet and then he chokes."

Joe had heard Tommy's comments. "I just missed the shot Tommy. Worry about your own game."

"Hey Joe, I think I'm the person in the lead."

Tommy was playing mental games with Joe and Joe knew it.

Tommy was first to hit at the 255-yard 5th. Not a particularly hard hole, the 5th is straight away, fairly open and with a large forgiving green. Tommy took out a 4-iron. He took a few practice swings trying to make sure he kept up the pressure. When he hit his shot, it went left into the trees about 200 yards out.

Russ was up next. Russ took out a 3-iron. He hit a nice shot with a slight draw landing just short of the green and then running up to within twenty feet of the cup. Joe was last to hit. Joe took out a 5-wood. He didn't want to over swing so he took the club back about three quarters of a swing.

When he hit his ball, it went very high and straight down the fairway. It landed on the front of the green rolling to the back left of the green.

The three started to walk down the fairway. Russ said to Joe, "Let's see how he gets out of this one."

"Keep an eye on him. Tommy has a tendency to improve his ball position if you know what I mean."

"I'll watch him," Russ said.

Joe kept walking up to the green. Russ walked behind Tommy keeping a safe distance from him while being able to see what Tommy was doing. Tommy looked around the trees, then in the tall grass but couldn't find his ball. Every few seconds, Tommy would look up at Russ to see if he was looking. Russ didn't take his eyes off of Tommy.

"I don't see it," Tommy exclaimed.

"Then you'll have to take a penalty," Russ said. "And go back and re-hit."

After looking for ten minutes, Joe said, "What's going on Russ?"

"Tommy can't find his ball. He'll have to take a penalty and then go back and hit another drive."

"Tell him to move it along," Joe said impatiently.

Russ talked to Tommy and then Tommy started to walk back to the tee box. When he did, Russ started to walk up to the green to wait by Joe's side.

"Oh, here it is." Tommy pointed past the area where he had been looking. He walked over to the spot he had been pointing at and set his bag down. Neither Joe nor Russ could see Tommy's ball on the ground. Russ started to walk over to where Tommy was standing and when he did, he could see a ball next to Tommy's bag. Russ just shook his head, turned around and walked to Joe.

"Did you see his ball over there Russ?"

"I can't say it wasn't there before. I didn't see it from where I was standing, and I don't think he looked there when he was looking before."

"So it might or might not be his tee shot?" Joe asked.

"I can't say. I should have walked with him back to the tee."

"It's not your fault Russ. Tommy's an opportunist. He'll do anything to win."

"Your speaking from experience, I take it."

"He's used gimmicks and tricks and cheating in the past. In the first qualifying round of this tournament he was D-Qed for dropping a ball from his bag. He's really sneaky," Joe said as Tommy hit his ball on to the green.

Joe was furthest from the hole. He putted first. The green had a slope in it from right to left. Joe had to aim pretty far right of the cup to compensate for the break. He hit his ball softly. It ran down the slope and using the break, cut back to the cup. The ball slowed approaching the cup nearly stopping just short, but momentum carried it one more roll forward and the ball dropped in.

Tommy putted next making the uphill ten-footer. Russ was last to putt. He dropped his putt right into the center of the cup for a birdie.

On the 161-yard 6th hole, Tommy was first to tee off. He took out an 8-iron. After three practice swings, he hit his ball. It went right into the trees. A few seconds later, Tony came walking out of the woods right around the area where Tommy's shot went in. Tommy said, "I didn't see anyone out there. I thought it was safe to hit."

Tony looked back and saw Tommy on the tee. He turned and walked the other way to the next tee.

"Maybe he was taking a leak or something," Joe said.

"They're already off the green," commented Russ as they all looked down the fairway.

"You're up Russ," Joe said.

Russ took out an 8-iron. His shot landed on the green about twenty feet from the cup. Joe was last to hit. He used a 7-iron and came up just short of the green ending up on the fringe.

When they walked down the fairway, Russ stayed right with Tommy. He wasn't going to let Tommy get away with anything. As they approached the area where Tommy's ball had gone into the woods, they could clearly see where someone had walked out of the woods by the footprints in the wet grass. Tommy looked around, "Here it is. It looks like Tony stepped on my ball."

Russ walked over with him and looked at the ball. It looked like it could have been stepped on as the ball was pretty far down into the grass.

"It could just be in a hole Tommy."

"I think I should get some relief," he declared.

"No way. You have to hit it where it is or take a stroke."

Tommy wasn't going to take a stroke so he hit it from where it was. He had trouble getting his club head to remain straight and when he hit his shot, the ball went to the right of the green stopping about ten feet off the green. He chipped on from there to within five feet of the cup.

Joe and Russ both made birdie. Tommy had to settle for a bogey. On the 7th hole, Tommy and Joe both shot par and Russ got another birdie. Walking up to the 8th tee, Joe said to Russ, "You're playing pretty good Russ. You might be able to make some gains on Tommy today."

"I've probably gained a few strokes on him, and you."

"Me? I had a bogey on the 4th."

"Yeah, but you were ahead of me when we started Joe."

"I think we're about even right now Russ. And Tommy's still a few shots ahead of us."

"Maybe his game will continue to be erratic and he'll drop a few more shots," Russ said as they reached the tee box.

The 8th tee looks out into space beyond the green. The fairway is very narrow. On the left side of the green, the fairway drops off to the 11th tee. Beyond the green is a very steep drop off of over a hundred feet. To the right is a tall stand of pine trees separating the 8th from the 4th tee. Russ was first to hit.

Russ selected a 9-iron. He took a few practice swings and then hit his ball. It caught one of the overhanging limbs on the right side of the fairway ricocheting into the 4th fairway.

"Finally, a bad shot," Tommy said as they watched it land.

"I can still get it up and down from there," Russ said confidently."

"We'll see," Tommy responded.

Joe hit next. He took out an 8-iron. He had decided to take a little off the swing and when he hit his ball, it landed on the front of the green thirty feet from the cup.

Tommy took out a 9-iron. He swung real hard as he hit the ball. It went very high, over all the overhanging limbs landing on the back of the green. They had thought Tommy's shot had gone over but to their surprise, it had hit on the back of the green, which they couldn't see from the tee box, with backspin ending up six feet from the cup.

Russ used a 7-iron to bump-and-run his ball through the pine trees and onto the green. He had a little over ten feet left for par.

Joe was first to putt. He pushed his putt up to within a few feet of the cup. Then Russ hit his putt right into the center of the cup for a par. Joe did the same. Tommy made his putt for a birdie.

The threesome walked over to the elevated 9th tee. Looking out, over the water, they could easily see the whole green below the clubhouse. Tony and his group were putting. They watched as Tony made a long putt from the right side of the green to the cup forty feet away.

"Looks like Tony made a nice putt," Russ said to Joe.

"Tony is a pretty good putter," Joe said in return.

"I know, I played with him once before and I remember he was pretty good around the green."

"You're up Tommy," Joe said to him as Tony and his group walked up to the clubhouse.

Tommy had the honors. He selected a 7-iron for the 169-yard shot. Tommy's drive went long ending up on the side of the hill above the green.

"Too bad Tommy," Russ said to him.

"I can still get par."

Russ took out his 7-iron. He took a few practice swings and then hit his ball. It landed on the left side of the green a few feet from the cup.

"You're in a groove Russ," Joe said to him.

"Yeah, I'm playing pretty good."

Joe hit next. He selected a 6-iron from his bag. He hit his shot right on the green running beyond the cup and stopping about eight feet away.

"Looks like we have a birdie putt coming up Russ," Joe said as the walked down the hill.

They got to the green. Tommy was first to hit, as he was a few feet off and on the side of the hill behind the green. He chipped on ending up a few feet from the cup. Russ and Joe both made their putts for birdie. Tommy made his for a par.

They walked up the hill to the clubhouse to record their scores for the front nine. Harry was standing at the scorer's table outside the clubhouse.

"How'd you guys do?" Harry asked.

"Russ is tearing the course up," Joe said.

Harry turned to Russ.

"Yeah, I shot 19."

"19? That's pretty much a two on each hole," Harry said extending his hand to Russ.

"Sometimes you're just in a good place," Russ responded.

Harry turned to Joe, "And you Joe?"

"I shot 23."

"That's pretty good also."

"How did Tony do?" Joe asked Harry.

"He shot 22."

"I knew he'd play pretty good here," Joe said.

Harry turned to Tommy. "How about you Tommy?"

"I shot 26."

"Not playing your usual game Tommy?" Harry said to him.

"I had a few bad shots. Plus, I think someone stepped on my ball on one of the holes."

"Stop making excuses Tommy," Russ said. "You had your chances."

"I was just a little tight when we started out today. I don't know what got into me."

Joe did, but he didn't say. The three turned and walked to the 10th tee.

"See you when you're done," Harry said as they walked off.

Chapter 39

As Russ and Tommy walked away, Joe saw Carol standing back by the clubhouse patio. He walked over to talk with her.

"Hey Carol."

"How you doing Joe?"

"Pretty good. I shot a 23."

"And Tommy?"

"He shot a 26. I think the upper I gave him made him impatient and agitated. He had a tough time staying focused."

"Great. Do you think you still need my help?"

"Nah. The pill seems to still be working. I think I'm tied with Tommy right now and if he keeps playing the way he has been the last few holes, I should be ahead of him by the end of the day."

"So, you'll be in the lead?"

"Not really. Russ Ford is on fire. He shot a 19, and Tony shot a 22."

"Want me to distract either of them?"

"Not yet. Russ didn't have a real good first round so he's not on top yet. Tony on the other hand might be a problem."

"Don't worry about Tony, Joe. I know just what to do with him."

"What are you going to do?"

"Better you don't know. Let's see how he finishes up."

"He's in the group right in front of us."

Joe pointed to the 10th green.

"There he is walking off the green now."

Carol looked in the direction Joe was pointing.

"I see him. I'll see you later."

Carol walked down the path on the right side of the 10th and then across the 18th fairway. When she got across the pond, she walked up the hill. She would intercept Tony in a hole or two.

Joe walked down the hill to the elevated 10th tee box. Tommy and Russ were ready to hit. From there, they had to hit back over the water to an elevated green 160 yards away. In front of the green was a very steep hill of over fifty feet. On the right side was a sand trap. Any golfer ending up in the trap would have trouble seeing the flag as the trap sat well below the hole. On the backside of the green was a steep hill going up to the back of the 8th green. The 10th hole required absolute accuracy in distance.

Russ hit first. He pulled out a 9-iron. After a few practice swings, he delivered a smooth swing launching his ball very high towards the green. The ball easily cleared the pond and settled on the green about twelve feet from the cup.

"Nice shot Russ," Joe complimented him.

"Thanks."

Next, Tommy took out an 8-iron. He put his ball on the grass, electing not to use a tee.

"Taking a little extra club, Tommy?" Joe said.

"I just don't want to be short."

Tommy took a practice swing and then hit his ball. It went long landing on the hillside past the green. Then, it bounced backwards eventually rolling to a stop at the edge of the green.

Joe hit last. He selected an 8-iron. After lining up his shot, he took two practice swings and then hit his ball. It landed on the front of the green rolling to the left twenty-one feet from the cup.

The threesome walked down the hill, across the bridge and up to the 10th green. Tommy was first to putt. He lined his shot up and then hit his ball. It went long and rolled off the front of the green all the way down the hill.

"Stop, Stop, Stop," Tommy yelled at his ball but it kept going.

He walked back to his bag and took out a lob wedge. Then, he walked down the hill to his ball. He couldn't see the cup from where he was standing. He took a practice swing and then hit his ball. It went very high landing on the front edge of the green. It had enough backspin on it bringing the ball back down the hill a few feet away from where he was standing.

"Damn it," was all Tommy said.

Then, he hit his ball again without taking any practice swings. This time, it sailed up and over the flag. Again, it had backspin on it. When the ball came to rest, it was six-inches from the cup. Tommy climbed the hill and saw where his ball had stopped.

"Should have been there on the first shot."

"That was a nice shot though Tommy," Joe said.

"Yeah, for a fourth shot. Now, I have a tap-in for a double."

"Sometimes crap happens Tommy," Russ said as he walked over to his ball.

Joe hit next. He sank the putt and then Russ did the same. The group recorded two birdies and one double bogey. Tommy was not happy.

They walked to the 11th tee box, which is 113 yards and straightaway, fairly easy. Russ hit his tee shot on to the green, as did Joe. Tommy again hit his ball over the green.

As they were walking away from the tee box, Tommy said, "What the heck is going on with my game? I go up a club and over hit it, I go down a club and over hit it."

"You seem a little aggressive Tommy," Russ said.

"I feel a little hyper, or tight. Maybe I just need to settle down."

"I've got some Motrin if you want some," Russ said to Tommy.

"Can I have four?" Tommy asked him.

"Sure."

Russ took a bottle of pills out of his bag. Tommy took them with a bottle of water to wash them down. Joe watched wondering what effect the Motrin would have on the uppers he had given Tommy when the round started.

The 12th hole is the second longest hole on the course. It is 200 yards long and fairly open. Russ played conservatively and got a par. Tommy got par. Joe tried to get aggressive and put his drive into the trees on the right side of the fairway. He was right behind a tree and had to layout to get back into the fairway. Then, he hit his third shot on to the green and was able to one putt for a bogey.

On the 13th, Joe and Tommy both shot par. Russ resumed his good play with another birdie. On the 14th all three golfers shot par. Coming up to the 15th, Tommy said, "Thanks Russ for the Motrin. I'm feeling better."

"No problem. It looks like you're settling down a little."

Tommy and Russ hit their drives to the edge of the green. Both balls were within a few inches of each other about thirty feet from the cup. Joe, having observed both of them on the green, took out his 5-wood for the 197 yard shot. He took a few practice swings and then hit his ball. It went left over by the big tree just off the green. For the second time on the back nine, his shot came to rest behind a tree.

Joe tried to hit his club backwards as if he were a lefty trying to get away from the base of the tree and on to the green. He was unsuccessful. His ball only went a few feet. He had to take another shot just to get on the green. He landed his wedge shot five feet from the cup stopping it in its place.

Russ was first to putt as he was just outside Tommy's ball. He hit his putt a little left of the hole. The ball ran across the green narrowly missing the hole. "There Tommy, that should give you some idea of what you need to do," Russ said to him as he marked his ball.

Tommy lined up his putt and then hit. His ball did the same thing as Russ's ball, stopping right next to Russ's ball mark. They both tapped in for par. Joe put his ball down behind his marker and tapped in for another bogey.

They walked up to the 16th which is a 146-yard straightaway hole sharing the hourglass shaped green with the 7th on the front nine. The challenges on the 16th are staying away from the big sand trap on the left side of the green and keeping away from the overhanging trees on the right side of the fairway.

Russ hit first. His shot went a little long on the drive landing on the back of the green. Backspin brought his drive back to within eight feet of the cup. Tommy hit next. His shot landed on the left side of the green. It looked like it might drop into the trap.

"Stop right there," Tommy demanded.

His ball stopped right at the top of the little hill leading to the trap. It didn't roll backwards.

Joe hit last. His tee shot landed off on the left side of the green, closer to the cup on the 7th green's cup than to the 16th. He would have a long putt for a birdie.

Joe putted first. His ball went around sixty feet stopping four feet from the cup. Tommy putted next. He could have chipped from where he was but elected to putt. His choice of putter worked out well, as his ball found the bottom of the cup for a birdie. Russ two putted for a par.

The three walked up to the 17th tee box, and as they were walking past a port-a-potty, Carol came out. She walked over to Joe who stopped to talk with her.

"Did you find Tony?"

"Sure did. And his game has definitely gone down hill."

"What did you do?"

"I told you I'd be able to distract any golfer you thought might need distracting."

"Ok, what did you do?"

"I showed him these."

She pulled up the front of her top exposing her breasts.

"They always work Joe."

"I'll bet."

"You don't have to worry about Tony again. Last time I checked, he bogeyed four holes on the back nine."

267

"When did you flash him?"

"On the 11th. I was right here by the fence. No one else saw me other than Tony and he couldn't take his eyes off me. He just stopped and stared."

"Well, I guess thanks are in order."

"You're welcome. Anyone else you want me to distract?"

"I don't know how the other golfers are doing. Russ Ford is playing pretty good but he's in my group."

"See if he's going to the reception later. I might be able to help out with him there."

"Ok. I'll find out. I've got to get going."

Joe walked off to the 17th tee. Tommy and Russ were ready to hit. Russ hit first. His ball landed on the center of the green. Tommy followed suit. His ball was left center on the green as well. They both were a little over ten feet from the cup. Joe took out his 9-iron for the 138 yard shot. He put his drive right next to the other two.

When they putted, Russ made his. Tommy and Joe both missed and settled for par. They walked over to the 18th. This was the final hole and it was over water. At 184 yards, with sand traps on the left front and left rear, and a steep drop-off on the front of the green, it was not the easiest hole.

Russ hit first. He placed his 5-iron shot right on the center of the green. Tommy hit next. His 4-iron went a little long ending up above the hole on the sloping green. Joe took out his 5-wood. He choked up on the club a little and hit a soft shot. His ball landed on the right side of the green. He would have to compensate for the slope of the green in order to make the fifteen foot putt he had left.

Tommy took two putts to find the bottom of the cup. Joe took two putts as well. Only Russ was able to master the 18th for a birdie. They shook hands and walked up the hill to the clubhouse.

Harry was there to greet them. "Well?" Harry said as they approached.

Russ spoke first. "I shot a 23 on the back along with the 19 on the front for a 42."

"That's fantastic Russ. You're leading by a long shot."

"Thanks Harry."

"How about you Joe?"

"I shot a 28."

"Not bad."

"With the 23 on the front, I ended up with a 51."

"And you Tommy?"

"I had one really bad hole, the 10th. Then I settled down and got a 27 on the back. That with the 26 on the front, I shot a 53."

"How did Tony do?" Joe asked Harry.

"He fell apart on the back. Four bogeys and a double on the 18th, I think he found the water on his drive," Harry said shaking his head.

"Really?"

"Yeah. He had it going for a while. Now, he's a ways back."

"That's good news for us," Tommy said.

"He's still in it," Joe came to the defense of his friend.

"You remember how he played when we played Bass River a few weeks ago with him Joe? He'll fall apart over there tomorrow."

"We'll see."

The three recorded their scores with the starter.

"I'm going to put my clubs in the car and then go to the restaurant for the reception," Russ said to Joe.

"I'll join you Russ, let me put my clubs away." Joe jogged out to the parking lot to his car.

Russ turned to Tommy, "You coming Tommy?"

"In a little. I see Carol over there. I think I'll talk to her for a little. Then, I'll be in."

"You got something going with her?" Russ asked him.

"Only if I can get her to come out to my car," Tommy said as he walked over to talk with Carol.

Joe and Russ walked across the street to stow their clubs and then go have a drink.

Tommy walked up to Carol.

"How'd you do Tommy?"

"OK. I shot a 53."

"How did Joe do?"

"He shot a 51."

"He beat you?"

"Only today. I'm still ahead of him for the tournament."

"And Russ?"

"He was on fire. He shot a 42. He's in the lead three shots ahead of me for the tournament. I'll have to play good tomorrow to catch him."

"He's leading? Hmm. And you're in second," Carol said as she dropped a scorecard she had in her hand. When she bent over to pick it up, she made sure Tommy could see down her shirt. Tommy did look and he immediately noticed she wasn't wearing a bra.

"I've got to put my clubs in my car. Want to walk with me?"

"Sure."

They walked across the street, past the practice putting green and past the cart barn. Tommy's car was at the back of the parking lot. When they got there, he put his clubs in the back.

"I've got a few beers here in a cooler Carol. Want one?"

"Sure."

270

"Let's sit in the back and have one. We can go in to the reception later."

Carol reached into her pocket and took out a blue pill. She got into the back of the SUV. Tommy popped open the beers and then reached under her shirt. When he did, she dropped the pill into his beer. In a half hour, the pill did the trick.

An hour later, they joined the others in the restaurant for the reception.

Chapter 40

Joe and Russ walked into the restaurant across the street from the clubhouse. As Russ came through the door, Martin Yates announced, "Here's the Tournament Leader, Russ Ford. He shot an unbelievable 42 today to take the overall lead by three strokes over Tommy Anderson."

Everyone clapped and a few cheered.

Martin looked around the room trying to see if he could see Tommy Anderson. When he didn't see him, he said, "In third place with a composite score of 187 is Joe Campbell."

Joe received a big ovation as well.

Joe and Russ went to the bar. Joe ordered a beer for both of them. When the beers came, Joe said, "Here's to you Russ. You played unbelievable today."

"Thanks Joe. I was kind of in a zone today."

"You showed us all what a good short game looks like."

"Thanks. Tommy played pretty good on the back nine once he shook off the jitters."

272

Harry had come up behind the two, "Tommy Anderson? Jitters? Come on."

"He was rushing and over hitting every shot on the front nine," Russ said.

"Who knows with Tommy?" Joe said. "Maybe he was on something from last night or something."

"You know something about Tommy, Joe?" Harry asked.

"Only that he's more active with the women than any guy I know. And who knows what he takes to keep up with that pace."

"You're probably right."

Martin Yates and his wife Helen came over to congratulate Russ.

"Russ, your score is the best ever recorded here at the course according to the people in the pro shop."

"No kidding?"

"Yeah. They said the lowest ever reported and verified had been a 46. You shattered that one," Martin said.

"Thanks Martin. I played well."

Harry said, "Martin, can I speak with you for a minute outside?"

"Sure Harry."

"Helen, why don't you buy Russ and Joe a drink? I'll be right back."

Martin and Harry went outside.

"Martin, I know you have a beef with Tommy Anderson. He finished in second place overall after today. Can you set aside any conflict you have with Tommy until after the tournament ends tomorrow night?"

"I understand Harry. I've got my business involved in this thing as well. We all want to project a positive image."

"Thanks Martin. Let's get back inside."

They were about to walk back in when Martin noticed Tommy Anderson walking across the street from the parking lot. He was tucking his shirt into his pants and zipping up his fly. Carol Tindle was walking next to him composing herself as well.

"Well, at least that prick won't be trying to hit on my wife tonight," Martin said nodding in Tommy's direction to Harry.

"Let's get this thing over," Harry said opening the door allowing Martin to go in first.

Tommy Anderson came in a minute later followed by Carol. Carol's face was a little flushed, and Tony, who had been seated in the corner, saw her come in with Tommy. Joe, sitting a good distance away from the door noticed too. "She must be working her magic" he thought to himself.

Harry stood in the middle of the room and announced, "Ladies and Gentlemen. Can I have your attention?"

The chatter started to subside.

"I'd like to recognize an unbelievable accomplishment today by Russ Ford. He shot a 42 on this course. His score was nine strokes better than the closest golfer. His composite score for the three tournament rounds played to date was 182, three strokes better than Tommy Anderson who is in second place. Please give Russ another round of applause."

Everyone clapped and shouted.

"Tomorrow is the final round for the Mid-Cape Open. We will start play at 9:00 am at Bass River Golf Course. All golfers should be on course for 8:00 am. Martin Yates has the pairings for everyone and your starting times for tomorrow. Please see him when we conclude the ceremonies," Harry said as he pointed to Martin.

"Following play tomorrow afternoon, we will have a reception and awards ceremony at Sundancers to conclude the tournament. I hope everyone attends. Ok everyone. Get a good night's rest and we'll see you tomorrow at Bass River."

Martin was handing out tee time sheets to all of the golfers. While he was doing that, Helen sought out Tommy.

"Tommy, want to take a walk outside?"

"I just came in Helen."

"I want to reward you for your accomplishments."

"I already did," Carol said as she turned to face Tommy and Helen.

"Helen, you know Carol?"

"I've seen her around."

"I've already taken care of Tommy, Helen, if you know what I mean." She licked her lips.

Helen made a frown, turned and walked away.

Tony had been watching all the action. He approached Carol and Tommy.

"Hey Carol. How you doing?"

"Tony. How did you play today?"

"I was doing just fine until someone took my mind off the game. Then, I couldn't do anything right."

"Oh, what happened?" She played dumb.

"When I was coming up to the 12th tee, I saw a woman inside the bathroom fencing showing her breasts."

"Oh really?"

"Really. And she looked magnificent."

"Any idea who it was?"

"We both know who it was, don't we Carol?" Tony had a smile on his face.

She tried to ignore Tony by turning back to Tommy but Tony didn't take the hint.

"So Carol, want to talk a walk with me outside. I'd like to get a closer look."

"You pig."

"Hey, you just came in from doing Tommy out in the parking lot. I'd be careful about calling someone else a pig."

Tommy turned and swung at Tony. Tony caught Tommy's fist in the palm of his hand rebuffing Tommy's attempt at chivalry.

"Tommy, Tommy. When are you ever going to learn?"

Tony pushed Tommy's fist away.

"You don't want to try to take me on Tommy. If you think Martin hurt you, you'll really get hurt trying to take me on."

"You need to apologize to Carol, Tony."

"Apologize? I want to do more than that," Tony said turning and looking at Carol.

"You'll never get any of this Tony," Carol said and hissed at Tony.

Harry saw the commotion. He and Martin ran over.

"Tony, Tommy. Take it outside if you have to settle something."

"We're not settling anything," Tony said. "I'd kick that little prick's ass."

"You're all talk Tony," Tommy said.

"Tommy, I owe you one. And Carol, I know what you were doing out there today. Don't play stupid."

Carol had a contrived look of bewilderment on her face.

Harry had everyone separated.

"Martin, take Tony to the bar and buy him a drink. I'm going to get Tommy Anderson out of here. He's a powder keg waiting to explode."

"Why don't you let me escort him out?" Martin said to Harry.

"Because you might do more than just threaten him."

"Who me?" Martin said as he turned the palms of his hands up.

"Yeah, you."

"Come on Tony, let me buy you a drink," Martin said as he put his arm over Tony's shoulder. They joined Helen and Joe at the bar.

"Drinks for everyone," Martin said motioning to the bartender to give the group another round.

Martin picked up his drink, "What was that all about Tony?"

"Something happened out on the course today and I was just trying to get to the bottom of it when Tommy tried to punch me. He's no match for me."

"Me either."

"I said that to him also."

"Oh, you know about my run-ins with him?"

"Yeah, I know all about it."

Helen tried to pretend she didn't hear the two talking but Tony kept looking at her. Oh, he knew all about it.

"Thanks for the drink Martin. I think I'm going to go over to Sundancers for a while. It should be a little quieter there," Tony said finishing up his drink.

Joe stood, "Tony, I think I'll join you. I've got to make a stop for a few minutes and then I'll meet you there." Joe did have something to do, plus he was just a little uncomfortable watching Carol work.

"Suit yourself," was all Tony said.

The two left Martin and Helen at the bar at Blue Rock.

Joe took a slight detour stopping at his attorney's house.

"How'd you play today Joe?"

"Pretty good. I'm still in the hunt."

"Good for you. Come on in and sign the agreement letter. Then, I'll fax a copy to USA's attorney. I've already got the $1,000,000 in escrow. If their Board approves the deal this weekend, we should be able to finish closing the deal Monday."

"Any way this thing might fall apart?"

"Only if their Board doesn't approve the deal. Their attorney said the deal should be a slam dunk."

"Great. Call me if anything comes up."

"Will do."

Joe left Mark's house continuing on to Sundancers.

Chapter 41

Joe pulled into Sundancers parking lot. It was pretty empty. He walked in. Dee saw him coming and got him a beer. Joe took up the stool next to Tony.

"I thought you guys would be staying at Blue Rock tonight."

"Too much drama over there," Joe said.

"Yeah. Tommy Anderson started a commotion. I just thought it would be in everyone's interest to leave," Tony said as he took a drink of his beer.

Dee motioned with her head to the dark corner of the bar room where a guy and a woman were seated. It was Tommy Anderson sitting with a woman whose back was to them.

"Oh crap, can't we get away from that dirt bag," Tony remarked.

"He's over there with someone. I didn't see them come in," Dee said, "but maybe she'll keep him under control."

"I wouldn't bet on it. Speaking of control, you won't believe what I saw Carol doing out on the course today," Tony said with a smile on his face.

"What was she doing, showing her breasts?" Joe said jokingly.

"How'd you know?"

"It's a long story Tony."

"So you knew she was going to be there flashing the golfers?"

"She was trying to play mental games with some of the golfers out there to help me."

"You? What the heck are you talking about?"

"If you must know, Tommy has beaten me at everything we have competed in since we were in high school. I was talking with Carol about it a few weeks ago and she told me it's a mindset I need to develop if I wanted to beat Tommy. She went on to say both physical and mental things could be utilized to affect the outcome of a situation to achieve a desired result. Her showing her breasts today was one of the ideas she said would affect play."

"Well, it worked. I couldn't think of anything but her breasts after she flashed them on the 12th hole."

"You sure she was flashing you and not Tommy?"

"I'm not really sure. If she wanted Tommy to see them, she was early. He was in your group, the one behind mine. But either way, I saw them."

"And now you want to touch them?"

"Wouldn't you?"

"I have."

"Then you know what I'm talking about."

"I guess."

"I saw Tommy and Carol at Blue Rock, and now it's probably Carol over there letting him put the move on her."

"I think it's the other way around. She's putting the move on him. That's another one of the things she talked with me about. She said she could tire him out so he wouldn't perform well playing golf the next day. I guess she's following through on her theory."

"You gonna say anything? I thought you and she were kinda exclusive?"

"Sort of exclusive, but hell no, I'm not saying anything. If Carol's right, Tommy will play like crap tomorrow. Then one of us might have a chance at winning."

"Maybe you should have had her focus on Russ Ford?"

"I'd rather Russ win tournament and I lose but beat Tommy. That's how she said she could help me out."

"So she's doing this for you?"

"I guess."

"Kinda a weird way to show you some love isn't it?"

"I don't know. Maybe. But it works for us."

Dee came over. She had overheard some of the conversation.

"Joe's got a lot going on in his life Tony. You should ask him about his software business."

"What's Dee talking about Joe?"

"Oh, I developed a computer software package over the winter and I'm building a business around it. It looks like it's going to work out."

"No kidding? Joe Campbell, a software geek."

"Yeah."

"And possibly a rich one," Dee added.

"Well, I hope it all works out Joe."

"Me too."

"I'm going home to get a good night sleep. Maybe I'll play better tomorrow," Tony said picking his keys up off the bar and leaving.

When Tony had left, Joe said, "Dee, I didn't want anyone else to know about my business just yet. There's a lot of things going on and I'm not supposed to talk about it."

"I thought you said it was your business Joe? You do landscaping? You sell software? What's new?"

"I got an offer on it early this morning and I have to keep it quiet until the deal gets approved and the papers get signed."

"Did you sell it?"

"I really can't say just yet Dee. The company that's interested is a public company and they can't let this kind of news get out until after the deal is closed."

"So you're selling your software?"

"I can't say."

"I hope you're getting a lot of money for it Joe."

"Oh, you can bet if I'm selling it, I'm gonna get a lot for it."

"Wow. You would be my first millionaire male friend Joe."

"Wouldn't that be nice?"

"Real nice. You'll have everyone woman within twenty miles after you."

"Hmm." Joe said as he picked up his beer and took a drink.

"You might want to get closer to Carol. She's got a bundle and might be able to tell you a few things about being rich."

Dee looked to the dark corner of the room. Tommy and the woman were all over each other.

"Maybe I will," Joe said looking in Tommy's direction.

A short time later, Tommy and the woman came out of the corner. It wasn't Carol. It was Joe's ex, Jessica. Tommy was having trouble walking a straight line, and was draped over Jessica's shoulder, "Come on Tommy, let me take you home."

"Can I spend the night?"

"Sure."

Jessica looked in Joe's direction as they left, winked and smiled. Jessica and Tommy might be doing to Joe what Carol was so good at, distracting him.

Joe sat there stunned. Tommy had definitely gotten to him.

"What's with you Joe? You look like you just saw a ghost?" Dee said to him.

"That's my ex, with Tommy."

"Really?"

"Yeah."

"Does it bother you? Are you gonna do anything?"

"What can I do. I haven't seen her in a few years. He must have remained in contact with her and now he's got her here to get back at me."

"You think so?"

"What else could it be?"

"Maybe he just hooked up with her at the golf tournament. I heard some of the girls talking last night and they said they were going to the tournament today. They were talking about hooking up with the single golfers for a party."

"Was Jessica there?"

"Not that I remember. But the place was pretty busy. She could have been there."

"I hope she doesn't show up. I've got enough to focus on right now and don't need another distraction."

"Looks like she's focused on Tommy anyway."

"Yeah, I saw. I'm heading home Dee. I've got to try to get some rest. Tomorrow's a big day."

"See you tomorrow Joe. Have a good round, and don't let yourself get distracted by silly stuff."

Chapter 42

Joe arrived at the Bass River Golf Course early. Even though his tee time wasn't until at least 10:15 am, he wanted to be there when Tommy Anderson showed up. It was eating away at him that Tommy had been at Sundancers the night before with, of all people, Jessica.

Joe hung around the clubhouse having a coffee and talking to some of the other golfers as they arrived. Tony showed up around 8:00 am. He got a coffee and doughnut, and then joined Joe.

"You ready to play Joe?"
"I hope so, but I didn't sleep much last night."
"Too much anticipation about winning?"
"No. I couldn't sleep because I couldn't stop thinking about Jessica."
"Your ex? Where the hec is that coming from?"
"That's who Tommy was with at Sundancers last night."
"I thought he was there with Carol?"

"So did I. Then, when they got up to leave and came out of that dark corner, I saw it was Jessica."

"No kidding?. I wonder what happened to Carol?"

"Last I saw her, she was at the bar at Blue Rock talking with Martin and Helen Yates."

"You know what he's doing Joe?"

"I know. He's trying to get under my skin."

"That's right. And I'd say he's winning."

"I can't help it. She looked so good."

"It's all about Tommy. Tommy wins at golf. Tommy gets the nice girl. Tommy gets laid."

"Alright already."

"He's playing with your mind Joe. If you give in, he'll surely beat you today."

"He's still got to play well to win. It's not only me. He has to beat you, Russ and everyone else."

"Joe, Tommy might not really give a crap. Or maybe he just wants to beat you."

"Got any ideas Tony?"

"Sure. You could whack him with a club. Poison him. Put extra clubs in his bag and get him D-Qed. Accuse him of something. You need to be creative Joe."

"Carol said the same things. She even offered to help."

"I know. Remember I told you I saw her help yesterday."

"That was only one thing. She told me how to drug him. She said sex would deplete his strength plus keeping him up doing it most of the night would make him tired. She had lots of ideas."

"They need to be your ideas Joe."

"I guess I better come up with something soon, because here comes Tommy."

They both looked out the window. There was Tommy Anderson walking to the clubhouse from the parking lot with

285

Jessica holding his hand. Tommy stopped by the bag drop and set his clubs down. He and Jessica continued walking. When they got right in front of the window where Tommy could see Joe and Tony sitting, he turned to Jessica, said something and then put his arms around her and kissed her. As he did, he let his hands drop to her butt where he squeezed her a little so they could see. Then, Jessica turned and walked back to the car and left.

Tommy came in and ordered a coffee. He stood at the counter waiting for it. Russ Ford was right behind him ordering also.

"Ready to play Tommy?" Russ asked.

"I don't know. I stayed up most of the night having sex with a beautiful woman," Tommy said it loud enough for Joe to hear.

"I know what you mean Tommy. I went home with Carol Tindle last night and she screwed my brains out."

"Ah, Carol is good at that."

"I thought you might go home with her. I thought I saw you come into the restaurant at Blue Rock just before the reception last night."

"Yeah, I was out in the parking lot with her for a while. But then she said she had something to take care of last night. Guess it must have been you, Russ."

"If it was, she sure did."

Tommy picked up his coffee and walked over to Tony and Joe.

"Ready to play guys?" Tommy asked.

"More than you are." Tony said.

"You jealous Tony?"

"Of what?"

"Because I slept with Jessica last night?"

"You're just saying those things to get to Joe."

"Oh, that's right Joe. Jessica used to be married to you."

Joe stood up as if he were going to hit Tommy.

"Go ahead and take a swing Joe. I probably deserve it. After all, she is fantastic in bed."

Joe's face turned red. He was about to unleash his temper when Tony said, "Let's get out of here Joe. We've got a tournament to finish." He put his big hand on Joe's arm and led him away.

"Why didn't you let me hit that prick?" Joe said to Tony.

"There's a time and a place for everything Joe. This isn't the time or place to get even with Tommy Anderson. Be patient. Plus, if you read the form you signed when you entered the tournament, it said any player demonstrating poor character, conduct or language could be disqualified."

"It actually said that?"

"Yeah. And I'll bet Tommy had notified the tournament officials to be on the lookout for poor conduct when he came in. That's probably why he's been taunting you."

"You think?"

"I don't put anything past Tommy Anderson."

"Ok. Then I'll keep my composure."

"Just be patient Joe. Look for opportunities."

"I will."

The two walked outside. They got their putters and went to the practice green.

At 8:30, Martin Yates and Harry Adams were standing with the starter. They all had clipboards in hand.

"Ok everyone. Today's the last day of the Mid-Cape Open. Someone is going to win the tournament today. The winner will be the person with the lowest cumulative score from last weekend's rounds, yesterday's round and today."

Martin pointed to the scoreboard easel next to the starter and continued, "Right now, Russ Ford is in first place

287

with a cumulative score of 182. Tommy Anderson is in second with a 185 and Joe Campbell third with a 187. The rest of you can find your name on the board. You'll all be paired in threesomes again today. In case of a tie, we will repeat the holes going backwards until there is one winner. When you make the turn today, please remember to report your score for the front nine to the starter. We want to keep the player board up to date. Also, each golfer will be allowed about twenty minutes at the turn to grab something to eat. After the last group has finished today, we will be holding the final reception and awards ceremony at Sundancers. We'll be playing from the back tees today gentlemen. And one last thing, yesterday, we had a few complaints about bad conduct on the course. Remember, you can be disqualified for bad conduct, and if you're not sure what you're doing is bad, then assume it is. Try to keep it clean. Good luck gentlemen. Let's get the last round started."

Martin called out the names of the first three golfers.

Chapter 43

Most of the golfers stayed by the 1st tee to watch the first few groups tee off. It was pretty clear the golfers were nervous. A few golfers hit to the left, a few into the sand trap and a few went straight. Nerves were definitely on display for the final round.

By 10 am, all but the last two groups had teed off. Martin called the second to the last group.

"Davis, Simpson, and Williams. You're on the tee next."

Sean Williams said, "That's us."

He, Len Simpson and Tony shook hands on the tee box.

Len was first to hit. He placed his ball on a short tee. Then he took a few practice swings with a 4-iron. He addressed his ball and hit. His drive went straight, right at the green 204 yards away. He was safely on board on the par three.

Sean Williams was up next. He took a 3-iron out of his bag. After a few practice swings, he hit his drive just over the green on the left side.

Tony was last. He selected his 5-wood. Even though it might be a little too much club, Tony wanted to make sure he didn't have to kill the ball to make the green. His swing was smooth. He took a little off the back swing and when he made contact, the ball flew right at the flag. It landed a few feet short of the cup and rolled to within eight inches of the cup.

Joe, Tommy and Russ had been standing behind the 1st tee watching.

"What a shot Tony," Russ commented.

"Good shot Tony," Joe added.

"Just lucky," Tommy said.

Tony turned and gave Tommy the middle finger with his gloved hand.

Russ said to Joe, "Tony and Tommy don't like each other I take it."

"Tommy's trying to get to Tony like he tries to get under everyone's skin," Joe said making sure Tommy didn't hear him.

"He ever do it to you, Joe?"

"He already did this morning."

"What he do?"

"He spent the night with my ex-wife and then had her drop him off this morning. He made it a point to kiss her and put his hands on her ass so I could see him do it. That's the kind of stuff Tommy Anderson does to get under someone's skin."

"If he did that to my wife, I'd kick his ass."

"Well, she isn't my wife anymore."

"Doesn't matter. If I knew he was doing something to get to me, I'd be pissed."

"I am. I'm just biding my time."

"You going to get him?"

"We'll see."

Martin Yates then announced, "Ford, Anderson, and Campbell. You're on the tee."

The three picked up their clubs and walked out on to the 1st tee at Bass River Golf Course. The last group in the final round was about to tee off.

Russ Ford led off. Russ selected a 4-iron from his bag. He took a few practice swings and then hit his ball. It landed safely on the green about fifteen feet from the cup.

Tommy was next to hit. He took out a 5-iron. After two practice swings, he addressed his ball. He took his club back a long way. His swing was very rapid making contact and sending his Pro-V1 ball very high. It landed ten feet short of the green and plugged right there.

"I got robbed," was all he said throwing his club at his bag.

"Should've used a 4-iron," Russ said.

Then it was Joe's turn. Joe took out a 3-iron. He took a few practice swings. As he hit his ball, he took a little off the swing. It paid off. His ball landed even with the cup rolling another ten feet on the green.

"Nice shot Joe," Russ complimented him.

"Thanks Russ. It's all about playing within your game," Joe said being sure Tommy could hear him.

Tommy just walked to his bag; picked up the club he had thrown, put it in the bag and started walking. He stopped at his ball, then took out his wedge and put his second shot three feet from the cup.

Russ picked up right where he had finished the day before. He drained the fifteen-foot puttfor a birdie. Joe missed his putt by inches and then tapped in for par. Tommy made his putt for par.

At the 2nd tee, a short 310-yard par-4, Russ took out his driver. He would try to drive the green if he could keep the shot under control. When he took his practice swings, he didn't like the feel of it and switched to a 3-wood. When he hit his ball, it went 260 yards right down the center of the fairway ending up just short of the green.

Tommy Anderson saw the opening. "Should have used your driver Russ. This green's reachable."

Tommy put his ball on a tee. He took two big practice swings and then hit his ball. At first, it looked good but as the ball went further out, it started to curve right. It missed the green by twenty yards and rolled into a patch of wild flowers.

"That's why I used a 3-wood," Russ said with a smirk on his face.

"Can't win if you don't try," Tommy came back at him.

As Russ walked past Joe, he said, "Now, he's trying to get under my skin."

"Don't say I didn't warn you."

Then, Joe teed his ball. He took a few practice swings with his driver and hit his ball 290 yards right center of the fairway. His ball ran up onto the green stopping twenty-five feet from the pin.

"Nice ball Joe," Russ said.

"Thanks."

"That's what Jessica said to me Joe, nice balls," Tommy said to Joe trying to get a reaction from him.

"You can't get to me Tommy, even using Jessica."

"Oh, really? That's not what she said. She said you overreacted anytime anyone paid any attention to her."

"That was a long time ago Tommy."

"I'm glad you don't mind Joe. I'm going to celebrate with her again tonight after I win this tournament. She was fantastic last night and I'm going back in for more."

Joe wanted to give Tommy a taste of his driver but decided not to. He put his driver away, picked up his bag and began walking to the green.

Tommy was furthest away from the hole. He took out his wedge and landed his shot on the fringe. The ball rolled a few feet on the green twenty feet short of the pin. Russ was next to hit. He used a 7-iron to bump-and-run his ball up to the flag. It almost went in and stopped a foot past the cup.

Tommy took two putts to get in. Joe and Russ both made their putts. Joe got an eagle. Russ got a birdie.

As they walked to the 3rd tee, Harry Adams walked up to them with a clipboard in hand.

"How you playing Joe?"

"Ok. I just got an eagle on number two."

"Great."

"Russ has two birdies so far."

"And Tommy?"

"Two pars."

"Isn't he playing well?"

"He's spending so much time trying to get under everyone else's skin, I think it's affecting his game."

"I know what you mean."

"How's everyone in front of us playing Harry?"

"Par or bogey seems to be the scores so far. I haven't heard of anyone making a run yet."

"Oh, it'll come."

"Probably. Well, good luck Joe. I'll check in with you in a few holes."

"See you later Harry."

Harry left. He'd catch up with them again in a few holes.

On the 425-yard 3rd hole, a par-4, Russ got a par; Tommy and Joe both got a bogey. Both players didn't compensate for the prevailing breeze when making club selections and missed the green in regulation. Then they both two putted. There was a reason why the 3rd hole was the number one handicap hole on the course.

At the picturesque 4th hole, a 356-yard dogleg right par-4, all three golfers shot par.

The 5th hole had a big bunker on the left side of the fairway leading up to a two-tier green. Russ played the hole conservatively and then two putted for par. Tommy had hit a good long drive, and then hit his wedge on to the wrong level of the green. He needed two putts to get into the cup. Joe hit a safe drive and then a nice approach shot. He landed past the cup. His first putt missed going in and caught the down slope of the green rolling to the lower level. He was fortunate to make the return putt back up on the top level and into the cup. He saved par.

The 6th hole presented another opportunity for the big swingers. At 312 yards, the par-4 could provide the better golfers with another eagle opportunity. The hole is picturesque with the Bass River in the background. Russ hit first. He took out his driver and swung away. His tee shot landed on the lower tier of the green rolling up the incline and stopping eight feet from the cup.

"Great shot," Joe said to Russ.

"Thanks Joe. I thought this hole might give me an opportunity to create some distance."

Tommy took out his driver. He took a few big swings and then hit his ball. It started out on the left side of the fairway and then faded back to the center of the green. His shot landed, rolled a few feet and remained on the lower tier of the putting surface.

"Let's see if you can match those," Tommy said to Joe trying to intimidate him.

Joe took out his driver. He hit his shot straight landing it 290 yards away. The ball bounced forward coming to a stop five feet off the green.

"Not everyone's a good long ball hitter Joe," Tommy taunted him.

"I do ok." Joe tried to neutralize Tommy's harassment.

They walked up to the green. Joe was first to hit being just off. He took out his putter.

"You think you can run that ball up to the top level Joe?" Tommy kept it up.

Joe didn't respond. He walked up to his ball, lined it up and then hit it. It raced over the lower tier and up the hill. As the ball approached the cup, it started to lose speed. At the last second, it dropped into the cup for an eagle.

"Yeah!"

"Nice shot Joe," Russ complimented him.

"Thanks Russ."

Tommy was on the lower tier of the green and next to putt. He looked at the line three or four times and then addressed his ball. His putt ran up the incline and right past the cup. It stopped ten feet on the other side of the cup, just past Russ's marker. Tommy was still away. He looked at the putt once and then hit it. It lipped out. He tapped in for a par. Russ made his putt for an eagle.

Russ looked at Joe, "Eagles soar."

"And turkey's don't," Joe added.

Tommy didn't respond. He merely picked up his clubs and walked to the 7th tee.

Chapter 44

Russ still had the honors at the 7th tee. It was a short 129-yard par-3. While considered a fairly easy hole, golfers tend to use one extra club due to the wind to make the green in regulation. Being able to hit the ball straight was required given the closeness of the trees on both sides of the fairway.

Russ took out a 9-iron. He took a few practice swings and then stood behind his ball. The wind was blowing from left to right, so Russ aimed a little into the wind when he addressed his ball. He had a nice smooth swing as he hit his ball. His drive went right down the center of the tight fairway landing on the green. The ball stopped three feet from the cup.

"Looks like another birdie opportunity," Russ said picking up his tee and turning around.

Joe was next to hit. He selected an 8-iron from his bag. After a few practice swings, Joe hit his ball very high and the right distance. It came to rest seven feet from the cup.

Walking away from the tee, he said to Russ, "Looks like we're both shooting for birdie."

Tommy took out a 9-iron. He didn't take any practice swings just as the wind had subsided. He addressed his ball and made a nice smooth swing. His ball took off with a little bend to the flight landing on the right side of the green fifteen feet from the hole.

All three golfers were in good shape and Tommy was first to putt. He drained the fifteen-footer right into the middle of the cup for a birdie. Joe shot second. His ball almost didn't drop when it circled around the cup and then dropped in. Russ tapped his short putt into the hole. All three had a birdie.

Walking to the 8th tee, Tommy said to Joe, "Russ is burning the course up. If he continues like he has so far, I don't know if I can catch him."

"Anything can happen Tommy."

"Maybe. But Russ is in another place right now and he was already ahead when we started the final round."

"Maybe it's time to get a little more aggressive."

"Maybe."

They walked out on to number eight. The hole is the third most difficult hole on the course. Even though the par-5 8th isn't overly long at 488 yards, it can play difficult. Russ was first to hit. He took out his driver and after a few practice swings, hit his drive over 300 yards down the left side of the fairway.

Joe was second. He hit his drive about 280 yards down the left side of the fairway. Tommy was last to hit. He took a few real big practice swings trying to get everything he could out of his swing. When he hit his ball, it blasted off. It went right down the center of the fairway, out driving Russ by 20 yards. Tommy had a smile on his face when he turned around looking at the other golfers.

"That's how it's done," Tommy said putting his club into his bag.

They walked down the fairway. Joe was first to hit the second shot. He took out his 5-wood. He blasted it 200 yards down the fairway and over the green by thirty feet.

Russ hit next. He took out an 8-iron and landed his ball twenty-five feet from the cup.

Tommy took out a 9-iron and mimicked Russ's shot almost exactly. Their balls were inches from each other about twenty feet from the cup.

Joe found his ball beyond the green. He took a wedge was able to put his ball about ten feet from the cup. As he was about to putt, he saw Jessica on the other side of the green. He pulled his putt a little left. As he walked up to his ball, he kept looking in her direction. She was motioning something to Tommy. Joe made the next shot getting a par.

Tommy and Russ both two putted for birdie. Instead of joining Russ and Joe to walk to the 9th tee, Tommy went over to Jessica, kissed her and talked to her. When he was done talking to her, she said, "I'll see you when you make the turn. I think you'll have a short break"

Tommy nodded in agreement and then walked up to number nine.

At 169 yards, the par-3 9th is a pretty easy hole. A golfer has to be aware of the water and the big sand traps on the left and front of the green.

Russ was first to hit. He took out a 7-iron and put his ball right on the green five feet from the cup.

Joe turned to Tommy, "You're right, he's in a zone."

Tommy hit next. He placed his 7-iron shot on the green as well, just a little further from the cup.

Joe wanted to make a good showing on number nine. The green had about fifty people standing above the hole watching the golfers come in. Joe selected a 6-iron for his shot. He took a few practice swings and then hit his ball. It went straight at the flag. His ball bounced once on the green and then hit the flagpole. It veered off a few feet coming to rest four feet from the cup.

All three golfers made their putts for birdie. As they walked off, the crowd clapped and cheered.

Joe went into the clubhouse to record his score. As he was walking up, Carol said, "How's it going?"

"Russ is going to be hard to beat. He's playing great."

"Want me to intervene?"

"I don't think you could get to Russ anymore than you already have. It hasn't helped me at all. He's real focused."

"Let me see what I can do."

"Whatever. I've got to go in and turn my score in."

"See you later," Carol said and she walked away from Joe looking for Russ Ford. Five minutes later, she had found him and was walking out to the parking lot with him in tow.

Tommy recorded his score and then came out of the clubhouse. He walked briskly to the parking lot and got into his SUV parked over by the back of the lot.

Joe was hanging around the clubhouse when Harry found him.

"How'd you do Joe?"

"Pretty good. I shot a 29."

"That's pretty good."

"But not good enough. Russ shot a 27. He was already ahead of me by five strokes for the first three rounds."

"So he's playing good?"

"I'd say he's playing great."

"What about Tommy?"

"Tommy shot a 32. He isn't playing very well for him. If he continues the same way, he'll be out of it. How did the guys ahead of us do?"

"No one is close except for Len Simpson. He started out four strokes off the lead and shot a 29 on the front. So, he's six out."

"Then, Russ is going to have to collapse for anyone to catch him," Joe said shaking his head. I'm just going to have to stay with it and hope Russ falters."

"Well, you're playing with him so you'll know."

"I know."

As the two were talking, Martin Yates came into the clubhouse with his clipboard.

"How's everyone playing Harry?"

"I was just talking with Joe about it. Russ Ford is in first by six strokes over Tommy Anderson and Len Simpson. Joe is seven back. Everyone else is pretty much out of it."

"Have you seen Helen?" Martin asked Harry.

"Not recently."

"She was coming in here during the break to get something to eat. She's been helping me out with the crowd control on a few of the holes."

Joe spoke up. "I think I saw her walking in the direction of her car when I walked up to check-in.

"Where's Tommy Anderson?" Martin asked in an annoyed tone.

"Tommy went out to his vehicle after checking in. He asked me how much time he'd have before starting the back nine and I told him a half hour," Harry said to Martin.

Martin threw his clipboard on the table and headed for the door. "That prick is probably out in the parking lot with my wife," Martin said as he stormed off.

"Oh boy. This isn't going to be good." Harry said to Joe. Then Harry started to run after Martin.

Martin was way ahead of Harry.

"Martin, wait a minute."

It didn't matter to Martin. He knew Tommy was out there somewhere with Helen. His blood boiled as he ran as fast as he could into the parking lot. He ran up and down the rows looking in as many vehicles as he could. He spotted a man sitting in an SUV near the back of the lot alone. Or at least he thought the man was alone. Then he noticed a head of hair rise and then drop out of site. It happened again as he ran up to the vehicle. He opened the door yelling.

"You prick. What the hell are you doing with," he stopped in his tracks.

It wasn't Helen in the vehicle, but Russ Ford with Carol Tindle.

"I'm sorry. I thought you were Tommy Anderson with my wife."

Carol stopped and covered Russ up. Russ said to Martin, "I saw Tommy and a woman a few minutes ago getting into an SUV over in the direction of the 10th tee."

Martin got the edge back again. "The 10th?"

"Yeah. I saw them five or ten minutes ago."

Martin closed the door and ran off in the direction Russ had indicated.

Harry was out of wind and had stopped half way across the parking lot when he saw Martin close the door to a vehicle and then run off in the direction of number ten. Harry turned and walked back to the clubhouse.

"Did you find them?" Joe asked Harry.

"I don't know. I saw Martin at an SUV in the back of the lot and then he ran off in the direction of number ten."

"I'd better get going to ten myself," Joe said. "We resume play in ten minutes."

"Just watch out over there Joe. I think Martin's really pissed off and he might do something to Tommy Anderson if he catches him with his wife."

"I can relate to Martin's anger Harry. I saw Tommy talking to my ex-wife a few holes ago. I hope Martin finds him."

"I hope not."

301

"See you later Harry."
"Ok Joe. Keep up the good play."
"I hope to."

Joe went outside, picked up his clubs heading to number ten.

Chapter 45

Joe stopped at the restroom, then got to number ten to wait with Russ and Tommy for Tony's group to reach the green. Joe took out his 3-wood and walked out on the tee.

"Tommy, did Martin Yates find you?"

"Sort of."

"What does that mean?"

"I was out in my vehicle during the break. When I got out to resume play, Martin ran up to me. The guy was winded. I don't know what he was after?"

"Yeah, you have no idea? Were you with his wife Helen."

"No. I don't where she was, and I have no idea what he wanted."

"He thought you were doing something with her in your car during the lunch break."

"I was doing something in my car during the break but it wasn't with Helen."

"I don't think I even want to know."

"Oh yes you do Joe. I was with Jessica."

"Screw you Tommy."

Russ turned to Tommy, "Yeah, I saw you get out of your vehicle Tommy. Looked like you worked up quite an appetite."

"You were out there Russ?"

"Sure was. Carol Tindle said she wanted to give me a reward for my good play. How could I refuse?"

"Isn't she a little old for you Russ?" Tommy asked.

"A few years, isn't that what cougars do?"

"So you think she's a cougar?"

"Absolutely. If you saw her work me over, you'd know she's definitely a cougar."

"You're up Russ," Joe said as he stood off to the side of the tee."

Russ put his ball on a tee. He took out a 3-iron and took a few practice swings. When he hit his ball, it went to the right and then got a bad break and rolled into the trees off of the sloping fairway.

Tommy said to Russ, "Watch out for those cougars in the woods Russ."

"Ha. Ha." Russ said sarcastically putting his 3-iron away.

Tommy hit next. He hit his 5-wood 240 yards down the right side of the fairway of the par-4 258-yard hole curving just enough to navigate the dogleg in the fairway. He ended up ten feet short of the green.

Joe hit last. He used his 3-wood. He hit his drive on the left center side of the green. His ball stopped thirty feet from the cup.

Russ had to lay out from the woods, as he didn't have a clear shot to the green. His third shot went long coming to rest on the fringe at the back of the green. He chipped on for his fourth shot.

Tommy chipped on, almost dropping the chip shot. His ball stopped two feet from the cup. Tommy and Joe both tapped in for birdie. Russ made his putt for a bogey five.

The three golfers walked up to the 11th tee. Tommy could feel the momentum changing with Russ's poorer play.

"The lunch break didn't agree with you Russ?" Tommy taunted him.

"Not really," Russ replied. "I had my fill."

"Too bad it didn't involve lunch," Tommy continued at him.

"I don't need to have lunch Tommy. I'm not as old as you are. My stamina lets me do what ever I want. And, didn't you say you spent your lunch break out in your car?"

"Yeah, I did. And she was great."

Joe was trying to keep out of the conversation and pretended he didn't hear the two of them jostling for manhood. "You're up Tommy," Joe called out.

Tommy took out his driver and crushed a 310-yard drive up the hill of the 406-yard par-4. He had a bounce in his step when he walked back to his golf bag.

Joe was next to hit. He hit his drive about 270 yards into the hill where the ball came to stop. He'd have an uphill 130-yard shot to make the green.

Russ hit last. He originally had his driver out and at the last minute, changed to a 3-wood. He hit his drive straight landing it 150 yards short of the green and at a flat spot in the otherwise uphill fairway.

"Why'd you change to the 3-wood Russ?" Joe asked.

"I didn't want to end up on the hill like where you are Joe. And, I know I wasn't going to drive the green."

"You think being on the uphill would be a problem?"

"Maybe. If you miss your next shot, you'll go over by quite a bit. I'm just trying to get my game back under control."

Russ was first to hit his second shot. He took out a 9-iron. He ended up ten yards short of the green.

"What the heck was I thinking? It was an uphill approach with wind. Come on Russ, get it together."

Joe hit next. He used his 9-iron to land his ball safely on the green thirty feet from the cup.

Tommy took out his pitching wedge and easily managed to get his ball on the green in regulation stopping about twenty-five feet from the hole.

Russ chipped for a third shot using his wedge but miss hit the ball. It made the green, just barely.

Tommy couldn't resist.

"Russ, isn't that three so far?"

"So what?"

"So, if you don't make that long putt, you drop another stroke."

"You only picked up two strokes so far Tommy. I'd focus on my own game if I were you."

"I'm just saying."

"Well, keep your comments to yourself."

It was evident Tommy was starting to get on Russ's nerves.

Russ had to putt first. His first putt fell way short of the cup. Then, he ran his ball up near the cup and then tapped in for a double bogey.

Joe was next to putt. The 30-foot putt almost went in the hole. It just missed on the left side of the cup running past the hole a few feet. Joe was able to make the return putt for a par.

Tommy hit last. He hit his putt too hard but it still had a chance to drop. When it hit the back of the cup, it bounced up and stayed out a few inches.

"That should have went in," Tommy exclaimed.

"Too much adrenalin, Tommy," Russ returned the jab. "Still thinking about the lunch break?"

It was Russ's turn to make Tommy think.

"Let's see, I got a par, what did you get Russ?"

Tommy tried to turn the tide again.

"A double, but I'll get it going again."

Joe wondered at what length these two would go to one-up each other. They walked off to the 12th hole, a 500-yard par-5.

They were now two-thirds of the way through the final round. Tommy and Joe had picked up a few strokes on Russ but he was still in the lead. The good news from Joe's perspective was his two playing partners were doing all they could to distract each other and lunch didn't hurt either.

And no one let up the bantering while playing the 12th. Joe, to be honest, was getting a little tired of it. It wasn't distracting it was annoying.

Chapter 46

The 13th hole was the second in a back-to-back set of par-5s. This one was 545 yards long. The hole was fairly straight with a ravine about three-quarters of the way up the fairway overlooking the green. A golfer who ends up in the bottom of the ravine might have a difficult time making par. The safest thing is to leave the second shot short on the top of the fairway short of the ravine and then hit a short iron to the green.

Tommy was first to tee off. He wasn't about to play cautious and hit another big drive. After he hit, he boasted, "Looks like I can make it in two."

Joe hit next. He hit a 250 yard drive straight up the center of the fairway.

"You can't get there with that one," Tommy taunted Joe.

"Don't worry about my shot Tommy. I'm playing my game."

Russ hit last. He had to get something going. Russ hit his driver a long way. It stopped over 300 yards out on the left side of the fairway.

They walked off the tee with Tommy mumbling something.

"Don't let him get to you," Russ said to Joe.

"I've competed against him so many times Russ, I'm used to his nonsense."

"Yeah, but I saw the look on your face when he talked about your ex."

"That does bother me. But there's really nothing I can do about it. She was a long time ago."

"Looks like you never really got over her."

"You know what it's like with your first one Russ. You really never get over that one. It's a feeling of failure somehow. I don't know if it's her, or just the sadness."

"I guess."

They had reached Joe's ball. He took out an 8-iron for his second shot. When he hit it, it landed right at the top of the fairway before the ravine.

Tommy had to keep at it. "See, I told you. Now you have to make a good third shot just to be in it."

Joe ignored Tommy's taunts.

Russ was next to hit. He took out a 3-wood and hit away. His shot looked good, heading right toward the green. It landed on the back of the green and rolled off.

Tommy hit next. He saw what Russ had done and elected to use a 5-wood. When he hit his ball, it went very high. At the outset, it looked like he had made the right decision but the shot fell short and rolled back into the ravine.

Joe was next to hit. As he stood at the top of the ravine, he could see Tommy's ball down in the bottom. Joe hit a wedge shot on the green stopping it eight feet from the cup. He'd have a birdie opportunity.

Tommy walked to the bottom of the ravine. He couldn't see the flag from where he stood. He walked up the hill to where Joe had hit and surveyed the back of green. He selected a large pine tree behind the green as his target line and then walked back down the ravine. Using a 9-iron, his shot came out in good shape heading right at the pine tree he had selected. The ball lost momentum and dropped on the green two feet from the cup. Tommy walked up the ravine to the green.

"Now, that's how it's done," he said boastfully.

Russ surveyed his shot from behind the green. He'd have to chip over a trap and land the ball softly in order to save the hole. He took out a lob wedge. When he hit his ball, it went high in the air and landed in the sand trap. Then he had to hit a sand wedge on to the green. Fortunately, he was able to sink the remaining 12-foot putt for a par.

Joe dropped his putt in for a birdie.

Tommy was last to putt. He missed the first putt and then made the second one. He ended up with a par on the hole.

As they walked off going to hole number fourteen, Tommy went right at Russ again. "Russ, looks like we're going to make a run at you after all."

"What's this 'we' stuff Tommy? Didn't you get a par also?"

"Yeah. But my par looked a lot better than yours."

"I'm still ahead by a few strokes Tommy. Joe might catch me, but I don't think you have it in you."

"It's time for the big guns now Russ. And that's either you or me."

"So you say."

They reached the 14th tee box. This one plays back over the same ravine as thirteen but it's only a 155-yard par-3. A golfer only has to hit a reasonable tee shot to avoid problems.

Joe was first to hit. He took out his 8-iron. When he addressed his ball, he put it a little further back in his stance than he normally would do on an 8-iron shot rationalizing a lower trajectory shot would ensure it wouldn't end up in the ravine. Better distance, less airtime. When he hit his ball, his rationale played out. The ball hit the front of the green and ran another twenty yards across the green stopping four feet from the cup.

Tommy hit next. He took out his 9-iron. Tommy's shot went very high landing in the middle of the green. He'd have another fifteen feet to make birdie.

Russ, having observed both of his competitor shots, decided Joe had the better strategy. He took out his 8-iron. As Russ shot, a gust of wind came up behind him. The effect was clearly visible on his ball. When it hit the back of the green, it carried well beyond the green and came to rest next to a stand of shrubs. He'd have a difficult time getting up and down from that position.

"Another poor shot Russ," Tommy kept it up.
"You still have to make yours Tommy," Russ shot back.
"Oh, I'm in a much better place than you are, Russ."
"We'll see."

Russ walked over to his ball. He couldn't get a good swing at it from where it ended up. He took his putter out of his bag and turned it backwards. Then, he putted his ball left handed out of the shrubs. The ball came out about ten feet but didn't make it on to the green. From there, he chipped on to within three feet of the cup.

Tommy was next to putt. His putt ran past the hole by a foot. He tapped in for par.

Joe was next to putt. He lined the putt up after having surveyed it four times. When he hit his ball, it went right in for a birdie.

Russ tapped in for another bogey.

"What's that? Five dropped shots on the back nine?" Tommy snickered at Russ.

"Hey, I'm still beating you by three or four."

"Maybe so, but I think Joe just passed you."

"And you," Russ said back at Tommy.

They walked off to the 350-yard par-4 15th. The hole played to a narrow fairway.

Joe was first to tee. He took out his driver and made a nice swing. His ball stayed true landing 270 yards down the center of the fairway.

Tommy hit next. It was time to put on the big game. Tommy hit his driver with a big swing. His ball jumped off the tee. It had a big bend in its flight ending up off the fairway on the left in deep rough.

"Trying to drive the green Tommy?" Russ asked him.

"Just playing my game," Tommy responded.

"Guess it's your turn to feel the pressure, Tommy."

"Don't worry about me, Russ. I'm in the hunt."

Russ just looked Tommy in the eye, and laughed.

Russ took out his driver. He hit a long ball landing 300 yards out. He'd have a short chip for a second shot. The three walked down the fairway stopping at Joe's ball.

Joe took out his pitching wedge. He took a big swing and overshot the green. His ball stopped 10 yards past the green.

Tommy hit next. His ball had been buried fairly deep in the 6-inch grass. He took out a 9-iron feeling he need a little extra club to navigate the rough. His swing remained on target all the way through propelling his ball right at the green. It stopped seven feet from the cup.

Tommy could be heard humming the music from Jaws as they walked up the fairway. "Da-Da, Da-Da, Da-Da, Dnt, Da."

Russ and Joe just ignored him. Russ hit a short chip shot. His ball landed on the green stopping eighteen feet from the cup.

Joe walked past the green to his ball. He used his 7-iron to bump-and-run his ball on to the green. It had a little too much mojo and ended up on the far side of the green twenty-five feet from the cup.

Joe was first to putt. He had watched his chip run across the green and had a good idea of the break his ball would take. On the return putt, he almost sank it. His ball stopped a foot past the cup. He tapped in for bogey.

Russ had a long putt to make for par. He surveyed it a few times and then addressed his ball. The putt fell short of the cup. He tapped in for a bogey.

Tommy acted cocky as he walked up to his ball. He'd easily make the seven-footer and pick up two strokes on Russ. He swung his putter. The ball went over the outside right of the cup but didn't drop. He had hit it too hard. It continued on another three feet. He made the return putt for a par.

As they walked off to the 16th Russ said, "Too bad Tommy. You could have made up some ground with that one."

"I picked up a stroke."

"Maybe, but you're still in third place."

"Three to go. I'll make it happen."

"So you say."

Tommy was first to hit on the 484-yard par-5 16th. The final three holes are pretty open. There was out-of-bounds on the right side. Tommy took his driver and safely put his ball 300 yards down the left side of the fairway.

Joe was next to hit. He took out his driver. After a few practice swings, he hit his ball. It went right and hit something hard in the rough. His ball took a big bounce further to the right landing in the street.

"Out-of-bounds, Joe," Tommy said with excitement in his voice. "Have to hit another one."

Joe teed up another ball. This time, his shot stayed straight 290 yards down the center of the fairway.

Tommy hit last. He placed his drive 300 yards out just past Russ's drive.

"Looks like the final three holes are going to be interesting," Tommy said as the walked.

Joe hit his second shot. He had taken out his 5-wood and placed the ball right on the green fifteen feet from the cup.

"Nice shot Joe," Russ complimented him.

"Gives me a chance to save par."

"Par isn't going to do it," Tommy said keeping up his taunts.

Russ was next to hit. He took out a 6-iron for the 180 or so yards left to the hole. He hit a beautiful shot. It landed on the front of the green coming to rest fifteen feet from the cup on the other side from Joe's shot.

Tommy was last to hit. He had paid attention to Russ's shot and selected his own 6-iron, but he wasn't as efficient with it as Russ had been. His ball landed short of the green by a few feet.

They walked up to the green. Tommy had to chip on. He landed his ball by the cup stopping it with a few feet remaining.

Joe had the first putt. It was a little longer than he wanted but he still had a chance at par. He took the shot and the ball found the bottom of the cup.

"Yes!" Joe shouted.

"Excited about a par, Joe?" Tommy said in a surprise voice.

"I saved par. That first drive could have put me out of contention."

"So you think you're in contention?" Tommy said.

"Yes, I am."

"He's working on you Joe," Russ said.

"I know. But it isn't working."

Russ made his putt for a birdie. Tommy missed his and had to settle for another par.

They walked up to the 17th tee. Russ said, "Let's see, that birdie ties me with Joe. How are you doing Tommy?"

It was clear Russ was playing role reversal with Tommy.

"Hey, I'm only two back."

"Yeah, with two to play," Russ said.

Russ was up first on the short par-4 328-yard 17th. The hole really didn't have any obstacles. Even still, Russ decided to play safe. He took out his 3-wood and hit a nice drive 250 yards down the center of the fairway.

Joe was next to hit. Trying to stay with Russ, Joe took out a 3-wood as well. He got the results he wanted. His shot wasn't as long as Russ's but just as accurate.

Tommy knew he had to make something happen. He took out his driver. After two practice swings, he hit a big drive. His ball rolled up on to the putting surface by five feet. He'd have a long putt, but at least he was putting for eagle.

Joe and Russ each hit short approach shots landing safely on the green. Russ had a fifteen-footer, Joe a few feet less.

Tommy was first to putt. He made a noble attempt to get eagle, barely missing the cup. He was able to tap in for birdie.

Russ and Joe both two putted for par.

Now the pressure was on Tommy. He was behind both Russ and Joe by one stroke with one to play.

Chapter 47

On the 18th tee, Russ looked over to Tommy as he was selecting his club.

"Got to have another good hole here Tommy just to stay in it."

"I'm feeling it," Tommy replied.

"Sure you are," Russ continued to try to get into his head.

"Just watch."

Tommy took out his driver. Again, he had a big swing. His tee shot was another long one carrying over 300 yards landing just short of the green.

"He might just do it," Joe said to Russ.

"Maybe. He's still got to make the shots," Russ replied.

Russ hit next. He continued to play it safe and used his 3-wood again. The shot achieved the same result as it did on the previous hole going out about 250 yards to the center of the fairway.

Joe was last to hit. As he took a few practice swings, it occurred to him he might actually have a chance at beating Tommy. He swung his driver as hard as he could. His ball took off down the left side of the fairway landing 290 yards out. It stopped just into the rough. He'd have a 60 yard chip shot left.

Russ hit his second shot from the center of the fairway. His wedge shot landed to the right of the cup about twenty feet away.

Tommy was next. He had a short chip shot into the green. A birdie would mean a play-off with one or the other, or possibly with both his competitors. He hit his ball. It landed on the back of the green leaving a thirteen-footer.

Joe chipped on from the fringe to within three feet of the cup.

Tommy, being away, surveyed his putt from every angle.
"If you miss this one, you're out," Russ tried to apply pressure.
Tommy didn't take the bait.
He stepped up to his ball and hit it right into the center of the cup. He had his birdie.
Joe and Russ each made their putts.

Walking up to Harry and the starter, the three handed in their scores. Russ shot a 68, Joe a 63, Tommy a 65.
"How'd we do?" Russ asked.
"Looks like it's going to be you three in a sudden death playoff," Harry responded. "Take a half hour and then it's back to eighteen for the first playoff hole."

The three picked up their clubs and walked to the clubhouse.

318

"You ready for a playoff Joe?" Russ asked.

"Sure am. I've never been this close before." Joe responded.

"Let's go get something inside. We've got a half hour before we have to be back on the tee," Russ said.

"I'm for that," Joe replied.

The two walked into the clubhouse. When they did, Joe stopped for a minute watching Tommy heading in the direction of his car. Joe and Russ went into the restaurant attached to the clubhouse.

"Joe, want a beer?" Russ asked.
"Nah, just a Diet Coke."
"Trying to stay focused?"
"Something like that."

Russ ordered a draft for himself and a diet coke for Joe. He brought them over to a table Joe had selected by the windows. Joe was looking out the window shaking his head.

"What's up Joe?"
"Nothing. I was just watching Tommy get into his car in the parking lot. I think he's in there with someone. I thought I saw a woman in a red sweater with him."
"Maybe he's out there with Jessica again?"
"It wasn't Jessica. She's got blond hair. He's out there with a brunette."

As they were sitting there talking, Martin Yates and Harry Adams came over to them.

"I'd like to go over the playoff format with you if I can." Martin said.

"What about Tommy?" Joe asked.

"We can wait until he's here." Martin responded.

"That might take a while." Russ said looking out the window.

319

"Where is he?" Martin asked.

"He's out there with someone in his car," Russ said pointing to Tommy's vehicle in the back of the lot.

"What's with that guy?" Martin said. "I caught him out there with someone during the lunch break."

"You thought he was with someone else as I remember," Harry said.

"Yeah. I found out a little while later he was out there with Jessica, Joe's ex," Martin said and then turned to Joe, "Sorry about that Joe."

"Well, he's out there with someone else this time," Joe said.

"Probably with the same one I saw him with earlier," Martin said.

"No. Jessica didn't have on a red sweater when I saw her," Joe said.

"Didn't Helen have a red blouse on?" Russ asked.

Martin looked around. He was looking for someone. He stood and walked to the end of the room looking into the pro shop. He didn't see who he was looking for and headed for the door. Harry saw Martin moving at a fast pace.

"Martin, you were going to review the playoff rules with the golfers," Harry said grabbing Martin's arm.

"Let me go Harry. I know that prick's out there with Helen."

Martin ripped his arm away from Harry and ran out the door. He ran across the parking lot with Harry a few steps behind him.

Martin ran right up to Tommy's vehicle and pulled the door open for the second time on the same day. This time, Tommy was lying on his back seat with a woman under him. They both had their pants down and were going at it.

Tommy turned his head when the door opened, "What's the hell's going on?"

320

"That's what I want to know," Martin said as he swung at Tommy. He connected with Tommy's jaw.

Then Martin looked at the woman's face. It was Carol Tindle.

Harry got there just as Martin punched Tommy. He tried to pull Martin out of the open door.

Tommy jumped right out after them, pulling his pants up as he got out.

"What the hell's your problem Yates?" Tommy demanded.

"You've been doing my wife Tommy and it's time somebody put you in your place."

Tommy stepped aside and pointed inside his vehicle. "I don't see your wife, Yates."

Harry looked in along with Martin. Then, Harry said, "Martin, Helen's not in there. That's Carol."

"I know. I can see that."

"So why did you punch Tommy?"

"He's been with my wife."

"I don't know about that Martin, but you might want to apologize," Harry said pulling him away from the SUV.

"I'm not apologizing to that prick for anything. I know what he's done with Helen."

"Hey, I'm not doing anything to your wife Yates. You need to talk to her."

"Come on Martin. We've got a few things to do to finish up this tournament," Harry said. "Tommy, we're going to go over the playoff rules in a few minutes. You might want to attend."

Martin turned and followed Harry back to the clubhouse. As they walked back inside, Helen and Jessica came walking out of the ladies room laughing.

"What's so funny?" Martin asked Helen.

"Oh nothing. Just girl talk."

321

It was clear to Helen that Martin was very mad. He wouldn't tell her what the problem was so she asked Harry.

"What's Martin so mad about?"

"He had a confrontation with Tommy Anderson out in the parking lot a few minutes ago. Martin punched Tommy."

"Why?"

"He thought you were the woman out there in his car with Tommy and Martin lost it."

"What?"

"I heard him tell Tommy he knows about some of the things you've done with Tommy behind his back. For some reason, he thought you were at it again with him in his SUV during the break."

"Oh boy. Now what do we do?"

"Nothing right now. I think I've got him to focus on finishing out the tournament. Beyond that, I can't say."

Chapter 48

A few minutes later, Tommy Anderson came into the clubhouse. He had a fat lip on the right side of his face with a little blood coming out of the corner of his mouth. He walked over to where Russ and Joe were sitting.

"What happened to you Tommy?" Russ asked him.

"Nothing. Things just got a little out of hand out there."

"Really? The women beating you up now?" Russ chided him.

"No. Martin Yates took a swing at me."

"Looks like it connected?"

Tommy rubbed the back of his hand on his mouth. The blood was visible on his hand then.

Harry walked over to the three, "We're going to cover the rules for the playoff. I don't want any problems," He said looking in Tommy's direction.

"Don't tell me Harry, tell Martin," Tommy insisted.

Martin Yates came over with a clipboard in hand. He read from a sheet in the stack of papers on the clipboard.

"Playoff Rules. Should a playoff be required to determine the winner of the Mid-Cape Open, all players tied with the cumulative low score from all four rounds will compete in a sudden-death playoff starting at the 18th hole and working backwards on the course until only one player remains with the lowest score. White tees will be used for the playoff. Should more than two golfers be in the playoff, only golfers recording the lowest score on each playoff hole will continue on to additional playoff holes. Do each of you understand these rules?"

The three golfers all shook their heads in agreement.

"Ok. Then we will resume play on number eighteen in fifteen minutes. Joe Campbell, you will tee off first having scored the lowest score for today's eighteen holes followed by Anderson and Ford. Any questions?"

There were none.

"Ok guys," Harry said. "Let's get out there."

They all went outside. Russ, Tommy and Joe picked up their clubs and walked back to the 18th tee. All spectators who had previously been scattered throughout the course following their favorite players or groups, were now concentrated at the single hole.

Joe took out his driver. He walked up to the white tee and put his tee and ball down. Moving to the white tees shortened the hole from 352 yards down to 339. It wasn't much, but it might help Joe out.

He took a few practice swings and then hit his ball. It went pretty straight down the left side of the fairway landing 280 yards away. Joe put his driver in his bag and stood at the back of the tee watching the other golfers.

Tommy took out his driver. He took two practice swings and then addressed his ball. He took his driver way back and then swung as hard as he could, making contact. His ball jumped off the tee going 320 yards down the left side of the fairway.

Russ hit last. His drive went out 300 yards right down the center of the fairway. The three picked up their bags and began walking. The spectators clapped in appreciation for good golf; Russ waved, Tommy tipped his hat and Joe nodded his head. Joe felt a little embarrassed with this much attention. He tried not to make eye contact with any of them.

When Joe stopped for his second shot, Carol was standing just off the fairway. She yelled out to Joe.
"Make it Joe."
He turned and looked at her. She said, "I did what I could to help you. You'll have to do the rest on your own."
All Joe could say was, "Thanks."

Then he took out his pitching wedge and hit a nice approach shot. It landed on the green stopping five feet from the cup.

Russ hit next. He had his wedge in hand as he addressed his ball. He took his club back about half way and made a soft swing. The ball only went about fifteen feet high and settled on the green about twenty feet from the cup.

Tommy, whose shot had almost made the green, took out a lob wedge, as he had to navigate over a sand trap to get on to the green. He took a few practice swings and then hit his ball. It went well past the cup and then came back to the hole as he had quite a bit of backspin on the shot. His ball stopped four feet from the cup.

"Looks like we all have to make our putts," Tommy said.

Russ was first to putt. Tommy walked over and stood next to Joe while watching Russ.

"I don't know Joe. Russ might miss this one. Then it'll be just you and me. And you know what that means."

"You're so sure of yourself Tommy, aren't you?"

"Let me see. Have you ever beaten me?"

Joe ignored him. Russ had lined up his putt. When he hit his ball, it curved a few inches to the right and then dropped right into the center of the cup. He was first in with a birdie.

Joe was next to putt.

Tommy said, "Looks like it'll be me and Russ," he was still trying to get under Joe's skin.

Joe lined up his putt to the right side of the cup. He made a smooth swing and his ball fell into the cup.

Now it was Tommy's turn. He had a four-footer. When Tommy lined up his putt, he looked up and Carol was standing directly in his line from his ball to the cup but on the other side of the hole. Joe noticed Tommy looking. He thought about prior conversations he had with Carol and thought she might be making good on one of the distractions she had told Joe about previously.

Tommy didn't flinch. If Carol did anything, Joe didn't see it. Tommy's putt dropped into the cup.

"Yes," Tommy said as his putt fell in.

They walked off the 18th hole still tied. Tommy kept up his attack on Joe.

"You'll have to do better than that on the next one Joe. I'm planning on driving the green."

326

"Go right ahead Tommy. You have always had a flair for the dramatic."

"Bet your ass I do."

They walked past the 17th green and back down the fairway to the tee box.

Chapter 49

The 17th hole from the white tees is 319 yards long. There are only two concerns about this hole. The first was Highbank Road runs all along the fairway on the right side. The second was the green is a small green and it does not have much room behind the green for error, as the entrance to the golf course is about twenty-five feet in back of the green. There are sand traps on the backside of the green to catch any golf balls hit too far.

Joe still had the honors. He placed his ball on a tee and took a few practice swings. He hit his drive a long way out and at the end of the drive, his ball found the rough on the right side of the fairway.

Tommy said, "Wow. That was close."
"That's OK, just so long as it stayed in bounds," Joe responded.

Tommy was next to hit. He had taken out his driver intending to reach the green in one. He took a few practice swings and then hit his ball. It took off but went left into the wide-open area left of the green. If he had hit a straight drive he'd probably have been on the green. Instead, he had to settle for a second shot thirty yards left of the green.

"Playing safe Tommy?" Russ teased.
"It just got away from me a little," Tommy said.
"Now you have to make a good chip or you'll be watching."
"Who says you're going to be any better?"
"I do," Russ said as he put his ball on the tee.

Russ took a few practice swings with his driver. He hit his ball. It went fairly high and straight at the green. The ball landed on the front edge and rolled to the back of the small green coming to rest at the edge of the green and fringe.

"Nice shot Russ," Joe complimented him.
"Thanks."

They walked off the tee and down the fairway. Russ and Joe stopped by Joe's ball. Joe did in fact get lucky. His ball was in the rough, ten feet from the street, but playable. The ball was sitting up pretty good in the grass so Joe took out his 7-iron for a bump-and-run shot. He lined the ball up to go on to the green on the right side and to then use the slope and move to the left. He hit his shot. The ball didn't gain much height. It bounced six times before reaching the green. Then, just as Joe had planned, the ball curved to the left towards the hole. It came to rest nine feet from the cup.

Tommy was thirty yards left of the green. He took out his pitching wedge for the shot. After a few practice swings, he hit his ball. It went long hitting on the top of the ground between the road and green. The ball ricocheted off something and bounced into the street. Tommy was out-of-bounds. He dropped a tee to mark his spot before he went to retrieve his ball.

He went out into the street, picked the ball up off the curb, and went back to his dropped tee. When he dropped his ball, it ran down the hill by the trap. He tried again. This time, it ended up in the trap. On the third try, the ball did the same thing again ending up in the trap. He got to place his ball on the top of the mound. Then, he hit his forth shot with his wedge. The ball looked like it would go into the hole saving par but at the last second, it curved and missed the hole ending up three feet past the cup.

Tommy was upset.
"I can't believe it didn't go in."
"Happens to the best of us," Russ said.
"No. It happened to me. I should be winning this tournament."
"Doesn't look like that's going to happen now," Russ said to him.
"You still have to make your putt."
"I've got two shots to eliminate you Tommy. You're toast," Russ said with a smile on his face.

Russ was next to hit. His ball was right at the cut line for the fringe. He took out his driver and walked over to the ball. He lined it up and then took a practice swing with his driver. He intended to hit it very easy and use the mass of the driver club head to carry through the fringe to create a straight shot. He hit his ball and in fact, the driver did the trick. The ball stayed on line ending up three inches short of the cup. Russ put the driver in his bag and took out his putter. He walked over and tapped in for par.

Tommy had been eliminated. As he was leaning on his bag, you could visibly see the air leave his body, and his head dropped.

Joe still had to make his putt. There wasn't much left to the shot as the ball had come to rest below the hole about

330

nine feet away. If Joe could drop this putt, he'd win the whole tournament. Joe lined up the shot for the center of the cup. He hit softly. His ball rolled very slow and stopped short of the cup. Then, he tapped it in for a par.

Tommy was now carrying on in Tommy-fashion, dramatically. He used a lot of profanities cursing his game. Russ and Joe picked up their golf bags and started walking to number sixteen for the third playoff hole. As they walked, they could hear Tommy still upset behind them standing on the 16th green.

As they walked along, Carol came over and walked next to Joe.

"Well, you don't have to worry about Tommy any more."

"Thanks God."

"What happened?"

"He hit OB. Had to take a penalty. Then, he couldn't get the ball up and down."

"So it's just you and Russ?"

"Yeah. But, you know what? I don't mind if I lose to Russ. He's a nice guy and I've enjoyed playing this round with him."

"Are you saying that because of Tommy?"

"No. Russ is ok in my book."

"You could still win Joe."

"Yeah. I'd take it if it comes my way. It's just that beating Tommy was enough."

"Don't you want to win the money?"

"It'd be nice. But I've got this big deal in the works and I think it's going to come in. That will be a lot of money. That'll be nailed down by the end of today."

"Good for you Joe. I'm happy for you."

"Thanks Carol. You know, I could use someone to bounce ideas off of who knows about money."

"I could refer you to someone I use."

331

"I was thinking about you Carol. You've got experience and I was hoping you'd give me some advice."

"Oh thanks Joe. But I rely on my accountant. I am many things, but not an expert on money matter."

"Your accountant handles your investments?"

"He handles everything, me, my accounting, the investments."

They both laughed.

"No really, Andrew Dunn is a very versatile man."

"Andrew Dunn? Wasn't he in business with Sam Sterns, Katherine's husband?"

"Yeah. They owned Sterns and Dunn."

"How did you come to do business with him?"

"When Katherine was alive, she referred me to him. I took my business there and have been with him ever since."

"I'll have to keep his name in mind."

"Let me know if you want an introduction."

"Ok. Well, I've got to get back to playing."

"Go get 'em Joe."

Joe walked on to the 16th tee. It was down to him and Russ Ford. Joe had the honors. He took out his driver. After a few practice swings, he hit his drive down the right center of the fairway about 270 yards out.

Russ put his ball on a tee. He took a few swings and then hit his drive 310 yards on the left side of the fairway. The ball came to rest a few feet into the rough.

They walked down the fairway in silence. Joe hit his second shot first. He used his 5-wood for the second shot. It went straight landing on the edge of the green. He'd have a thirty-foot putt attempt for birdie.

Russ took out an 8-iron for his second shot. He hit his ball very high out of the rough landing it on the green a few feet in front of Joe's ball.

They walked up to the green. Russ marked his ball, and Joe was first to putt. He looked at it a number of times and then addressed the ball. It started out right at the hole and then missed by a few inches. The ball came to a stop a foot past the hole.

Russ now had a chance to win the tournament. If he could make his putt, he'd win. He had watched Joe's putt closely. Russ lined the ball up on a line similar to the one Joe had used. Russ hit his ball. It looked like it would miss to the right and then it looked like it wouldn't make the hole. As the ball slowed, it started to turn left. The ball stopped right at the cup. Half of the ball had to be hanging over the cup. As Russ walked up to tap it in, the ball dropped.

He had a birdie and the tournament.

Joe walked over to Russ extending his hand. "Nice shot Russ. You deserve the win."
"You played pretty good too Joe."
"Thanks Russ."

Harry and Martin walked over to congratulate Russ and Joe. They all shook hands. Harry held Russ's hand in the air declaring him the winner.
Russ in turn, held Joe's hand up as well.

Harry said, "If you'll come over to Sundancers in the next half hour, we'll have the presentation and awards ceremony. It'll be followed up with a reception. Good job Russ."
"Thanks Harry. I'll be there right away."

Harry walked back to the clubhouse. He picked up the leader board easel and put it into his car. Then he got in and drove to Sundancers.

Joe was walking off the 16th green, took his cell phone out of his golf bag and turned it on. He had a message from his attorney. Joe called in for the messages.

"Joe, its Mark Goldstein. The deal's done. We got the approval from USA's Board of Directors a little while ago. Congratulations. You're a millionaire!"

Joe closed his phone. He had a bounce in his step and a big smile on his face. He put his clubs into his car and drove to Sundancers.

Chapter 50

Joe parked in the nearly full lot at Sundancers. He got out of his car and went in. The bar was packed. Most of the golfers were in there already celebrating. Dee saw Joe come in. She came out from behind the bar and gave him a big hug.

"Too bad you didn't win Joe."
"It's ok. I finished second."
"But you could have won."
"I don't mind losing to Russ. He played a good game."
"Why are you being so gracious about all this Joe?"
"I sold my software business."
"No kidding?"
"Yep."
"Did you get what you expected for it?"
"That and a whole lot more."
"Really?"
"Yes. Millions."

She put her arms around him again, hugging him and giving him a big kiss.

Carol Tindle had arrived ahead of Joe and was seated on the opposite side of the bar. She had observed the interaction between Dee and Joe. When Dee had gone back behind the bar, Joe stayed by the door talking to some of the other golfers.

"Dee, what was that all about?" Carol asked.

"I just wanted Joe not to feel bad."

"About what?"

"He didn't win the tournament, but he won big time with that software company of his."

"Oh yeah. He talked with me about it a little today."

"I told him he should talk to you if the deal panned out. You've got a lot of money and he'll need someone he can trust to give him advice."

"Thanks Dee."

"You're welcome."

"So he's ok with the tournament?"

"See for yourself."

Dee pointed at Joe at the other end of the bar. He was buying Russ Ford a drink and making a toast. The two were laughing and having a good time.

Harry and Tony came out of the kitchen. They heard the commotion by the door and went over.

"Good Job Russ," Harry shook his hand again.

"Thanks."

"How'd you do Tony?" Russ asked.

"I shot an 80 today. It would have been asking a lot for me to play the same as I did last weekend."

"Just the same Tony, you did well," Harry complimented him.

"Thanks."

"So Joe, I didn't get to see you over at the course after I finished playing. We had to get back here to make sure things were set up for tonight. How'd you finish?" Tony asked.

336

"It came down to a three way tie. Russ, Tommy and me were in a playoff. We all tied on the first hole. Then Tommy had a bogey on the second playoff hole. That ended his day. Then, on the third playoff hole, I made par but Russ made his putt for birdie."

"So you beat Tommy?"

"Yeah. I guess I did."

"Where is the creep?" Tony asked.

"The last time I saw him, he was standing on the 17th green complaining about his play," Joe said.

"His SUV was gone when I went to my car after play," Russ added.

"Maybe he's too ashamed to show his face here tonight after all the grandstanding he did all week," Tony remarked.

"Let's just hope he doesn't show," Harry said as he motioned his head in the direction of Martin Yates.

"I thought Martin was going to kill him halfway though the round today," Joe said.

"I know," Harry commented. "I had to get Martin refocused on the tournament. At one point, Martin slugged the guy when he thought he was up to no good again with his wife, Helen."

"There might be more there than you think," Tony said raising his eyebrows.

"I don't even want to go there," Harry replied. "Dee, give all the golfers a round on the house. They did a good job during the tournament."

Joe and Tony talked with the other golfers for a while. After an hour of drinking, they were getting a little loud. Joe walked to the back of the bar and to his surprise, he saw Jessica sitting at the corner of the bar talking with Tina Fletcher.

"Hey Jessica," Joe said sheepishly.

"Joe."

"You know Tina?" Joe asked.

337

"You remember I went to school down here don't you?"

"Well, yeah."

"Actually, Tina's younger sister was one of our classmates. Remember Donna Santore? Tina's name was Santore before she got married. She was a few years ahead of us in school."

"A few," Tina said. "I'd say a dozen."

"Yeah, I remember Donna Santore. She was a very pretty girl."

"It runs in the family," Tina said.

"That's how I know Tina," Jessica said to Joe.

"So what brings you back to this area Jessica? Last I remember, you left with some guy and then divorced me."

"Tommy Anderson gave me a call recently and said I should come back for a visit. He said things have changed here and I might like it. My relationship with Bob didn't work out."

"That's too bad," Joe said, but he didn't mean it. "So, are you waiting for Tommy to show up here?"

"He said he'd meet me here about a half-hour after the tournament ended. That was an hour ago. I don't know if he's going to show up or not."

"Tommy's day didn't end very well. He's probably off somewhere drinking his sorrows."

"I don't know," Jessica said. "He was pretty specific I should meet him here tonight."

Tina joined the conversation. "Anytime Tommy asks a woman to show up in public somewhere, it can't be good. He usually asks a woman to go home with him."

"He must have something up his sleeve," Joe remarked.

Dee had overheard some of the conversation. She stood behind the bar in front of the women and Joe, "Well, it looks like you're going to find out what Tommy was up to. Here he comes."

Tommy Anderson was walking, or rather, staggering in though the door.

Chapter 51

Tommy looked around and saw Jessica seated next to Tina. They were talking with Joe and Dee. Tommy worked his way around the bar knocking into a number of people along the way. When he got to them, he was already slurring his words.

"Jessica, there you are. I've been looking for you for hours."

"I've been here for over an hour Tommy. Where were you?"

"I stopped in at Riverside after leaving the course. I ended up having a few pops with some of the guys over there."

Dee knew about the issues between Helen and Tommy. She said, "Were you looking for Helen by any chance Tommy?"

"Helen? Why would I want to find her? I've already been with her. She's ok for a quickie but I'm looking for something a lot nicer."

Right after Tommy made his remarks, a fist came around from behind him, decking him. Tommy went down like a ton of bricks. No one had time to react before Martin was all over Tommy. He punched him numerous times. Finally, Harry ran over and put his arms around Martin from behind stopping the action.

"Martin, what's gotten into you?" Harry asked.

"I heard him talking about Helen. It wasn't nice. He was saying he had been with her and something about a quickie. You know what that means."

Tommy cleared his head and stood up. "Not what we did together Martin, what she did to me."

Martin tried to break free of Harry to come after Tommy again, but he couldn't.

"Tommy, I think you should leave," Harry suggested.

"Hey, I paid to be in the tournament. I'm here for the award ceremony and reception. If anyone has to leave, it should be him. I didn't start it."

He had a point. Harry turned Martin around and got him to walk to the back of the room with him. They had a very animated conversation and then Martin went into the kitchen. Harry came back over to the group, "Tommy, Martin will leave you alone while we're handing out the awards. But when we're finished, I highly suggest you get the hell out of here or Martin might kill you."

"Is he threatening me Harry?"

"It's more of a promise since you have been doing things with his wife. And I'm not sure anyone will come to your aid, Tommy. Especially when they find out its true."

"Like I told Martin, Harry, I didn't do anything to Helen. She did it to me."

"You can mince your words any way you want Tommy, but you're screwing with another man's wife. And he knows about it. We're going to hand out the awards in a few minutes, then hold the reception. You should be out of here within an hour."

"You can't force me to leave."

341

"But I can refuse to serve you." Harry looked to Dee and made a cut-off motion and pointed at Tommy. He might be able to stay for a little while but he'll be thirsty doing it.

Harry walked to the stage with a microphone in hand.

"Ladies and Gentlemen, today we concluded the first Mid-Cape Open. All of the merchants sponsoring the tournament want to thank you for your participation. The event was a huge success."

Everyone clapped.

"I'd like to have Russ Ford come up here."

Russ stood and walked up to Harry. Harry picked up a trophy and read the inscription, "First Place, The Mid-Cape Open."

There were cheers and clapping in the audience.

"Russ, you're the first winner of this tournament. Congratulations."

Harry handed him the trophy. Then, he picked up an envelope from the table, "In this envelope is a check for $5,000 for winning the tournament. So what do you think you'll do with the money? Go pro?"

Russ opened the envelope. He took out the check and declared, "Harry, I'd like to donate this check to Save the Animals Foundation here on the Cape. Can you see to it?"

"Are you sure?" Harry said.

"I'm sure. This has been a blast. But it can go to a better cause than me."

Everyone clapped and cheered.

"Thanks again everyone for coming. We have a buffet set up and the bar is open."

Everyone started for the bar. A few of the golfers got on line for the buffet. Fifteen minutes after the awards, things had settled down. Tommy had taken up a stool next to Jessica. He asked for a drink but Dee wouldn't serve him. Tommy looked across the bar and saw Joe and Russ having a drink together. They were both smiling and telling stories to the other golfers they were drinking with.

"What's Joe so happy about? He lost, or hadn't he noticed?" Tommy asked.

Dee was in front of Tommy, "Didn't you hear? Joe had a huge success today."

"What, he finished second?" Tommy slurred.

"Yes he did."

"So he's celebrating?"

"He sure is."

"Oh, I get it. He beat me."

"Tommy, it has nothing to do with you. Joe became a multi-millionaire today."

"What are you talking about Dee?"

"Yeah, what are you talking about Dee?" Jessica asked incredulously, and with raised eyebrows.

"You can read about it in the papers sometime in the next few days guys. Now I think it's time for Tommy to get out of here."

Dee pointed to the door.

"Come on Jessica. Let's get out of here."

"Why don't you go by yourself Tommy? I think I'll stay and see if Joe will talk to me."

Jessica sat at the bar for a little while watching Joe. He seemed to be having a good time with some of the other golfers. After a little while, Carol and Tina both came up behind Joe. They sandwiched him in between them and began giving him kisses.

Carol whispered something in Joe's ear. He smiled at the two women.

Carol and Tina turned and went back to where they were sitting to gather their things. When they walked away, Jessica walked over to Joe.

He turned to look at her.

"Joe, what's all the talk about you becoming a millionaire?"

"I sold my software business today."

"What software business?"

"Something I had been working on for some time. A big company made me an offer to buy my company and I took it."

"I never knew."

"I took an interest in computers after you dumped me Jess."

"Joe, I was in a bad place."

"So what do you want Jess?"

"Maybe we can go somewhere and talk."

Just then, Carol and Tina came back to Joe. Tina overheard Jessica trying to get Joe to go somewhere with her and said, "No you don't miss tight ass. He's ours."

Carol took one arm and Tina the other. Joe didn't resist. They led him to the door and off the three went.

Jessica just stood there stunned.

31166560R00199

Made in the USA
Charleston, SC
08 July 2014